THE
Looking-Glass
Lover

THE
Looking-Glass
Lover

A NOVEL BY

Ursula Perrin

Little, Brown and Company

BOSTON   TORONTO   LONDON

FIRST EDITION

The characters and events in this book are fictitious.
Any similarity to real persons, living or dead, is
coincidental and not intended by the author.

Library of Congress Cataloging-in-Publication Data

Perrin, Ursula, 1935–
The looking-glass lover :
a novel / by Ursula Perrin. — 1st ed.
p. cm.
ISBN 0-316-69961-6
I. Title.
PS3566.E6944L6 1989   89-2803
813'.54—dc19   CIP

10   9   8   7   6   5   4   3   2   1

Designed by Marianne Perlak

FG

Published simultaneously in Canada
by Little, Brown & Company (Canada) Limited

PRINTED IN THE UNITED STATES OF AMERICA

How still! how still! Through the mirrors
of strangers white shadows swim
. . . Or is that ghost myself . . . ?

Anna Akhmatova
"A Shadow"

Prologue

. . .

May Night Conversation

Barbara: Do you remember when we were seven?

Claire: No.

Barbara: Aw come on, yes you do. When we were seven you had a birthday party and we all drove up for it. Daddy was at Fort Holabird. I remember the drive, it was terrible. Dora got carsick in the back seat and threw up all over me. Mother dabbed at both of us with a little lace-trimmed handkerchief. Still, I stank, I mean really stank. Then when we arrived, there you were, the birthday girl, Miss Pristine. You were all decked out in a pink dress your mother had made for you. It had smocking and rows of silvery blue cross-stitch above the smocking. You wore a rosebud wreath on your head.

Claire: What?

Barbara: It's true, you had a little wreath on your head and long shiny blond hair. Oh, I adored your mother and I was crazy about your father, too. Boy, did you have it all.

Claire: Me? Come on, grow up. There's a price to be paid for being a good girl.

Barbara: Yeah? What?

Claire: You don't have any fun.

Barbara: Did I have fun?

Claire: Didn't you? You did all those crazy things. You got thrown out of summer camp! You had a high-school boyfriend who had actually been in jail! You had an outrageously poignant love affair with a married man. You had all the fun and you got all the attention.

· 3

Barbara: You got published first.

Claire: You got more reviews.

Barbara: You got Gordy.

Claire: You've had a hundred men.

Barbara: Not quite a hundred.

Claire: You've actually kept track? Revolting! I'll bet you write about them, too.

Barbara: Of course, don't you? Oh that's right, you don't.

Claire: "She said smugly!" It's odd that we both turned out to be writers. Must be a glitch in the family protoplasm. My father always claimed that we were descended from E. T. A. Hoffmann. How's your novel coming?

Barbara: I never talk about my work.

Claire: We ought to do it, you know.

Barbara: Do what?

Claire: Trade lives.

Barbara: Yum. Do I get Gordy?

Claire: You get my writer's block.

Barbara: We'd learn to hate each other.

Claire: Are we friends now? Tell me something, do you ever think of him? Jason? I don't mean professionally, I mean . . .

Barbara: (*coldly*) No. Listen, we've got to go, it's late. You're not upset about that little scene in the kitchen are you? I think of Gordy as . . . just another cousin. Thanks for everything, it was great. Oh wait a minute — here's Jason's office address. As a publisher I think he's tops. Go ahead, give him a call, what have you got to lose? Thanks again! It's spring, I love spring, don't you? It's so soft and spermy.

Claire: It's sad. I always think of spring as sad.

Barbara: Oh Claire, you are . . . (*voice trails off*).

(There is the sound of car doors slamming, a car horn toots, a car moves away. From another part of the house music begins to play — Scott Joplin's "Maple Leaf Rag." Claire stands up and claps her hands over her ears.)

· I ·

Barbara

1

Last night I dreamed that Jenks died and I felt sad but relieved. A tall, thin minister stood in back of the bier holding his hands up in blessing. I recognized him at once, it was E. T. A. Hoffmann in long clerical robes, a white collar and a shock of red hair. His complexion was sallow, my dream invented a mushroom wart for his chin. Then a book appeared in his hands, he clapped it shut and said, "Dearly beloved, too bad. This marriage is hereby dissolved." I tried not to cheer. I turned away thinking, That's that. Hoffmann went up in a puff of smoke.

And then in an instantaneous dream transition I was in the back seat of my Uncle Henry's 1953 Chevrolet and Gordy Parker and I were making love. Out of pure delight I bit into the white freckled skin of his shoulder and saw with satisfaction that a row of dark vampire dots had sprung up, alert as flowers. The blood tasted warm in my mouth and when I lay back, exhausted, I saw his face over me, watching: pale, drained, horrified. No, it wasn't Gordy it was Jenks. As if this face — sweaty, aghast — were transparent, a beamed camera image or something ectoplasmic, it slowly faded upward and away into nothing, almost nothing, a dancing sunbeam filled with dust. Ashes to ashes and dust to dust, I wonder if Jenks is dead.

Of course he's not dead, he's in Duvernoy, New Jersey.

A breeze rustles the leafy branch outside my open window and lifts the grayish curtains and the sunbeam dissolves into morning, late May, in the year of our Lord, whatever, one of endless many forever and ever, Amen.

THANK YOU, LORD, FOR LETTING THE SCHOOL YEAR BE
OVER.

(Except now of course there'll be summer school.)

Ah, Gordy.

Good God, Gordy Parker, my cousin Claire's husband.

Time to get a new boyfriend.

The smell of burned toast wafts into the bedroom from the kitchen two floors below. The toaster is on the fritz and I am on the prowl. I hear my son, Cliff, aged twenty and screwed up, singing a Lou Reed song as he slams the refrigerator door: "It's such a perfect day, I'm glad I spent it with you . . ." Well, I'm not. Last year he spent three months at a rehab center overcoming his drug addiction. He's a sweet kid when he's not high. Gordon Parker, I can't believe it. He has the most marvelous back.

Oh God oh God send me a new boyfriend. Someone sexy and not too smart, just let him like going to bed. Not Gordy, please don't let it be Gordy. Someone uncomplicated and nice. Someone who likes to snack in bed after making love — for example: caviar on buttered toast triangles with a chilled bottle of Piper-Heidsieck — Viva la compagnie! sitting back on propped-up pillows. Someone who doesn't like Mantovani, I can go with country, though, or the Stones. Not another narcissist, I'm bloody sick of narcissists or these guys on a power trip. How come I have such dumb bad luck?

Oh, believe me, Kind Sir, as I lie here in my bedroom (the bed sinks, the ceiling sags, the drapes hang crooked from wobbly rods, the furniture is battered nineteen twenties, we bought the house furnished, the owneress had died), believe me, Gentle Jesus meek and mild, if you send me a new boyfriend I will not lay so much as a little finger on Gordon Parker. Will not bat an eyelash or wiggle a butt. I like my cousin Claire, though I used to hate her when we were kids — she was one of those skinny perfect-looking blond brats so ladylike you wanted most of all to push her into a large stinking mud puddle — I was fat, sloppy, smart and I adored Claire's father. I used to have dreams about Claire's father, my mother's half brother, my handsome Uncle Nils. Claire looks like my mother. I look like . . . nobody.

A kid bawls somewhere outside my window. "Maaa . . ."

I sit up. "What, for God's sake? Don't you know it's my vacation?"

"Telephone, Ma! It's Aunt Claire!"

I run out to the hall in my sleep shirt and take the receiver off the hook. The receiver is sticky — chewing gum? grape jam? — so I put it up to but not quite on my ear. The telephone sits next to the banister on a thin-legged little table that also has a glass Cinzano ashtray upon it heaped with my daughter Alicia's cigarette butts. She sits up here and talks to her boyfriend and smokes. She smokes and cries and Cliff smiles and blinks. "What's up, Coz?"

She tells me in her clear, cultured, amused voice that it's after ten o'clock, I should be at work. I smile and at the same time straighten out the oriental hall runner with my bare pointed toe.

"Listen. Today's my day to clean." Claire laughs. She knows I never clean. "Why aren't you off for the shore? It looks like great sailing weather."

And again — darn! — I see Gordy's back in the boat last summer, lean and white as he bent to turn a wench — oops! winch! — oh Barbara, Barb, Bobbie, you're a wicked creature. Ah ha. Claire's staying home this weekend, not going down to the shore, and therefore requests the pleasure of my company this afternoon at tea. She'll use her silver service no doubt, and we'll sit on her wide back veranda that has Doric columns and a Chippendale railing. Tea in her translucent white china cups

· 11

with fluted gold rims. Thin slivers of lemon, sugar cubes. Claire's house is heaven or drawing-room comedy; my house is hell or burlesque. I groan, hope she'll understand, but today I am going to just hang out. I corrected one hundred exams this week and I feel as blind as Milton. *Ciao,* then, Claire baby.

Tea.

Christ.

What I need is a shot of gin.

· · · 2 · · ·

My name (to retrogress for a second) is Barbara Ledyard Bigelow and I live in the pleasant town of Comstock, New Jersey. I stand five-five in my stocking feet, weigh one twenty, have green eyes and black hair and good pink color. I wear my hair cut short and curly — it is just starting to go gray. I am forty-one years old, poor and good-looking, with three children of my own, and an ex-lover's kid as a boarder. My husband — such as he was — took off seven years ago on a very long drunk but before he left he paid up the mortgage from his Aunt Macy Small's bequest. He left me the kids as well as the house. My mother-in-law said his drinking was all my fault.

His suits still hang in his closet, his shirts are still in the drawer. I was waiting for my son, Cliff, to grow into them but instead he grew past them, and anyway, he doesn't wear suits, he wears jeans or worn-out cords or his waiter's uniform — he dropped out of U. of Vermont last year and now lives at home and works at the Bull's Head Inn, a local pub.

Jenks's drinking was *not* my fault.

Jenks lives in a rooming house down at the shore with a bartendresse.

Why did I marry him?

I could have made something out of myself! I could have been somebody sooner!

This house is a tall, ugly, three-story Tudor with brick below and dirty yellow stucco and half timbers above. Since Jenks left, I've let the property go and now the trees and foliage have crept up past the halfway mark, making the first floor infernally gloomy. The house sits on a knob or knoll hard by the petulant Passaic, a river (so called — I grew up next to the mighty Mohawk, a real river and not just a "crick" as we used to say in upstate New York) that daily washes up on our steep grassy bank: spare tires, bloated condoms, dead cats and once a whole human hand — yes, folks, this is New Jersey, winter home of the Mafioso. The river is out in back. Down in front is a roaring roadlet that shortcuts between two major highways; west of us is a shady side street of lugubrious "older homes" (we are so high up we look down on their patchy rooftops) inhabited by many elderly cat lovers squeaking it out on Social Security or old-timey practicing Catholics with hordes of snot-nosed brats. To the east, just below us, the Erie Lack-awanna, a commuter railway, creeps wearily toward New York City.

In fact, this knoll is an island and I sometimes think my life here is daily as hard a battle for survival, demands as much cunning and skill and fortitude as that of any Crusoe washed up on any shore. For money, I teach history (five days a week) at the Barstow School for Girls (upper school, grades nine through twelve). After hours, I write novels. My income as a novelist peaked last year at $4,800. I have a short, sleazy, lecherous agent and a publisher, Trend-Dee Books, that also owns a baseball team. Despite my best efforts at teaching and writing, I am often broke and reduced to cadging small change from my lovers — poverty tends to make one opportunistic, even in bed.

My cousin Claire lives in this town, too. I had spent a lot of my life avoiding Claire (we exert a magnetic force on each other — alternately fascinated and repelled, we have been through whole cycles of bumping together and fleeing apart) so that when Jenks told me the Parkers were living in Comstock, New Jersey, a town we were then considering, I groaned. How can I explain? Sometimes, someone you have known since early childhood becomes a kind of mirror and, looking at her, what you see is yourself as she must see you: aged six, sad and dumpy, or at fourteen — an angry adolescent with a rash of pimples on your forehead, or an overweight college girl, teary and morose, recovering from a first love affair. You know that this mirror has recorded all your hideous vulnerabilities and, worse, it has a memory that is deep, unforgiving, inconvenient.

Still, Comstock was a good commute to Wall Street (Jenks was still gainfully employed then) and he liked Gordy, who was an old friend, and besides, Jenks's law school training or his job at Shearling, Swain and Cravatt or the influence of his awful old mother, Dragon Lady, made him bring up "social life" or "seeing people," which, in our bumbling young-married years, we hadn't yet hit upon. We moved to Comstock but so ingrained was my obstinate habit of nonviolent obstruction that even six months after we'd settled into the Plumleys' house, I still hadn't called Claire Parker.

For one thing, the Parkers seemed so at ease in their world. Wherever you went in Comstock you heard about the Parkers — the marvelous parties they gave, the elegant house they'd bought, the amusing things they did: the night Gordy hired a three-piece band to play an anniversary song for Claire from their roof; the birthday Claire hired a chauffeured Rolls-Royce to drive Gordy to house calls and the hospital.

Whereas Jenks and I were still deplorably poor. Each month's mortgage payment on the house was a hurdle that left us winded; our secondhand Volkswagen ate money just sitting still; and all year round the outward flow of capital to our pediatrician's office resembled the Mississippi River on its spring rampage.

"Aw come on, Barb," Jenks said one March night as the wind rattled the loose leaded panes in the "den," an awful room. (I had left the moth-eaten moose head on the wall as well as the old yellowed photo of Otis Plumley in felt hat, checkered shirt, knickers and high boots holding up a string of fish.) "Why don't you just give 'em a call?"

"Who?"

"Hey, Barb, okay, Barb, let's leave out the fact that Claire's your cousin and Gordy's an old friend of mine. Let's just be crass and think about this summer." (Here he cast a frowning glance at the tinkling window, which seemed about to slither musically into bits.) "You really want to spend a hot, humid New Jersey summer next to our plastic wading pool?"

"Whatever are you getting at?" I said crossly.

"At the rear of their house," Jenks said, "the Parkers have a lovely long inground swimming pool."

I sighed and promised to call.

"You will?" Jenks said.

"Anything for my kids," I said.

"Great!" he said happily and yawned and slouched down into Otis Plumley's recliner so that the sheaf of documents he was studying slid out of its manila folder and down his long legs onto the floor. He grinned at me and tapped his foot. "Now why don't you come over here?" he said. "It's almost bedtime."

Jenks was very bright and wholly unambitious, and after we'd been married a year or so (I was pregnant with Cliff) it occurred to me that Jenks didn't give a damn about The Law. For a while I tried to get him to do something else — something that might interest him — but I never found out what this interest was. There was scotch, of course, and there was sex (and how marvelous he was in the sack) and oh, he told a good story. He liked to sit with a glass in his hand and regale a crowd. After I called Claire she asked us to dinner and she said while we both pottered in the kitchen afterward, "Jenks is so funny! I love the way he told that joke. By the way, the key to the pool gate is on a long nail next to the garage door up under the wisteria vine. Come over anytime."

"Thank you," I said humbly, "we'd adore it."

You see what I mean? It was hard not to hate this person. She had everything! What didn't she have? She had money and looks and brains and it was appalling how nice she was and how good her manners were, and I thought to myself, I'll bet she is loyal and true and all that stuff. Also, she had Gordy, who (to tell the truth) I'd always had this thing for, and all through dinner that night, they sat making eyes at each other — enough to make you barf, right?

Now of course everything's changed.

She has that sad, bad, trapped look, and when I ask her how the writing's going, she snaps, "What's there to write about?"

So every now and then, just as a tease, I tell Claire about Jason. Love! Adventure! Passion! Just what she needs.

Friends, it's like feeding a lineful of chum to a bluefish.

A scream!

Hastily tumbling down the dusty stairs from the third floor, barefoot, in white shorts and a T-shirt, I see from the second-floor landing that my son, Cliff, has bound up Nesta Dwyer, our sixteen-year-old boarder, in the black wriggles of the extra-long phone cord. Cliff is sitting on her midsection with the phone plunked between his yellow-and-blue running shoes. He is grinning and dialing while Nesta flails her long white shapeless legs. I bet she is getting some sort of erotic thrill out of this. I hope he isn't making a long-distance call.

"Hey you! Cliff Bigelow! What do you think you're doing? Get off her immediately. Nesta, for Pete's sake, stop that hollering." She stops at once, such an annoyingly good girl you want to thwack her, and Cliff slams down the receiver and rises, slowly unwinding his home-style lariat but grinning all the while. Oh what a gorgeous kid he is! (However, one must be stern: thus, sternly:) "What is going on here, Clifford?"

"Nes here hogged the phone for an hour and a half, Ma. Honest to God, I politely asked her to get the hell off but she wouldn't."

"You exaggerate," I say, "because I was on the telephone myself less than a half hour ago."

"So what, it was still a long time. When's her old man coming to get her anyway, she's a regular pain, aren't you, Nes," he says, smiling and tenderly stubbing her in the small of the back with the shoe's blunt toe, "Nes the Mess."

"Shut up, you," she says, sitting up and fluffing out her sticky black shoulder-length hair. You could fry an egg in the oil from a single strand. Sometimes I think she has taken a secret oath not to look or smell good. Nesta is big bosomed and overweight and I should feel sorry for her but she is so determinedly unattractive. She wears spotty shirts and long droopy dark skirts, toeless leather sandals and dirty lavender socks. Her father, Peter Dwyer, was a marvelous man but he went to Paris on a Guggenheim and left me Ernestine — she looks like her mother only her mother is much thinner and lives with her second husband in Oahu.

"Nes," Cliff says in a deep sad voice, "it really destroys me to tell you this but, my dear, you have a distinct, er, smell. Now up in my room I just happen to have an unopened bottle of Old Spice after-shave . . ."

"After-shave!" Nesta says. She gets up like an old lady, staggering slightly as she rises. I see, bemused, that there are two pink spots in her pale cheeks — the exercise has done her good.

". . . which for only five dollars — five small buckolas — half of its retail value . . ."

"You . . . you *jerk,*" Nesta says, "you greedy jerk, you mangled gene, you bent chromosome without a home!" (Say, she is pretty good: soon she'll fit right in.) She walks by me with dignity, waddling only slightly under the long black skirt that makes her look like an apprentice nun. She has dead white skin and dark brown eyes.

Cliff booms after her in his sonorous bass: "When in clothes my lady goes, / Everybody holds their nose."

"Show-off!" she calls back. "Rot-burger! Maggot-pie!"

"Say, wait a minute, Nes," I interject pleasantly toward her wide receding back, "you're talking about the scum I love."

"Right!" she says, stopping at the kitchen door and holding her head up. "Scum-dumb. College dropout!"

Ow! That hurt. I can see Cliff fumbling for a comeback. Oh why did Peter leave her with me? I wonder who he sleeps with in Paris.

"Shut up!" Cliff yells as Nesta plunges into the kitchen. He turns to me, red-faced. "Jees, what a loser that girl is, Ma." I know — I should have asked Peter for more money, she eats like a shark. "I try not to let the guys know she lives with us. I mean, she looks weird and she acts weird. Just because her mother ran off, honest to God, half the kids in town have mothers who ran off."

"Fathers, mostly," I say, "let's get it straight. *I* am still here."

"Yeah," he says humorously, "I know. You had to take the rap when old Jenks got sick of us."

"Wrong," I say firmly. "You know that's wrong. Your father was not sick of you, he was himself sick."

"Yeah, Ma, sure, Ma. That's Lecture Number Ten. We had it once a week in Group at the rehab center — 'Adult Children of Alcoholics.' Kin I use the Tank tonight?"

"I thought you were working tonight."

"I'm doin' the lunch shift today so's I'll be home at four. How about it?"

Notice the speech pattern? Pure New Jersey! Cliff has gray eyes under straight black brows and would be such a great kid if he could get his life together. He wears a blue headband around his too-long black Navaho hair and often, as this morning, appears in his faded jeans without a shirt — mainly to show off his long, lean, tanned upper torso. Once, downtown, I saw my own son, all six feet two of him, sauntering along down Main Street. A new Chrysler station wagon chock-full of teenaged girls pulled up alongside but Cool Cliff just grinned and loped off with a kindly wave — they whistled and yelled and beat on the car door with their hands. Handsome Cliff! Girls have been calling him up at home since sixth grade.

"I think I told Alicia she could have the car, Sonny" (my old pet name for him).

"How come? The Bear's got wheels, don't he?"

"Doesn't he. Where's Alicia? Why don't you ask her?"

"Aaah, she's still zonked. Notice how she sleeps all the time? Pro'ly she's pregnant again."

"Oh shut up," I say, waspish once more. "Go up and ask about the car if you want but leave off on Nesta, will you? She's a paying guest. Also, I have a chore for you. I want you to take the big hedge clippers and lean out of the windows and chop. Do it today. It's getting really depressing around here."

"Always was," he says gloomily, and this stabs me in the heart. Well, after all, I have tried. Lots of things didn't work out but you-know-who was in there pitchin' every minute. In her own way, of course. "But I'm always true to you, darlin', in my fashion." Old song from another era. Jenks used to sing it to me when we went out on dates. He had a convertible, a good build and parted his curly auburn hair on the left. He had gone to Princeton and was attending Harvard Law School and I wouldn't sleep with him until we got married. That's how it was back then if you were serious about someone.

· · · 3 · · ·

I don't know why my life has turned out the way it has. One of my college professors — not the one I slept with — said I was brilliant and full of promise. I think of this walking into the living room with its sagging brown leather sofas glumly facing each other in front of the large, ugly, baronial brick fireplace. How I hate this house! I dream of incendiary action and a Winnebago rising from the flames. A week's worth of junk mail and newspapers lie scattered on the worn gold rug and someone has placed a thoughtful decoration in front of the gaping black hearth — a shiny pyramid of Schlitz beer cans. Last night's dirty supper plates abound — stale pizza crusts decorated with little black dots — mice turds. Isn't it time for the critters to leave for the summer home?

The kitchen is better but not much. Nesta refuses to clean up after herself, and since she eats nine times a day the drippings are constant. Here comes my treasure, my daughter Susan in her tennis whites, with a red-white-and-blue headband circling her golden brown hair and a marvelous flush on her tawny cheeks — my pet, my prize.

"Well, hi," I say, "how was the game?"

"Okay," she says, dropping into a chair and laying the tennis racquet on the round kitchen table. She lifts an arm over the chair's wooden back, exposing one blue-shaded armpit.

"Who'd you play with?"

"Oh, just Hal."

Good old Hal! I wish she'd get on to somebody else — this Hal irks me. "Did you win?"

"Of course, Mother, I always win. God, this place is a mess again, I can't believe it. I suppose the Loch Ness monster came out for her tenth munch of the morning."

"That's not nice."

"Why can't she clean up after herself? She thinks we're all her servants. I had the whole kitchen cleaned up before I left."

"I'll speak to her. How's Hal?"

"The same. We played singles first and then doubles with the Connell twins. I'm really getting sick of Hal. We were sitting around later and Hal said in front of them that his mother says you're eccentric."

"Say what?"

"Mrs. Pendleton says you're eccentric."

"Oh yeah? Well I may not be married to a big-time rich crook like Peewee Pendleton, but I don't think I'm eccentric! . . . Do you think I'm eccentric?"

"Doesn't eccentric mean, like, off-center? If it means that, yes, I think you are. Like, Ma, things around here are often chaotic and not orderly."

"Oh, I lack form, huh? Is that what you're trying to tell me?"

"I don't know. It's not really important except that Hal said it to be catty. Anyway, I think Mrs. Pendleton is weird." Susan strips off her square brown sunglasses and sits chewing a plastic earpiece, looking at the ceiling. "The leak's getting worse, did you notice?"

"Oh yeah?" I look up. "So it is. No, I hadn't noticed."

"If we don't get the ceiling fixed it might fall down."

"The sky is falling, the sky is falling."

"Well, okay, if you want the real truth, I think you are. Eccentric. But I don't care, not anymore. I accepted it years ago. You can be what you want to be, Mother."

"Why that's damn fine of you, Susie-Q. Only let me tell

you something: there's not much I've done that I wanted to do. Did you know that?"

She shrugs. "Figures. Life is a bitch."

I think it's sad that she is seventeen and cynical, but on the other hand, I agree. "You bet and you better remember that."

She narrows her green eyes and says, "You're crabby and I know why. You haven't had a steady boyfriend for six months."

"Look who's talking! I wouldn't call Hal a boyfriend. That kid is the biggest crap-out I've ever met. Susie, you don't have to go out with him, you know. I mean, my God, you're bright and pretty — why him?"

Susie's head droops and she leans her gold-downed temple on a hand. Her coloring is different from mine — more like her father's — but she has my straight nose and my up-tilted eyes.

"I don't know, he's okay. I don't like him as a boy, I like him as a person. He's not, you know, pushy."

"Yeah? I think he has different tendencies, if you know what I mean."

"I don't care," Susie says, not looking at me and moving some toast crumbs around the table top with her fingertips, "he's just a friend. There's no pressure. I like going places with him, that's all. I don't want to screw around like Alicia."

"Susie, don't say that about your sister, you don't understand."

"Oh, Ma!" she looks at me fiercely. "For God's sake, Alicia's been screwing around since she was fourteen."

"Well, don't tell me about it!" I shout, and slam the coffeepot down on the burner. "I don't want to hear it, there's nothing I can *do* about it."

"Okay, okay, I'm sorry. So just leave me alone. You want me to get pregnant too?"

"Not right now but I hope you will someday. Someday when you're married."

"I am never going to get married, Ma. Never. You think I want to live like this?" Her face is contorted, ablaze. "You think I want to live the way Nesta's mom did and then look what happened to Nesta. Or look at Marcy's mom — all those kids and she's even older than you are and they are even poorer than us. Well I don't want to get married and have a bunch of kids and get stuck with them on no money."

"Well what do you envision, living alone forever?"

"I don't know. What do you envision — living alone forever?"

I turn away from her to watch the perk pot come to a boil. Aw heck, maybe I should have married Al Meyer and his Maserati, thus providing a "normal" male role-model for my kids. Anyway, they were all for it, thinking there would be more spending money, plus opulent ski trips to Colorado. I kinda liked Al, but he was, I don't know, encumbered. He had this enormous family, all very religious, and I didn't exactly fit in. He was such a nice guy but there was his sister Lorraine in her tweeds and the clink-clank-clunk of her jewelry and her gossip about goings on at the temple, not to mention the two brothers, the brothers' wives, their cousins, his cousins, but I liked his parents, a plump couple shaped like a pair of rosy tops who stood in the doorway with their arms around each other to greet me, they thought he was finally going to do it, forty-four-year-old Al has this girl, "so she's not Jewish, so she's not a girl, exactly, but at this point, Lorraine, who's complaining? He should live alone forever?" They liked me, I liked them, the kids adored Al, only . . . I don't know. I started feeling uneasy. Every time I find someone I think I like I start feeling uneasy.

"Listen, Susan," I say, "men are okay, some are even very nice. But you know what?" I pour us two mugs of coffee — black, bitter, strong, full of used-up grounds, a metaphor of my life. I carefully carry the mugs to the table and set one down in front of her. "You've got it kid, so use it. It's the Family Talent I'm speaking of. At least one artiste in every generation. Your great-grandfather, you know, was quite a famous photographer."

"Yeah?" Susan says sneerily, "and then who?"

"Why, uh," (I say modestly) "there's . . . ME."

"Sure, Ma," she says, "that's why we live in this *dump*. That's why we've got so much money. Ya know," (she narrows her eyes . . . she knows where to get at me) "nobody reads anymore, so why do you waste your time writing these novels? I mean, it's wholly unproductive. You could do something useful with your life."

Now why is it this makes me feel kicked in the head? Momentarily, I hate her — yes, hate her, my very own daughter. Here I have passed on to her the Family Talent and look how she repays me — just call me Queen of Leers! Besides, I have no reply. I don't know why I write books. At first I wrote to get away from the kids and Jenks, so I could sit in a nice quiet room by myself. Then it became a habit. I decide to ignore this silly ignorant child and forget it.

"What I do is my business," I snarl, "and as for you, you're going to be an actress someday, and don't forget it, forget it, forget it."

"Oh Ma," she says, "eject! Your tape is stuck."

"And then, when you're an actress, starring in a play by Sam Shepard, *then* come and talk to me about money. Meanwhile . . ."

"Yes?" she says, warily waiting for the kicker to come.

"Don't let the OTHER THING get in your way." I sit down

across from her and watch her face. I see that I have her interest at last.

"You mean sex," she says, shrugging and swiveling her face away from me.

"No," I say, "not sex. Love! Love is what gets in the way. Sex is just sex, it's love that's the all-time killer."

I watch her fondly, she doesn't lift her head. Strange advice for a mother to give, what? But who should know better than me? I like men — in fact one of the themes of my life has been looking for the perfect man. First of course there was the ab-original *ur-Vater,* my dad, Herbert Ledyard, M.D. My mother left him when I was thirteen and without question he deserved it. Boring? Oh my God. I should know, I was the one that got stuck with him. For four years I came home from high school every night — to him. Four years — honest! — of nonincestuous bliss. He never touched me . . . he never knew I was *there.* He had this way of being in a room with you or a life with you and not really being there at all. I tried different ways of getting his attention — I was good! I was bad! I got perfect grades! I got failing grades! Nothing mattered, nothing made any difference and so, when I was seventeen, I left home. Then guess who was labeled "Miss Persona Non Grateful"!

In due time, at nineteen, came the slightly older man, my famous first disaster, Jason, and following him, my infamous second disaster, Jenks, and ever since (I am more or less usually serially monogamous) several species of lesser disasters. But hey, it's not that I'm fussy. If only they didn't (each one) have some hideous basic flaw, like brainlessness or a penchant for Monday night football. Or if they're great they're taken, like, say, Gordy Parker, who I've liked since I first met him on a football weekend years ago. I drank too much that weekend and got sick in his car and he courteously handed me Kleenexes whenever I vomited out the car door.

"Ma?" Susan says, putting down her coffee mug and looking up at me so clear-eyed and innocent I tense, knowing a bummer is coming. "The thing I don't understand is this: how come you never divorced Daddy?"

Time to go to work! Ah my novel, blessed isle of peace. I frown and stand up and shake my head. "I don't know," I say. "Maybe because I never felt married, or maybe because divorce is so expensive."

And that's no lie. I pick up my mug, sip, then wend my way down to my dank basement workroom. I have an old desk, a typewriter, a table lamp, a palisade of bookcases and, for company, about fifty sleeping crickets. Next to the typewriter lies Claire's last book of stories, peacefully snoozing under its fuzzy coat of whitish dust. She certainly does write well, if you happen to like precision engineering. If she dropped one comma you would hear a fatal *crack*, like a piece of high-speed gravel hitting a windshield or a mirthful heart (mine) bursting with glee.

· · · 4 · · ·

On the humid Tuesday after Independence Day, in sensible black shoes and a modest dark red cotton dress only slightly sweat-stained under the arms, I become my other self (or one of them): Mrs. Bigelow, history coach to Barstow Summer School for dawdlers, doodlers, dreamers, dummies and defectives, also for students wishing to make a score of 800 on the College Board History Achievement Test.

This morning, the first of the summer session, we have a 7:30 breakfast meeting with the new headmaster, Eugene Quirt, Ph.D., in what used to be the refectory — ten years ago, the school still took in boarders. Now it is a day school and the refectory has become the Reading Room. The breakfast is basically a cheerleading session, with Gene piping into his megaphone at one end of the long table while Ida Cross Berryman (Latin) pours coffee from the silver urn at the other. Miniature Danish pastries are being passed around on a large doilied plate and Jennie Lou Wong (Science) is distributing paper napkins. The napkins are left over from the faculty Christmas party and show, in blotched colors, Santa laying a finger aside his rubicund nose. Gene makes merrie up in front, tells us what a wonderful, devoted group of people we are (i.e., underpaid) and then lets us have it with the bad news: Althea Miller will be with us again this session.

General groans. Jennie Lou Wong, standing next to me, mutters, "Shit."

Dr. Quirt — Gene — holds up one big meaty hand (the first thing he told us about himself was that he used to be a running back for Princeton). He's a large man with thinning brown hair and a wide smile. Big booming laugh. Big commanding voice. And a pea brain no doubt, but let's be fair, they say he knows how to raise money and the big problem at the Barstow School is lack of same.

It rained early this morning but now a bright sun breaks through the haze. The long refectory windows are filled with dazzling sunlight and the glossy shimmer of fresh-washed rhododendron leaves. I have a sudden nostalgia for a childhood self I never was — I want to play hooky. God, how very much I don't want to teach this summer. Oh for just a breathing space, a little time away from the endless purposeful march of history or its limping straggle, depending on your point of view, I've always favored the latter.

What, then, would I do today? Maybe drive into New York, go to a sweetly dim bar, pick someone up. Not just any guy of course (herein lies the problem) but someone acceptable on my terms: he would have to have a dong. Donglessness is grounds for elimination, as is inexperience, also narcissism. Oh wouldn't I like someone tall and nice-looking who doesn't think he is doing it by himself? So many of them (you do wonder what their wives are like) fall into two groups. There is the A group or "Oh do I feel guilty!" group and they do it, but they feel so bad doing it that they do it mainly to get it over with. Then there is Group B, the Narcissists. They do it but only to please themselves. In fact, my second time with Fred (also the last time) I pointed out that there was someone else in bed with him and he brooded for half an hour then walked out. See, he knew I was supposed to concentrate on him — his needs, his feelings. He loved flowers but it turned out that he liked those spare angular Japanese arrangements when I like big blossoming bouquets.

"Sorry, Gene, what was that you said? My mind" (heh-heh)

"must have wandered." Quirt's pale sempiternal eyes beam at me. Does he know? I'll bet he does. Some kind trustee or other no doubt filled him in on my horrid habits, but the kids like me and (this is my job protection) I can get them to do their work. He genially inquires how well, generally speaking, last year's seniors did on their history achievement tests, information I am smart enough to have right in front of me, printed out on 3x5 index cards — they did all right, scores very much in line with or better than (I am consciously droning, let him think I'm a drone) similar schools, the Hilliard School, for example, in nearby Glenoaks, and more blah-blah-blah-de-blah, this is a prodigious waste of my life, in my opinion. Hunched over my cards, squinting, mumbling, I am trying to give the impression that I am the very epitome of sexless pedantry, however, I do detect something a trifle ironic in Quirt's tone when he talks to me. So what, what can he do about it? Generally, even in these highly uncircumspect times, I have kept my social life off school property and out of town. In the last five years, a kind of sub-rosa singles culture has emerged out here in the 'burbs, but after Al I got disenchanted. I stopped going to Pal Joey's and the Lion's Paw. It was embarrassing to pop up at these bars with a date and find my kids with theirs.

Now we are sitting around courteously sipping black coffee — Jennie forgot to bring the Cremora — and someone, Mr. Harris (good old B.B. of the Music Department), leans back in his chair. Looking up at the Beefsteak over his glasses, he says, "But what on earth are we to *do* with Althea Miller?"

Bravo! There's a brave man. Quirt says (softly, sadly), "I don't know. Let's try our best one more time. Her family, as all of you know, has been very supportive of this school."

Meaning: $$$$. The Millers are Old New Jersey, something people outside of this state think doesn't exist. The Millers live in Short Hills and summer in Belle View, down at the shore.

The Millers have produced two governors and a couple of senators and Miller Community College. They have also produced Althea, who is fat, lazy and incorrigibly stupid. I can't imagine Althea sailing off Belle View, though you might be able to use her for ballast on a larger vessel. The meeting is over at last. Quirt raises his hand as if giving a benediction: "Good luck!" When I pass him, I shuffle coolie-style, drop my head and hunch, but it doesn't work, he says, "Ah, Mrs. Bigelow!" His voice is so rich, it sounds as if he dines on bloody beef and lunches on marrow. "I wonder if you'd favor me with an audience sometime this week, shall we say . . ." He reaches inside his navy blue blazer and brings out a small notebook, pops it open with a flick of his thumb. ". . . Thursday at three-thirty?"

I straighten up and respond regally: "Of course. I hope we're going to discuss my salary." When in doubt attack, although I offset the aggression with a sweetly feminine smile and a playful bat of my lashes the way in nineteenth-century engravings you'd see slaves cavorting on a dock around someone playing a concertina.

He winks. "I do think, Barbara, it's a bit early in the year for salary negotiations." Ha. Next I suppose it'll be a kindly, paternal pat on the ass. "But there are just one or two things I'd like to talk about. See you on Thursday, then."

I nod in obeisance then stride into my classroom, wanly grinning. Say. What is this? How can this be? Althea Miller is in my first class. I had her all last year, why isn't it Trilby Potter's turn? But Althea stuns me, getting something right in the first five minutes. We are talking about Charles II of England, called "a trimmer," and I ask where the metaphor comes from. A slant of light passes across Althea's fat flat features; she blinks her furzy lids and rolls herself up off the desk —

the word loll was invented for Althea — and says in her adenoidal murmur, "Sailing?"

"Right!" I say and think of Althea lolling around in a Snipe in Belle View Bay and such is the persistent drift of my thoughts this morning that I think of Gordy Parker. What I see is a boat with Gordy in it and there, by God, is Claire standing on a dock. Gordy's sailing away. Is it forever? Is this symbolic? Or maybe this is only my nasty mind again, inventing a situation that doesn't necessarily exist.

Driving home, I ponder my life. Hmm. It's not exactly the life I had doped out for myself when I was in college. Yes, indeed, I met Jenks — and Gordy — at the same Princeton football game. I was a senior at Vassar and for two weeks before that game I had spent most of my time drinking. In my dormitory room I would lie curled up on my unmade bed drinking sherry out of a paper cup, staring out of the window, watching the light dwindle, and all the ordinary soothing balms I'd used for pain most of my life — reading, thinking — were of no use. I had had a terrible heartbreak. People smile at young love affairs but the pain I had of this one had not been bearable and I guess in some ways I never recovered. I was a different person afterward. Something was destroyed, some ability to trust, to give, to take risks.

Still, that Saturday in October at Palmer Stadium the trees were gold-green, the sky was cloudless, intensely fiercely blue, and the sun shone like a blazing disc, an ancient barbarian buckle of wrought gold. It was hot in the sun so that you felt itchy in wool clothes. My date kept passing me his flask and I drank like a kid hooked on Robitussin, letting the scotch go down amber and fiery, hoping it would burn all the pain away.

He was a blind date gotten for me out of pity by a girl down my dormitory hall.

The game (at last) drew to an end and a slant of shade fell across our side of the stadium, and as if the stadium were a giant sundial began slowly encroaching upon the opposite side. I felt cold and sick. After the expansive air of the sunlit afternoon, there was something sad in this chill, a reminder of time, autumn, winter, loss, death.

A final point was scored, a cannon or something like it went off, the crowd roared then sighed and stood up, compressing itself into a funnel-like surge down the concrete steps. A drift of woodsmoke floated across the stadium and cut through the yeasty smell of spilled beer, and the Princeton band, straw boaters askew, drifted off the field in their disconsolate fashion — Princeton had lost.

I stood up, and fell down. My date looked amused, and then horrified. From somewhere out of the crowd my cousin Claire appeared with two men. Very soon I was wrenchingly, miserably sick and it was Gordon Parker who took care of me. We sat in his car — I kept the door partway open — and whenever I vomited, he patted my arm and handed me another Kleenex.

My date disappeared, Jenks took Claire to dinner, but the next week he called me up — I had no idea why. At first I thought Jenks was really in love with Claire and I was the next best thing. Later, after my ego had healed, I saw he was in love with me and I determined that I would marry him. In the first five years we were married, I had three children and Jenks had nine jobs. Soon Jenks himself was a full-time job. It seems ironic to me now — how I thought Jenks Bigelow would become my refuge.

· II ·

Claire and
Gordy

· · · 1 · · ·

"Come right in," Mrs. Nupp, Psychic, said briskly to Claire Parker, unlocking the screen door and flinging it wide. "We'll go sit in the kitchen — it's cozy there."

Claire blinked — the May sunlight was bright, the narrow hallway dark — and followed the woman's stout back. Fresh-pressed blue cotton dress with a yellow plastic belt right out of my childhood. And look at this kitchen. Same niche out of that time warp.

"Sit down," Mrs. Nupp said commandingly, "and we'll have some tea. Then you tell me a little about yourself. I have to have a few, you know, vibes."

The last word was jarring. Claire's whole sense of the woman and the dim little kitchen was small-town 1950s — not her parents' side of town either but Railroad Street down by the box factory. A rented, shabby-clean flat in a two-family house with a new "dinette set" in the kitchen (Formica table and chairs with awkwardly splayed legs made of bent aluminum tubing). What's that smell? Gas stove.

Mrs. Nupp set a steaming china teacup in front of Claire and herself sat down, folding her plump white hands complacently upon the table.

"Now," she said. "Tell me about yourself. You do something, right? But it's not a business, it's not a profession. Am I correct so far?"

"Yes," Claire said.

"You have a gift then. I sense . . . you write?"

"Yes," Claire said and thought uneasily, She looked me up.

"You have a gift, but you don't believe in *my* gift," Mrs. Nupp said, raising her thin penciled brows.

"I'm . . . not sure."

"You have a gift, so why can't I have a gift?" Mrs. Nupp asked boldly. Then forgivingly smiled. She had a shiny moon face, round pale eyes, and her blue-gray hair had been neatly set and sprayed. Two rooms away there was a noise (a snap followed by the crackle of static) and a TV came on.

"That's my husband," Mrs. Nupp said. "I could close the door."

"Oh no," Claire said, "it's all right."

"So. But something isn't right. You're not happy. Something's wrong in your work? No. Family."

Les gens heureux n'ont pas d'histoires.

"Your husband, but also the kids. Tell me about the kids. How many and so forth."

Claire took a sip of the tea — it was strong and heavily sweetened — and then put the cup down. "I have four children," she said, hesitated, but went on firmly, "I mean had. My oldest son died seven years ago. I have a daughter, Leslie, who's sixteen. She's a junior in high school and she's very athletic. I have a son, Todd, who's twelve. He's extremely bright."

"So it's the other one," Mrs. Nupp said, "the one you left out." Claire started — what did she mean "left out"? Mrs. Nupp, staring intently, leaned forward so that her large soft bosom pressed against her folded hands and Claire imagined she could smell the woman's warm skin — comfortable, old-fashioned aromas of Ivory Soap, laundry starch and fresh ironing rose from the neck of her cotton dress.

"Yes," Claire said and cleared her throat. "My other son. His name is Evan. We've heard from him but don't know where he is. If we could . . ." Then from the darkened front room came a terrible fit of coughing that went on and on like a locomotive out of control, ending in a gasping wheeze and the faint cry: "Marilou! Marilou!" Mrs. Nupp stood up and left the kitchen, shutting the door behind her.

Alone, Claire Parker felt overwhelmed by shame and weariness. Oh what am I doing here, she thought despondently. Maybe after all I am cracking up. She let her hand fall upon the table and, looking down, absentmindedly traced with her finger the pattern of the Formica — coffee-colored with creamy marble streaks and gold flecks. Who had a table like this one? Gordy, of course, in the Brookline apartment he shared with two other medical students. One night, he had cooked spaghetti for her and later, just for laughs, they went out to a small-town carnival in a hay-scented field near Weston. A hot black summer's night with the pink smell of cotton candy in the air and the exciting sizzle of strung-up electric lights. Kewpie dolls, a Ferris wheel, a merry-go-round — doleful lions, leopards, Lippizaners gliding by in stately rotation to the "Skater's Waltz."

That night they had their pictures taken together in a self-service photo stand that was enclosed by a tatty red velvet curtain. Their engagement eve — 1962. Claire was twenty-one, Gordon twenty-five: everything was going to be just fine. The Depression was long over so no one was worried about money. World War II was over, the Korean war was over, and no one would be silly enough (so they thought) to use nuclear weapons. Late fifties, early sixties, the Age of the Gilded Ostrich.

We loved each other, Claire thought, and we knew we'd have perfect children and we saw our married lives stretching out in front of us, one road going off between pleasantly patchwork hills into the yellow, sun-dappled distance: Oz.

This is crazy. I shouldn't be here.

The door opened and closed. Mrs. Nupp sat down and composed herself for a moment — a plump, forceful woman. She looked at Claire and half-closed her eyes. "You see," she said in a low voice, "there is something missing in your life. I don't mean your son. I mean something else and that is . . ." She opened her gray eyes wide and parted her lips. Her lips were thin and bright with pink lipstick. Claire expected a musical sound . . . la, la, la? . . . but Mrs. Nupp mouthed a word. What was it? Claire frowned. On the *V* Mrs. Nupp's small white teeth bit down into her pink bottom lip. Love! It was love! "Believe me," Mrs. Nupp whispered. "Please believe me. I can always tell. You must find love. Now give me what you brought."

Claire handed her Evan's shirt and at once felt her heart begin to pound.

This is awful! she thought. What will she say? She was suddenly afraid, her head hurt, her palms were ice cold, and as in a bad dream, where everything is very ordinary and very evil, she felt the kitchen walls bend and slip.

With a grip like cold iron, the woman grasped Claire's hands and cried out hoarsely, eyes closed, "Shut your eyes! Shut your eyes! Remember his face! See it! Feel it! What is it I'm getting? I'm getting something. . . . It's hot, but I can't breathe. Whew!" She coughed. "What could it be?"

Driving home, Claire thought to herself dully, A psychic! I'm a fool . . . and missed her exit off the Garden State.

· · · 2 · · ·

The Parkers' house was an old white house set behind a lawn, trees, and a circular driveway. The rooms were high ceilinged, cool and airy, there was a shady screened sunporch furnished with chintz-covered sofas and hanging plants; but after the first of May the family gravitated toward the long columned porch at the rear of the house — the Chippendale railing was great for perching, the back steps wide enough for impromptu games of gin rummy or hearts. Late that May afternoon, Claire went out to this porch with a colander of green beans to tail and top. Her daughter, Leslie, was playing tennis; her son Todd was collecting aquatic specimens at a nearby pond.

The screen door opened and closed. " 'Lo," Gordon said.

" 'Lo," Claire answered.

Gordon was carrying his scotch in a glass that said DAD in big, old-fashioned black-and-gold shaving-mug letters. Michael had given him the glass one year for Father's Day. Gordon had on his office clothes and a stethoscope dangled out of his pants pocket. Sometimes, when he came in a door or into a room, Claire thought, as startled as if he were a stranger, Why, he's handsome. His dark hair was going gray along the sideburns but still curled up at the ends, and his body — a handsome body — was thinner now than when he was young. It had acquired a tough, knotted, stubborn look; there was something less fluid, more rigid in the way he moved. It wasn't graceful-ness he lacked but spontaneity. Even his dark eyes had changed their expression, as if they'd been drained of vitality and what was left behind was mere doggedness.

He sat down on a creaking wicker rocker and said, "I am beat. I even yelled at poor Elaine today, so I decided to cancel tomorrow's patients and take the whole weekend off. When I yell at Elaine, I know it's time to quit."

"Poor Elaine, I'll bet she didn't deserve it."

"She deserves roses every day of the year. I couldn't function without her." He looked up at the peeling lath of the porch ceiling and said, "Did the roofer call back?" The ceiling was painted light blue, a tradition in New England where Claire had grown up.

"No, not yet."

"I think we're soon going to be desperate. There's a leak up in Leslie's room."

"And here come the bees again. I've sprayed and sprayed but they won't go away."

Carpenter bees had built a home in one of the big white columns, gouging it out, hollowing large arched entrances near the pediment — front and back doors.

"Sometimes," Gordon said, "I think this entire porch is going to fall on our heads."

"I guess you really had a bad day."

"Well, yes, you might say that. Fella had a heart attack in the office while I was examining him. He'd been telling me about his *father's* heart attack. I had to get him to the hospital and all that stuff, meanwhile something like twenty-two people were discommoded — everything all screwed up and Elaine rescheduling everybody. It was lovely. Your friend Sandy Lewis was the day's last patient."

"Was she awful?"

"No, in fact she was very nice. She told me she'd wait for me forever."

"She must be sick."

"She's fine, Jack is fine, the kids are fine, everybody's fine."

"She's an idiot," Claire said scornfully. "She's never been fine, she just doesn't know the difference."

"She knows. Do you?"

Claire thought, What about *you?*, but didn't say it. Instead she shrugged. If she dipped her chin an inch she could see the white rambler rose which fell like a snowy waterfall over the back fence. Gordy had planted the roses and the grapevines, she had planted the beauty bush and the flowering almonds.

"Oh," he said, "and Barbara called."

"Barbara? Which Barbara?" Claire knew at least three Barbaras.

Gordon frowned and flushed. "You know which Barbara. Your cousin Barbara."

"Huh. *Her.* Did you two have a nice chitchat? What'd she want?"

"To thank you for the nice time the other night."

"She calls you at the office . . . to thank me? That's marvelous! Someday she's going to cook dinner for us and I'll keel over."

Gordon abruptly laughed.

"And honestly," Claire complained, "I'm sick of talking to her. She's always prying. I get sick of her always wanting to know about my life. Doesn't she have a life of her own?"

"Maybe she thinks your life is better."

"Really. Could she possibly be that dumb?" Claire grimaced and thought, Now stop it. You're only tired. Out loud she said, "Nikki called this morning. She's coming east at Thanksgiving."

"She's not going to stay here, is she?"

"No, Gordon, don't worry, Gordon, she's staying with Mother."

"Thank God. Can I get you something from the kitchen?" He stood and she glanced up at him. Never exactly a classy dresser, lately Gordon just threw on clothes: he was wearing a glen plaid suit jacket with blue poplin slacks. Once she'd thought his lack of interest in clothes was a vanity, as if he knew how handsome he was and needed no special exterior props. Now Claire felt his haphazard dress was a painful way of saying, "So what? I'm shot."

"I'll have another glass of white wine, thank you. There's Almadén in the fridge." And wasn't that the oldest trick in the world, Claire thought, reminding her how interested Barbara was. But just how interested was she?

Two nights before, at the birthday barbecue supper she had given for Cousin Barbara's daughter who had just turned nineteen, Claire had caught Gordon in the kitchen kissing the girl's mother. In the pinkish twilight they were leaning against the refrigerator (and each other) under a hazy rainbow so redolent of alcohol that if she'd lit a match, she would have sent them both to heaven in a blaze similar to the fiery tail of an ascending spacecraft. They'd stood there, entwined, each with a drink in hand, the other hand groping or pawing, as she'd staggered through the swinging door with a trayful of dirty dishes. Claire, ever humorous in critical situations, had announced loudly over the heaped-up tray: " 'Lips that touch liquor / Shall never touch mine!' " and their heads, both dark, had separated, peeled away from each other (it was a warm evening) and turned, looking at her with the dazed expressions and limpid lit-up eyes of two animals caught in the glare of your headlights on a black back-country road. Claire felt she hadn't glared — only perhaps grimaced. She wasn't surprised, exactly. She'd always known that someday this might happen — Barbara was always mooning after Gordy — but she felt afterwards, as they both gamely, clumsily, tried to console her, like, well, murdering them.

Dammit. It had spoiled the party.

And she'd worked so hard!

And then, late, late that night she'd had an odd thought. It had drifted into her sleep like a little cloud and she'd playfully at first, then more seriously, grabbed hold. Let her have him. If she wants him so much, let her have him, it, the whole shebang. She was sick of it. Maybe they'd be perfect together.

Gordy came back out to the porch, kicking the screen door open, elbowing it shut, holding out her glass of wine. Claire took the cold dewy glass in her hand.

Gordy said, "What time do you want to go down tomorrow? We could leave early . . . say eight?"

"If we leave at eight we'll hit the rush hour at Perth Amboy."

"Well, what time would you like to go down?"

"I don't want to go down at all."

"You say that every weekend."

"Still, we go down every weekend."

"All right," Gordon said reasonably, "we can stay home. There's no reason we have to go to the shore every weekend. We'll be there all of August."

"I'm sorry," Claire said immediately, contritely, "I'm just feeling cross. Besides, Leslie told Andy Allen she'd crew for him on Saturday."

"Why don't we send her off and we'll stay home?" When he was younger Gordon had a sly, iniquitous sense of humor, and a fleeting remainder of this, like the ghost of a missing person, passed over his face. She turned her head away and remembered suddenly, just as fleetingly, how once after they'd been five years married he had gotten up from bed after they'd made love and had turned and looked down at her. She was lying on the rumpled Sunday morning bed exhausted and naked, with an arm shading her eyes against the sunlight. "What?" she'd asked, lifting her arm, but he'd only smiled down at her, so smugly and proprietarily that she'd sat up and punched him — it had come to her that he thought he owned — no, controlled — her body. He'd caught her hand in his and said, laughing, "You really hate letting go. What is it you think you're giving up?"

Hopeless, she thought now, we are hopeless, it is hopeless, and she said, "Oh why don't you all go down and leave me in peace up here? I'd so like a weekend to myself."

"All right, if you want. But what are you going to do alone, without us?" He said this teasingly, but his eyes had an anxious glimmer.

"One thing I plan to do is go see Ingalls and Conover."

"Both of them at once?" Gordon said ironically. "I doubt you can handle that."

"Ingalls is dead."

"Ah. This is the publisher Barbara mentioned? The Great Love? The youthful mistake?"

"The very same."

"So. We've established a dubious character here, but does he publish real books? Wait a minute . . . Oh, God. Isn't this Mother's big barbecue weekend? What shall I tell her?"

"Tell her?" Claire said. "Why I don't know. Tell her I loathe barbecues. Honestly. Sometimes you make me feel as if I married her."

"Well, you did."

"No, I did not. Besides, she never stops. She's always pulling and tugging and straightening and rearranging, trying to get us all into perfect shape. Why can't she understand? It's not her world anymore."

"It's not ours either."

"I know and I'm sick of it, whatever it is."

"So am I."

Claire jumped up and the glass she held tipped, spilling wine onto the colander of green beans at her feet. "Well, leave then!"

"Oh will you . . . look what you're doing! Sit down!"

"No, Gordon, don't talk to me like that! I'm not your dog and I'm not your patient. That's how you talk to me — as if I were one of your elderly patients. Stop being so ironic and careful. Don't you understand? Everything's going to hell here."

"Claire . . ."

"Look around, Gordon. Your kids are in trouble. Do you see that? Do you see how much trouble Todd is in? He has got to get out of here."

"Claire . . ."

"Don't you understand? He needs something else. This is no good for him. He's got to go away to school."

"I'll tell you what, let's talk about it after dinner."

"Will you be here after dinner?"

"I have to go back to the hospital for a meeting but . . ."

Claire snorted and slammed through the screen door. She went out to the kitchen and in a fury began fixing the elegant cold supper she had planned. She slammed a pan on the stove and got the shrimp out of the refrigerator for cooking. She got out a lemon and began slicing it, and as the shiny yellow fruit yielded its sharp oily fragrance, she nicked her left forefinger with the knife and immediately, a U-shaped triangle of dark blood appeared near the nail. Tears sprang to her eyes and she put the finger in her mouth. Gordon came to the kitchen doorway and looked at her, alarmed.

"What's wrong?" he asked.

She took the finger out of her mouth and slowly shook it, tears now streaming down her cheeks.

"Are the kids all right?" he asked.

She didn't answer.

"Claire," he said in a louder voice, "cut it out, will you? Either tell me what's wrong or go take a Midol."

"Oh shut up."

"Shut up yourself."

"You just told me to talk. Make up your mind."

"I'm too tired for this, really."

"Aren't we all."

"Is it Todd?"

"Yes, it's Todd. Remember last week when he came home all bruised? Well, he didn't fall off his bike. Some kids in his class beat him up. Leslie told me."

Gordon looked at a spot above her head. "I know," he said, and shrugged. "Kids."

"You know!" she cried. "You knew and you didn't tell me? Oh God, you are . . ." She couldn't find words and so, instead, she threw the knife she was using, an expensive Sabatier, across the room and it hit the plaster wall and harmlessly fell. Later, when she picked it up, she saw that the tip was bent. It would cost forty dollars to replace. Waste, she thought. It's all such a waste.

That night, at two A.M., Claire's telephone rang. She and Gordy had separate bedside telephones — calls for Gordy sometimes came at night through his office answering service and Claire, listening to the circular sound of the ringing, boring persistently through the dark summer air, waited for Gordon to pick up his receiver. At last she raised herself up on an elbow and groggily clamped her telephone to her ear. A woman's voice asked if she was Claire Parker — Claire H. Parker. "Yes?" Claire said, wide awake, heart thudding.

The woman's voice went on. She had something difficult to tell her.

"Yes?" Claire said again, straining to hear against the blood pounding in her ears. Tomorrow, the woman said, she should go to the Sixth Precinct Station House in Manhattan. It was on West 10th Street, in Greenwich Village.

"I don't understand," Claire said.

"Your father is dead," the woman said.

"Pardon?" Claire asked.

The woman repeated: "Your father is dead," and hung up.

Claire replaced the receiver and lay down, looking into the lumpy darkness. Relief. Oh my God, what a relief. Evan wasn't dead after all. Next to her, Gordon turned over under the sheet. "What's the matter?" he asked.

"Nothing," she said, "a joke, I don't know, go back to sleep."

Her father had divorced her mother, left the East Coast, and last she'd heard, eight years back, he'd died in a fiery car crash in Ohio. There had been a small family memorial service in Massachusetts. She hadn't attended. So. Anyway. It couldn't be. Rest in Peace, she thought, punched up her pillow and more or less promptly fell asleep.

· · · 3 · · ·

For many years, Claire and Gorden had thought of themselves as happy and blessed. Then, at the age of thirteen, Michael Parker, their eldest son, had died in a skiing accident. Three years later, his brother Evan had disappeared one dark January afternoon between hockey practice and dinner time.

It was Nora Purcell's turn to do the hockey practice car pool and when Claire finally called her, feeling fussily overmaternal, Nora told her that Evan had gone before she'd gotten there, the other boys had seen him walking down the hill, carrying his hockey stick and duffel. If only (Claire thought later) it hadn't been winter. If it had been June or April or October, she wouldn't have been left with the image of an exhausted kid sinking down in a snowbank and never waking up again. But lost in a snowbank in New Jersey? Off Route 78 or 24? Surely someone would have found him, picked him up, taken him home.

Which was the problem, of course. Evan often hitchhiked the couple of blocks across town between the skating rink and home and who knew what passing stranger, seeing an extraordinarily handsome boy — that thatch of white-blond hair, so evidently masculine and yet, at fifteen, the cheeks as gold-downed and rose-splotched as a girl's — who knew what passing stranger might have reached across the passenger seat of his car, flung open the door and said, "Hop in, kid." Always, when Claire had taken her children to museums or other outings in the city, she had held firmly to her son's arm — once, right in front of St. Patrick's Cathedral on Fifth Avenue, he'd been accosted by an aggressive foreigner.

So he was gone, without a trace. Two dour-faced policemen came to interview the Parkers and after the required three-day wait, a missing persons bulletin had been put out on him. The Parkers called everyone they knew and any place they could think of that a kid might suddenly have decided to go — it was exam week at Comstock High School and although Evan was a good student, the police had suggested to the Parkers that kids got funny notions at exam time.

They called Gordon's sister Muffy in Bernardsville. She was in the midst of a painful marital crisis and didn't at first comprehend what they were saying but no, she said at last, she hadn't seen Evan or had any word from him. They called Gordy's parents, who were spending a month in Florida. Gordy's mother sounded cross — there was a dinner party going on — and Gordy's father made light of the event — meaning to make things better, making them worse. When Gordy hung up the telephone, Claire had said, "How stupid," meaning: Your Awful Family.

They called Claire's sister in California. Nikki, who had been married three times, was living with a man half her age. He was a young French actor who had had a bit part in a Clint Eastwood movie but he didn't speak English well and he'd hung up on them. Nikki called back to apologize but she seemed a little out of it, high on something or other, and Gordon (who had never liked Nikki) hung up, saying, "That incredible nitwit."

They called Gordon's brother, Charlie, at his law firm office on K Street in Washington, D.C. Although Charlie was in the midst of a terribly complicated divorce — his own — he offered to fly up immediately.

"Oh no, Charlie," Gordon said wearily, "but many thanks anyhow."

Charlie called a friend of his who had had a runaway kid and sent them special delivery a typed-up battle plan — things to do, agencies to call, the names of several good private detectives in the New York area.

For a year after that, they had done all the things parents do when a child is missing. They hired a detective, a large, florid, white-haired, sad-eyed man well known in the business, who listened to them gravely, attentively. He had a large paunch and when he stood up his hands grasped his belt and hiked it upward — but he wasn't any real help — none at all.

The first year that Evan was missing they lived with a terrible constant fear, and then, not quite a year ago, just when Claire felt from the black look in Gordy's eyes that he had given up, and the detective had told them sadly that they could hope, of course, but that Evan must be "presumed dead," one morning a postcard had come in the mail. Claire remembered how lightly, disinterestedly, she had picked the thing up, looked at it, flipped it over. It was a picture of the Seattle space needle taken at night. The message, in ball-point pen, in familiar chicken-scratch handwriting, leaped off the pasteboard and stung her heart. It said, "Hi. I'm okay. Don't worry. Love, Evan."

Was it really from Evan? Together, each of them holding a corner of the postcard, Gordy and Claire ducked their heads, read, reread the card, decided it was. His handwriting, for sure. Hope revived. Claire cried, laughed, cried. "I'd like to kill him!" she said, waking up in the middle of the night and switching on the lamp. With her fist she struck her blanketed knee.

Why? Where was he and why had he gone?

Gordy flew out to Seattle, talked to policemen there, flew home looking exhausted.

Why?

There was no further word, life settled down again, more or less — less pain, more resignation. Only why didn't he call them or come home? Still, it was better knowing he was still alive, and he was older now, eighteen, not a baby anymore and had, presumably, survived thus far.

Claire, who had stopped writing, went back to work.

But nothing was as it had been before.

When you are in bad trouble, there are various things you can try. First of all, you can call on your friends. After Michael died, Claire's friends had taken her out to lunch — singly or together, once or twice, over the course of a year or so — and then they'd mumbled excuses and shoved off. Who could blame them? Their children were whole and well, they more or less loved their husbands, they were engrossed in the perfectly normal concerns of suburban motherhood: SAT scores and Mary's weight problem and what color to paint the dining room. And Claire sat like a stone among them, nodding, smiling, nodding, wishing they'd leave her alone, wanting to go home.

If your friends don't work out there is psychotherapy. After Evan disappeared, Gordon found a psychiatrist for Claire, but Dr. Macintyre had a bad habit of clearing his throat — small muted clicks came from behind his uvula — which of course Claire wouldn't have heard at all if she'd been able to say something. But she couldn't think of anything to say. She sat in the green leather wing chair in his office and twisted her rings or fingered the cool brass nailheads that secured the leather to the chair arms and her mind was a blank — not the clean slightly cloudy blank of a fresh-washed slate but the lowering blank of a sky before it storms, a sky that is thick with yellowish gray, like layers of steam escaped from a boiling vat.

She might have cried or screamed or spent a month breaking china but she didn't know how to do these things. She'd always been a good girl, the kind of little girl who is serious and kind and stubborn and shy, who keeps her hurts to herself and blushes when she laughs as if it were a crime or a shame to laugh. Well. Growing up, her family had emphasized self-control.

Once when she was eight, her mother had gotten for her a little beagle pup — they were a family that had always had dogs. One night, rather late, it had a strange sort of shuddering fit and then it lay down on its side and could not get up. Claire was terrified. Was it something she'd done? All night long, she lay curled on the floor next to the little dog, with its paw tucked into her hand, but when she woke up the dog was dead. She screamed. She couldn't stop screaming. Her father came into the room. He shook her. "Of course," he said in disgust. "If only you'd called us. It had distemper. How could you do this? This certainly was not intelligent."

As a family, they esteemed intelligence.

Claire knew she was intelligent. That wasn't the current problem. She could think. That wasn't the problem. Her mind, or that side of the brain in which intellection occurs, went ticking on with the stupid predictability of a well-wound clock. In a mechanical way, she functioned perfectly. She could easily run her household; she could balance her checkbook; she could read and comprehend works of considerable difficulty. She could even write — oh these boring heartless dead stories.

What couldn't she do?

She had lost the ability to laugh or tell jokes.

Music of any kind she found immensely irritating.

She couldn't make love, and she couldn't write about passion.

She had a husband, two lovely children, enough money, some talent, but nothing really mattered and she went through her days with the odd feeling that she was separated from life —

that between herself and the rest of the world there was a thick, unbreakable wall made of glass and this glass was both a shield and a barrier. She envied her cousin Barbara who could laugh and sing rock songs and sleep with almost any male and claim to enjoy it, and biennially produce a novel, which Claire would dutifully begin but never finish reading. There was something in these novels Claire found disturbing, something excessive and dark and baffling, like (she thought crossly) the root of an awful vigorous weed — the more you pulled and hacked at it the more it grew and before you knew it, it had taken over the garden — *your* garden.

After Gordy and the kids had left for the shore, Claire went up to her attic workroom. Seated at her desk, she rummaged listlessly through its center drawer, looking for nothing in particular. She found a used appointment book at the very back of the drawer and flipping the calendar pages (it was seven years old) she realized that the year she was glancing at was the last year in her life she'd been more or less normally unhappy or happy. She sat dully looking out of the attic window into the shining, twittering leaves of the mulberry tree. There was something she had to do today. What was it? Oh yes. Jason Conover. And after all, she would do something about the telephone call. Her father. Could it be? Why not? The Escape Artist of All Time. She stood up and purposefully went down to her bedroom to dress.

But Jason Conover, she thought. She twisted her hair up at the back of her head and pinned it. She put on a white piqué dress. The neckline of the dress made a deep *V* that showed her long neck and pretty clavicles. She put on small pearl earrings, a gold bracelet, slipped over her head a thin gold neck chain that fell into the deep shadowed *V* of the dress.

She looked at herself in the mirror — a stiff solemn face. She thought (as she always did), My chin's too big. She tried a small apprehensive smile. Better. Then she shrugged and turned away, stopped, looked into the mirror once more over her shoulder. At least her neckline was good.

Oh stupid, she thought. Stupid.

More hopefully, a voice in her head said softly, Maybe he's tall.

· · · 4 · · ·

The Sixth Precinct Station House was a new building with a simple brick base and a second-floor overhang of crushed stone interrupted by vertical concrete ridges. It was all very modern and accessible, like an elementary school. In Claire's imagination, the "policeman at the desk" would sit high up on a platform and look down in a menacing Kafkaesque perspective, but Officer Mayhew had a small table in the echoing stone and tile entrance foyer.

"Yes?" he said. She looked down at him. He sat behind a typewriter with a stack of large index cards on his left. He was a young man with a pudgy pale face stippled with acne scars that were oddly bluish, as if someone had pushed the point of a carbon pencil into a mass of bread dough. His blond hair was smoothly parted, his gray eyes behind rimless glasses were the eyes of an overworked teaching assistant at a prestigious university — cold, wary, red-rimmed. But he spends his life dealing with crooks not books. Crooks, kooks and victims; people in trouble.

"I hope you can help me," she began. "I live in New Jersey. Last night about two A.M. I got a strange telephone call. Someone was calling to tell me my father was dead. She told me to come here."

"What was your father's name?"

"Nils Hoffmann."

"Okay, how do you spell that, I don't think we have . . . no, nope, nothing on a Hoffmann." He riffled through the set of cards. "How old a man was he?"

She blinked, considering. "He'd be seventy-four."

He glanced down at a card in the splayed pile, picked it out with his fingernails. "Want to describe him? Just generally?"

"Oh, tall. Six two. Big-boned. Large features and wavy white hair. Blue eyes." And the curl of his lips — sardonic. And the tone of his voice — charming. Scathing. Professor Hoffmann. Appeared on the stage in many European capitals. Ex-head of the Theater Department, Gardiner College. "He had a long scar on one cheek." God. Which cheek was it? She couldn't remember. Wait. The left.

Officer Mayhew looked over his shoulder to an area partitioned off like a bank-teller's cage with chin-high opaque glass. "Hey, Burger, where's the slip we had on the D.O.A. yesterday at West Twelfth? Was that Klein and Williams went out? Hey, Williams? You want to talk to this lady over here?"

Patrolman Williams was a black policeman with a round face and a sympathetic look. His small almond-shaped brown eyes had tightly upcurled lashes. He held a Styrofoam cup of coffee in his hand and sipped from it as she talked. When she'd finished, he said, "Fits the description of the deceased only his name was Charles Wendell."

"Wendell?"

"W-e-n-d-e-l-l."

"Oh." She looked at him numbly.

"We went in 'cause some lady call, you know, say she worried about this fella Wendell. When we got there, he was dead. You lookin' for your dad?"

It was such a simple question, so naïve and heartfelt, that she regretfully smiled. "I don't know," she said. "I don't know if he's the one."

"We'll have to go uptown," he said. He pursed his lips and sipped coffee. "Any suspected homicide, suicide, that's a automatic PM. You want to sit down here for a minute? Officer

Klein and me, we'll take you soon as he gets in. You want some coffee?"

"No thanks," she said.

She sat in the back of the squad car. The springs were shot and the innocent odor of bananas rose up from under the floorboards. Officer Williams drove. He asked her, turning his head slightly, how she liked New Jersey. Fine, she said.

"Terry like New Jersey, too," he said, laughing at Officer Klein, a thin-faced young man with a dark drooping mustache. "He got a girl out there in the boonies." Officer Klein didn't respond. Claire bounced along on the spring-shot seat wishing there was something to hold onto, digging her nails into the corded edge of the vinyl. It started to rain. Water sluiced crookedly down the grimy car windows.

"You mean to claim the body?" Patrolman Williams asked.

"No," she said. The men watched her silently. They had taken up positions on either side of the mortuary desk. "Because," she said, looking down at the desk, "he abandoned us." It wasn't true — was it? — and the men looked at her steadily.

Williams said, "Okay. So you gotta sign a release then. Fill out these here forms."

She said, "I'd like to see his apartment."

Klein said, "It's sealed."

Williams explained, "That means you ain't supposed to go in and you can't take nothin' out."

She said, "I'd just like to see it. You see, when he left he took a lot of my mother's jewelry. He left her without any money. I'd just like to see if maybe some of her things are there. Maybe she can get them back."

The men looked at each other.

"What you think, Terry?" Williams asked. "Think it be okay?

See, miss, the apartment's not officially under us no more. It's under the public administrator's office. That's a whole separate thing. Legal and sticky, you know? I guess we could just drop by, Terry."

Klein said nothing, only looked at her with his black eyes and drooping mustache. Williams talked, Klein made the decisions. "Okay," Klein said.

They went back to the station house to get the keys and then drove to West 12th Street in the squad car. The house was old, the hall was dark, its pimply walls painted an oily tan color. She followed the policemen up the crooked stairs to the third floor. Apartment 3 had three locks on the door, the last one a police lock — when the key turned, it released the catch on an iron bar screwed into the floor that scraped as they pushed the door open.

The apartment was dim and smelled of food. The bamboo shades were down at the two back windows and the curtains, made of some coarse gray fabric, were pulled closed. It was a floor-through apartment, two large rooms, a small bedroom in between, a small bedroom to one side, everything shadowy, closed-up, with piles of papers everywhere and strewn clothes. At home, when she was small, he had been meticulous about his books, his clothes. Of course, her mother had done the picking up. At home, he had been something of a connoisseur of elegant modern furnishings — modern art, nineteenth and twentieth centuries, had been a special interest.

This place was furnished shabbily, with a few American antiques: pine, country. A dirty, sagging quilt was tacked onto the wall over a worn camelback sofa; there were rag rugs on the floor; a little rolltop desk; a dry sink near the front window was full of plants. A copy of an American primitive painting hung over the living room fireplace, a little girl in a red dress holding an apple.

She said, "Did someone else live here?"

"Not to our knowledge," Klein said. Williams amplified. "Neighbors said he lived alone. A quiet type. Kept to himself. Not even a TV."

They let her look through the drawers of the two bureaus, placed side by side in the tiny bedroom. Nothing that she remembered. Jewelry wasn't what she was after. She wanted to find some discernible trace of him and some evidence of his life with them — the life he had led before this life. However, there were no clues. No tucked-away snapshots of her mother, of Nikki or of Edward. She hadn't expected any of herself — they hadn't gotten along. The bureau held his underclothes, socks, handkerchiefs. The other smaller bureau contained only one drawer full of woman's clothing. Whoever the woman was, she obviously had not lived here full time.

She glanced into the closet — nothing that she remembered — and she had the odd thought that the ex-person she had seen in the morgue, the gray-faced, green-lipped corpse, was not, after all, her father. No. Impossible. The scar, become in death a livid lavender slash, was there. Growing up, her father had been for her (emotionally, at least) too much of a presence. Now she felt vaguely that there was too much missing.

"Thank you," she said to the policemen. "I guess there's nothing." They left, slamming the door behind them. THIS APARTMENT IS SEALED, said the official document taped to the door.

This is crazy, Claire thought. She walked the streets of the Village in a circle — Bleecker to Hudson, down Hudson, up Charles — stopping now and then to look listlessly in a shop window. She felt stunned and empty and something thudded inside her head as if it were a cracked bell wrapped in yards of thick muffling rags. When it started to rain again, she ducked into the doorway of a little restaurant and ordered chicken salad. The coffee was burned and the carrot cake so sweet her molars tingled warningly. Why did I order this glop, for heaven's sake? It's my German background. Growing up in a German family you suppress your feelings but doggedly eat your meals. Years later you find you are twenty pounds overweight but have malnutrition of the emotions.

But was that my father?

Of course it was he, Claire thought, sipping her coffee. Yet how strange. Was it possible that eight years ago it had all been mistaken identity? Or — really, how bizarre — had he staged his own death? And if so, why? A new life? Another chance? What was wrong with the old life, Father? We all worked to make it so perfect.

The restaurant table was covered with a green-and-white-checked oilcloth and plastic ferns hung in the dusty rain-streaked windows. Outside in the pelting rain a young couple ran by shouting at each other, the boy in a T-shirt wildly streaked as if with tears, the girl barefoot and holding her shoes as she ran. The girl was tall and her ankles under her long limp skirt looked strong and white.

Claire thought, Why would he want another life when he had it all anyway? It was all for him — the house, the cars, the parties, the flowers. Oh, those parties — we were introduced and handed around like little props. If you could try on lives the way you try on clothes.

I was how old when I found out?

Eleven.

Mama was in the hospital with pneumonia, in an oxygen tent. He was never home. I thought he must be at the hospital, too. Some nights he'd come home at two or three — my room was on the driveway side of the house and I would wake up when he pulled in, tires skidding on gravel. Nikki said, "He's got this girlfriend. Don't tell Mama, okay?" She smiled at me and went on painting her nails. Then she looked up again and said, "Listen. You've got to learn there's nothing you can do about it. Don't agonize. If she hated it so much she could get a divorce." Nikki was always my father's favorite. Every time she gets married she writes me a letter saying she's met the love of her life.

Wickham was a small town, everybody knew everything. When Edward came home from prep school I told him and he said with a bored look, "Yeah? What else is new? Where have you been?" And then a few minutes later (we were watching TV, an old 1940s movie) he started cracking his knuckles and then he said (with violins rising in the RKO background), "I'd like to kill him."

My brother Edward never married. He is a banker and lives in Paris. I wonder if he is a homosexual but we've never discussed it. We were never a family to talk about things. When he's in New York he takes me to lunch or dinner and we carry on the old family tradition — we don't talk about personal matters, we tell interesting anecdotes, reflect on the news, discuss books we've read. Edward is tall but black haired and gray eyed like my mother. There is a love and sadness between us — Edward and me — that is unexplainable. Yet, at the same time, Edward has my father's excellent eye, his sensibilities, his love of subtle discriminations. I wish he could be happy but I don't know if he is. It seems to me he is not. For all her marriages and affairs, I don't think Nikki is happy either. As for me . . .

Reaching for the purse she'd left on an empty chair, Claire

(instead) knocked it to the floor. It promptly coughed up a checkbook, comb, three lipsticks, a wallet, a packet of Kleenex and three sets of keys — her house keys, her car keys and the keys that she'd taken from under some papers on her father's desk.

· · · 5 · · ·

The publishing firm of Ingalls and Conover was located in a seven-story building on the west side of Union Square. Riding up in the building's tiny elevator Claire felt she must look bedraggled and sweaty; her bun of pinned-up hair was beginning to straggle downward, and the shoulders of her rain-spotted white dress stuck to her skin.

On the seventh floor, she stepped out of the elevator directly across from a receptionist's desk. Was this the right place? Everything at Ingalls and Conover looked temporary — there was a ladder upon a paint-speckled drop cloth and the walls were making a slow transition (left to right) from gray to mauve. The receptionist, a tall, plump, pink-faced blonde in purple pants and an argyle vest, was smoking and talking into the telephone. "Wait a sec," she said into the telephone and blew a stream of smoke out of the side of her mouth. "Who? No, he's not here anymore, he left a month ago. Who? She's not here either, she left in March. He did? He was? Oh. Well, do you think you could call back at a later time, we have quite a communication problem here. Well, I'm really sorry about that but there's nothing I can do at the moment. However, I'll certainly have someone call you."

"Whew!" the receptionist said, plunking down the receiver at last and sitting with a masculine hike of her pants legs. "It's mayhem here all right, maybe that's why I like it, you never know what's going to go next. Life in the break-down lane. Can I help you? You are . . . ?" She dipped her head downward revealing the dark part that rambled through her blond hair and ran a pointed fuchsia nail across the scribbled-over page of a notebook. "You're here to see him, right? He's not here, he's out having a late lunch. What time is it?" She craned her neck to look up at the round clock on the mauve wall. "Jeez, that late? Well come on in and sit down. Just make yourself at home, we're very informal here, it's not Alfred A. Knopf."

Claire followed the girl, who smilingly said her name was Etta, into the room where a row of three attached wooden folding chairs out of some Methodist church basement stood on center stage. Etta motioned, Claire uneasily sat. Climatically, the room was like a steppe with blasts of lacerating cold air moving east to west across incoming hall humidity. From this central room, she could see a circle of offices, all cluttered, book and paper laden, with sometimes a pair of crossed (male) feet upon the desk and sometimes a hunched female figure talking on the telephone and earnestly scribbling.

The trio of chairs was perhaps fifteen feet from an empty office slightly larger than the others. There was no one at the desk and through the windows — there were two — she could see streaks of silver rain and the blurred green treetops of Union Square. There were two black telephones on the desk — one was silent, the other rang and rang as if it were in pain and calling for help. The telephone fell silent at last — perhaps it had died. Time passed. Steppe life is monotonous. There was a tall, crammed bookcase to the left of the office door and Claire went up to it (this is ridiculous, what time is it? who is it I'm waiting for?) and pulled out a large book and immediately, as if the book had something secret to show her, it fell open in her hands to an old photograph of old New York. For a moment, looking down at the row of quiet brownstones, caught in a golden, soft-textured turn-of-the-century light, she felt queerly suspended, stuck in that gentle silence, as if time had indeed softly paused before shuffling on. When she and Gordon were first married, they had lived in a brownstone like this one, on East 15th Street.

That brownstone, long since crumbled into dust and memory, had been part of the row across from Stuyvesant Square. They'd rented the tall-ceilinged back half of the parlor floor and the only furniture they'd bought was a pull-out bed and a large gold-framed mirror to hang over the pretty red marble mantel. Claire had always thought the room resembled a dancer's studio with its floating unfurnished space, its long bare windows, its uncarpeted wooden floor and the large mirror that reflected the changing seasons as represented by a skinny but determined ailanthus tree that had grown up through the sour soil of the dank back courtyard.

They'd eaten their meals on a card table borrowed from Gordy's mother, the sofa-bed stuck at their most impatient moments. They'd bought a small cocker spaniel — rescued her from the hot, ammonia-scented, paper-littered window of a Third Avenue pet shop — and every afternoon, Claire walked Taffy twice around the square when she got home — she taught history in a girls' school on the Upper East Side.

They'd lived in the apartment three years. Two children had been conceived on the wickedly obstinate pull-out bed. It seemed to Claire that these early years of her marriage were so clear in her mind and everything later was a bright muddle, a mix of images and strange impressions. Really. Where was the man? What time was it?

There was a clock over the door — a twin to the clock in the hall — that smugly said three-thirty and then, to her astonishment, the officious clock faltered and at the same time the lights in the office flickered and typewriters paused and then the lights went out. A bolt of blinding blue flashed briefly in the east windows, followed by a crack of thunder that seemed to cleave the gray city air, turning it black. The lights came on again and it began to pour — waves of rain beat upon the windows. She heard the elevator doors open in the hall and turned her head. A strange tall figure stepped forward, rain hat pulled down and dripping tan raincoat wrinkled and sodden. He barked something at Etta, grabbed a stack of papers from her desk, then stalked toward Claire, glaring at her from under the hat. She saw the glint of glasses, a long pink face, a thin curling mouth. He seemed to be scattering papers as he walked and Etta the Receptionist flew along in back of him, calling out messages in a soothing, flutey voice and picking up papers. Behind Etta, shaking out his rain hat as he swiftly rolled forward, came another man, short and stout as a barrel, also in dripping raincoat, bald head gleaming, with brown-tinted glasses and a large cigar stuck in the corner of his mouth.

Etta retreated, both men passed Claire, glanced at her, then turned into the empty office. The short man flipped out his raincoat tails and sat down. Taking the cigar out of his mouth and waving it about like a baton, he said in a rasping voice, "Look, Jase, I'm not going to shit ya, this Blade Daggers babe has more holes in her head than an Appenzeller, famous rock singer or no. P.S. — her life's story is what in all kindness I can only call a monumental bore. Her real name, by the way, is Jane Brown. Thank God for the soaps — Jake's lifted whole chunks of junk from various daytime shows. She oughta be grateful. We're makin' her life outa art."

The tall man, meanwhile, had shrugged out of his sodden coat and tossed it onto a hook on the back of a door; he had removed the dripping hat and set it on top of the coat. Glancing at Claire, he removed his glasses and stuck them into his shirt pocket. Then he nervously combed his fingers through his straight brown hair.

In a voice like a rusted saw the short man said, "Her folks'll sue, of course, but what the hell, it's good for sales. Her mom is not and never has been a Percodan fan — she works part-time as a secretary to the local Lutheran minister. Her father is first vice-president of the Maple Grove, Iowa, Savings and Trust — he's been there for thirty years. He did not abandon Missus and Babe when Blade a.k.a. Jane was three months old. He does not have syphilis and frankly, as they say in the Old Testament, I doubt he's ever Known another woman. They're nice folks if dull. Her brother's an orthodontist in Cedar Rapids."

Jason Conover was tall and bony with a long droll face, a long thin nose and nearsightedly shuttered eyes that gave out only a shy beam of green; a loud sudden laugh — too ready; defensive, really — and an expression that Claire thought appealingly boyish and eager.

"What the hell is wrong with Val?" the short man asked. "I bumped into her on Madison Avenue last week and right there in front of E.A.T. she started in with a tirade you wouldn't believe."

At once Conover's expression altered into cold, glint-eyed wariness. "I would," he said stiffly, "believe."

"She flipped or what?"

"In a way," Conover said cautiously.

"Anyhow, she's mad as hell."

"Yes," Conover said and glancing out at Claire again, softly closed the door.

Ten minutes later, the door swung open, the short man stomped out and Conover leaned out of the doorway, motioning her to come forward. Inside the office he pointed toward the straight chair and strode around the side of his desk, caught his foot on something, stumbled, cursed ("Damn!"), reddened, sat down, slouched, brought his fingertips together and slowly wheeled his revolving chair around to face her, all the while keeping his eyes fixed on the desk top.

"So," he said. "You want to change your publisher."

His voice had a resonant, resinous cello-hum. He sat up straighter, placed his shirt-sleeved arms on the desk, looked up at her quickly from under thin brown brows. She thought it odd that he had on a blue button-down shirt and no jacket or tie, strange attire to go to lunch in.

Conover picked up a ball-point pen from the desk and tapped it softly on the edge of the blotter and cleared his throat. "I'm afraid I don't know your work but I do know your editor, Horace Upham. I have a very great regard for Harry. How is he?"

"Not awfully well," Claire said. She was sitting up primly and felt confusingly returned to seventh grade (not her best year) and this was the principal's office and she'd done something wrong — what was it? "He's going to retire soon and if he does" . . . she lifted a shoulder . . . "I'll certainly be without a publisher. There's a new editor in chief there . . ."

"I know," he said. He raised his eyes and immediately lowered them. "I've met him. Tom Greene."

"Yes."

The telephone rang and he picked it up and at once his voice changed, became ringing and clear and deprecatory. "Well, of course he can't do that and he knows it perfectly well. No . . . no . . . that wasn't part of our agreement. Not at all. Certainly not." He leaned back in the swivel chair and looked up at the ceiling and moved the chair slightly, impatiently, as he listened. "What? Oh come now . . ." There was a sneer in his voice. ". . . he can't really believe that. Well, have him call me then. Of course not today, I'm just leaving for the country. . . . No, not on Monday, I'm not here on Mondays. . . . Yes . . . yes . . . all right."

"Sorry," he said, putting the telephone down; immediately it rang again. This time, picking it up, his tone changed en-

tirely. "Laura, dear," he silkily murmured and he sat differ-
ently, too, turned away from Claire, half hunched over the
receiver. Girlfriend? Claire wondered and looked away. Or that's
the impression he wants to give. He seemed in some way to
want to impress her.

While he talked into the telephone she glanced around the
office. There was a wall of bookshelves to the left, books stuffed
into it every which way, and on the right hung a large empty
bird cage.

"Sorry," he said briskly, putting the telephone down. "Where
were we? Upham . . . Greene . . . Yes. Why don't you send
me the manuscript of your latest, and a copy of your first book
as well. It's stories you write, isn't it? Not poetry."

"Yes," Claire said, "short stories." She looked at him and
then looked past him — the air outside the windows had turned
black. There was a flash of light followed by a terrific clap of
thunder, and to her surprise Jason Conover leaped up, and like
a child squeezed his eyes shut and clamped his hands over his
ears. The lights flickered but did not go off, and slowly, warily,
like someone coming out of ether, he opened his eyes and
dropped his hands.

Claire, too, had stood up, and had gathered her wicker purse
to her bosom, protectively putting her arms around it. "What
a storm," she said and laughed shakily.

He was staring down at his desk. His hands, loosely folded
into fists, were lying upon a manuscript and she saw they were
trembling. "I don't know why," he said, "I've always hated
thunderstorms." He raised his eyes and, coming around the
side of the desk, said in a brisk, ringing voice, "I really must
leave now. We can go down together. Good gracious, have
you no umbrella?"

"It doesn't matter," Claire said, looking down vaguely at
her damp wrinkled dress.

"Yes," he said, soberly. She felt he was watching her with a curious, tilted, examining expression.

Outside in the teeming rain, they waited — self-consciously pressed together — under his black umbrella for a cab. At last an empty lit-up Checker swerved out of the traffic and crossed the rushing torrent of gutter water to pull up with a splash at their feet. Conover leaned forward to open the door for her. Getting in she saw that he had on sneakers.

"Goodbye," he said. Before he closed the door he put his wet pink face into the cab and softly asked, "Are you married? I mean to say, are you still married?"

"Oh yes," she said, hunched forward upon the seat, and without knowing why gave a despondent little laugh.

"Good," he said, "good," and nodded distractedly before slamming the door. When she looked out of the streaming window, he had turned in the other direction.

What a strange man, she thought. Something about him had frightened her. Getting into the elevator with him she had felt her heart beat in her ears. It was the kind of sensation she had when skiing, standing at the top of a ski run that she knew was beyond her skill — there was a sense of exhilarating challenge and a sense of fear. These last few years since Michael's death, Evan's disappearance, she'd become an excellent skier. She'd lost something that had always held her back — a sense of self-preservation. Now she took the hardest, iciest trails and she knew that time after time she was waiting for something to overtake her on some jagged gray icy mountain. So far, disaster and death had stubbornly avoided her.

"Where is it to, lady?" the cabbie asked. They were headed back into the lit-up stream of traffic.

"I don't know," Claire answered dreamily, then corrected herself and gave him the address of her parking garage. She settled back on the seat and looked out of the window. The city air, now a soft, billowing violet, was studded with blurred gold lights and jewel colors — red, green, gold — wavered and flashed like exotic fish caught beneath the gleaming surface of the wet streets.

Was Val his wife? And who was Laura? Oh, what business was it of hers?

Huddled next to him under the umbrella's sheltering arc Claire had felt a troubling sexual tension assert itself between them. He had cleared his throat three times.

Some Don Juan.

She sighed and plucked the wet dress from her thighs and reached up and pulled out hairpins to let the wet coil of hair fall down her back, separating the sticky strands with her fingers. So this was Barbara's great love, the man she claimed had ruined her young life. Of course that was years ago. And who knew the truth? There were always at least twenty-two sides to every story. Really, he seemed rather nice, hardly the classic leering Don Juan type, only bumbling and a bit shy.

Oh, Barbara! She was vulgar and ditsy and inclined to breathless exaggeration. Drama, drama, drama.

And, in his office, after the thunderclap, she'd seen, when he'd lifted his eyes, that they were a shocked black. And that moment, she had seen something in him that contradicted the commanding voice, the impatient stride — an anxiety that he had instantly veiled and that struck her as guileless and touching. She had wanted — what an idea! — to comfort him.

She laughed to herself so that up in the front seat the cabbie lifted his frizzed gray head and looked at her in the rear view mirror. He said to her sorrowfully in a Russian accent, "Missus! You would not be believing how today I am having worse day in my life." Then he told her — people always told Claire their troubles — a long tale of love and jealousy, passion and betrayal. Listening, Claire was sympathetic and amused. What

· 73

stories people made out of their own lives: every man a Vronsky, every woman an Anna Karenina. And why not? Still, some folks certainly overdid it . . . Barbara . . . her father . . . these self-absorbed melodramatic types. Their lives racketed by, like old-fashioned horse-drawn gypsy carts out of control. Drama, drama, drama. You stood there astonished, waiting for the smash-up. And always, they got out from under, walked away with a grin, leaving someone else to deal with the wreckage.

Not this time. She would tell no one about the events of the day. He, her father, had caused enough pain.

That night, lying alone in her great carved Victorian bed, Claire slept restlessly and dreamed of Jason Conover. In her dream, he was waiting for her near the elevator doors but the elevator did not stop, only carried her helplessly up to the next floor. When she stepped out she saw that the floor separating them was made of thick clear glass and the man smiling up at her wasn't Jason at all, it was her father.

· III ·

A Crisis
at
Barbara's

On Thursday, back from the Barstow School salt mines, I am in a rotten mood and to make matters worse, when I stare into the living room looking for this week's copy of *New York* magazine which someone has already heisted from the littered mail table in the front hall, there is my son, Cliff, stretched out on his back on the brown leather sofa, looking long and emaciated, with his bare dirty yellow-soled feet propped up on the sofa's arm, flopped over into a *V*, his face pale in repose, his mouth softly open and the whole room awash with the odor of beer. He is asleep, dead drunk, and he should be at work.

I stand at the side of the sofa and gently rotate his left shoulder. "Cliff? Clifford Bigelow? Can you hear me?" No, he can't. He is as one drowned and long under water. I start shaking his shoulder (it is covered with a ruby satin polyester shirt) and then pretty soon I am beating on him. He groans and turns on his side and says in his sleep, "Oooow."

Yeah, me too, buddy. I, too, feel like howling. Tired out, I sit tailor fashion on the floor and put my chin on my fist and ponder. Just what was it I did wrong? I tried so hard! I loved you! I read Dr. Spock until the cover fell off and so did the whole first chapter. You were my very first child and I loved you to distraction.

Cliff and I! We spent our days together completely alone, in a mother-baby world where space was measured by the inches between us and time by the arced span between feedings. I got up when you got up and slept when you slept and sometimes, if your father was out of town, whole days would go by, and I wouldn't see another soul or talk to anyone else. I read a lot then and it was an odd, bifurcated life: my mind so engaged — one airy blazing Oz or another in my head — and the warm, earthbound physical presence of your small sturdy baby body in the crook of my arm, suckling your dinner, your chin milky, your eyes a newborn's dark wandering blue. While you nursed I read novels, with the library book propped on two small cushions on the arm of a chair. And then, at a certain point in your lunch or dinner, looking down at you over the white moon-rim of my own blue-veined breast, I would see your eyelids flutter, they would change color, become a fatigued violet, and your eyes would roll, your head drop off to one side — asleep.

In the afternoons, we went for long walks, communicating all the while, you from under the carriage hood, cooing and gurgling, and I would tell you things: how much I loved you, what kind of day it was, what you would be when you grew up. When you were only five months old I taught you to sing. Holding you in my arms, I would hum something — an old show tune, a bit of Mozart, and you would arch your back and lift up your head and hit pretty close to the last note I'd give you. Astonishing! So much obvious talent in one so young. I told this once to a musician I knew but he only looked bored and nodded and said, "So what's the story, Barb? I mean on me." I don't know what went wrong. I guess I'd always planned for us a more or less outwardly conventional life and thought that whatever, my love would get you through. It wasn't enough. I wanted you to love life and instead you have totaled three cars and you told me one night that you weren't happy unless you were high or blotto. What was it you liked best in life? Being out of it. This was six months ago, after you came out of drug rehab. I don't know, I don't know. What is it that's wrong? You're so sweet and talented and amiable and screwed up.

Now Cliff groans again and in his sleep cries, "No, no!" and covers his head with his bent arm. He looks hopelessly immobile to me and feeling generally beat, I decide to go upstairs and take a bath.

My interview with Gene I, King of Barstow, went badly. He had all sorts of requests I didn't want to fill. First of all (he said, leaning forward over his desk and earnestly knitting his ham hands together) as regards the fall semester, how would I like to do a creative writing workshop for seniors? This would help counter the, er, unpleasant impression made on some of the, er, less-sophisticated parents by the exceedingly liberal content of my life-style which one Mrs. Dean, a mother and trustee, has described as purportedly "steamy." Mrs. Dean, a gaunt leftover from the Coolidge administration, with a whiskery iron jaw and many shares of IBM in her safe deposit box, is a direct descendant of Anthony Comstock, for whom this town is named and who lived here for a while. (Remember the Comstock laws? I'll bet you don't.)

How much, I asked Gene, would this extra assignment add to my already insufficient muniments? He looked regretful. "As a matter of fact," he said in his deep beef-juice voice, "I was rather hoping you'd do it as a professional challenge."

Get it?

Blackmail!

But that's not even all. Since Miss Burdett, the assistant physical education instructor, is concentrating on soccer and field hockey in the fall semester, she simply will not have the stamina to do the tennis team; and since so many parents support the tennis team; and since Gene has heard that I am an interested player (where'd he hear that?): how would I like to wear the "hat or shall we say visor" (ha ha) of tennis coach?

Sarcastically, and instantly trapping myself, I asked him if he wanted me to meet with the would-be creative writers at six A.M. — since the tennis team practices at seven.

"So you *will* do the writing!" he said, lifting his sage, shaggy, beaming head, and immediately, he stood and came around the side of the desk and took my hand, pumping it heartily, and then gently pressing it against his still-beating oxford-cloth-covered headmaster's heart. "Don't you see?" he said, gleaming dreamily down at me, his blue eyes brimming with empathy and his face burst-blood-vessel red, "This is a wonderful opportunity for you. If there is anything left in the fall sports budget after Christmas, we will certainly think about putting it toward Your Group. Meanwhile," he dropped my hand and put his own upon my shoulder and began sweatily steering me toward the door, "think of the inspiration you'll glean from these eager young authors."

I went to the teachers' washroom and did something I have trained myself not to do: I put both arms up against the Ly-soled white-tile wall and buried my face in my arms and cried. I am so tired. I am so damn tired. Oh what the hell, my life has turned to shit. The house is falling down, I can't pay the electric bill, despite thermal underwear and roaring brush fires in the fireplace we freeze to death in the winter. Pretty soon we will all have TB as in a nineteenth-century novel and lie around coughing up bloody sputum and drinking herb tea. We are poor, we are fucking poor and there isn't a damn thing I can do about it and when I get home, here is Cliff dead drunk on the sofa when he should be at work.

So I go upstairs to bathe, calm down and relax but of course there is no warm water, the hot-water heater hates me and sensing my mood has snidely decided to go on strike — it feels it should have retired years ago. I decide, therefore, to skip the bath, come down to the kitchen in a cotton robe and scuffs and a roaring bad mood. Cliff is up. That is, he is in a modified sitting position at the kitchen table with his head in his arms. Looking down, I am revolted by his stringy black hair and the fact that his pale blue headband is transparent with grease.

"Okay," I say, "what's up? Something happened, right?"

"Yeah," he says, lifting his head, blinking and shyly smiling. "I got fired."

"Oh yeah?" I say. "That is really great. What did they fire you for?"

"Well, ya know Jack, the assistant manager, I told you about him, right? How, like, he's this impossible asshole and also there is something seriously wrong with the guy 'cause he's, like, overly orderly, see. I mean, I been working there five months, right? Well, today he all of a sudden says to me, 'Hey, Cliff, didn't I tell you yesterday to get a haircut?' and I'm like goin' 'Hey, man, sure but I ain't got the dough, ya know? We don't get bread until Friday, besides, I had this same hair when you hired me and you said then it was okay.' So he goes, 'Well the Board of Health was here yesterday and they wanted to know who the kid with the dirty hair was, and didn't I know that long hair was against the state's sanitary rules?' See, Ma, I think he's lyin' through his teeth because he would of known that already, right? He keeps lookin' for ways to get me into trouble. So he says again, 'This is it, kid, go out and get it cleaned and cut,' and I say again, I can't on account of the financial straits are severe so he takes a fiver out of his pocket and crumples it up and tosses it at me — the way, you know, you toss a dog something — and he says, 'You can pay me back tomorrow,' and I say, 'Hey, listen, man, but no thanks, I guess not,' and he says, 'This is it, then, kid. You're fired,' and

I say, 'The hell with you, then,' and I step right up to the bar and I say to Mickey, 'Hey, Mick, I'm a customer now. I'll have a Kronberg and put it on my bill.' "

A Kronberg! What's wrong with Schlitz? There is a knot in my stomach that is queerly beginning to turn. "Why?" I ask.

"Why what?" Cliff asks. He has his head propped up on his folded fist and just rolls his head around slightly to look at me.

"Why couldn't you get your hair washed and cut?"

"Because, Mom," Cliff explains patiently, as if I am six and slightly backward, "I am twenty years old, practically twenty-one. I don't have to take his shit. Where the fuck does he get off telling me about my hair?"

"Then I'll do it!" I scream in a rage and I chop him on the back of the head with the side of my hand, so hard my hand hurts and he winces and puts his hand up to the spot and I get him again. "You dope! You loser! You bum! Get out, get out, get out! Who do you think you are, you snotty no-good! Who do you think you are, huh? You're throwing yourself away and taking me with you! I'm sick of you! I'm sick of your being drunk or sick or high, I'm sick of taking care of you. I'm sick of you! I want you out of here. I can't stand it any-more. Get out of this house!" and so forth and so on, and I am beating on his back and shoulder blades, yelling that he is a goddamn pauper that's who he is, nobody special, he has to take shit just like me, and this time I mean it, get out and don't come back and if you do I'll have the police pick you up. He is prancing around the kitchen with his arms up defending himself and I am getting in punches here and there — well, actually I'm not huge so I guess they really don't hurt but anyhow, I am hurting everywhere, as much as he.

Dimly, as beyond the footlights of a stage, I sense a dark, goggle-eyed throng lurking in back of the wide-open kitchen door. I am in the kind of rage in which the color red actually appears as a film over one's blurred vision. I want to murder this kid and he just stands there openmouthed, leaning against the wall, watching me.

"Go on!" I scream, "get OUT." When he doesn't respond, I run to the knife block nailed up on the wall and I take out the longest knife and rush at him. There is a funny look on his face, as if he is about to laugh, but instead his gray eyes turn round and gelatinous and there are gasps and scrambling noises from the half-hidden audience in the hall and all the while I am yelling, "OUT! OUT! OUT!" and waving the knife inches from his face. He backs out of the open doorway and runs for it. I hear his feet thudding up the stairs, then all is still. Blearily, I see Nesta's face. It appears as a scared white blob in the doorway, then withdraws. I stand there a moment all numb and drop the knife and sink into a chair. I think I am going to faint. I hear the pounding of feet back down the stairs — two and a half flights and then a giant thud as he hurtles the last six steps. Miles away the front door slams. Majestically, I move to the sunroom window and see my first-born, my son, flying down the hill in his ruby satin shirt with a khaki duffel over his shoulder that is leaking clothes so that scattered upon the driveway, like the trail of crumbs Hansel and Gretel left in the woods to show their way home again, are items of apparel — here a pair of boxer shorts, there a T-shirt, a white crew sock, a bandanna.

I go out the front door and slowly walk down the driveway picking up clothes and when I have them all bundled up under my arm I go back into the house. Nesta is on the sunroom glider behind my copy of New York magazine, looking pale and smug. Susan is curled up in a wicker armchair, smoking and crying. She wipes her face with the butt of her hand and then buries it in her upper arm and Nesta, big-bosomed Nesta, ugly as always in her nun's black skirt, takes a giant bite out of an apple, making it sound like the crack of doom, and gives me a triumphant look. So, her look says, you've failed again. I want to hit her but I need her money. Maybe, instead, I will just poison her food.

For two weeks I didn't hear from my son and I didn't miss him. I went on about my life teaching history, dragging home groceries and correcting papers over the nighttime crap, crackle and pop of sit-com rerun summer TV. One Friday night I had a dinner date with an old friend of the fall before — Ted. Nothing came of it. He's had a heart attack and he suddenly looked washed out and ninety-two. I didn't want to go to bed with him. Instead, I sweetly patted his hand.

I didn't think much about Cliff at all except at night in bed after everyone else was asleep, and then I'd lie there for hours remembering how he taught himself to read when he was four and was writing poetry when he was six. A sweet kid, too. There's an old white wicker plant stand on the sun porch and on it a big pink candle decorated with fake cloth rosebuds — Cliff bought it for me with his own money: Mother's Day, the year he was in fourth grade. I don't know, I don't know. What went wrong?

I broke the cow that day, too. In my rage that awful afternoon I had knocked over various things in the kitchen — a basket of laundry that sat on the counter, a stack of unopened bills, and a cream pitcher that I've always liked in the shape of a cow. Jenks had gotten it for me the day Cliff was born. I had had a long painful labor and after it was over I lay flat, drained and doped. Two candy stripers came into the room to make the bed up around me and I lay there with my arms stuck out over the covers feeling happy and mindless and thin.

Then Jenks came in with yellow roses and a stapled-up bag from the hospital gift shop. He sat down next to the bed. I was too weak and tired to sit up but I wanted to hold on to someone, something, so I reached up for a leather button on his tweed sports coat and I clung to that instead of talking and he said, necessarily leaning over, giving me a whiff of his grass-green after-shave, not moving his body at all but carefully shifting his hands and bringing up the bag, "Hey, I saw this thing in the hospital gift shop and I don't know why, it reminded me of you." It was the cream-pitcher cow, not a placid china cow but one that was a little defiant with its forelegs planted apart and its head atilt at a no-nonsense angle. It was cross-eyed and had brown spots. I stared at it and then started to cry. For months I'd felt like a great dumb cow, and I was tired of it. How was I to know true cowhood had only just started?

The next day Jenks brought me a slew of fashion magazines — Harper's Bazaar, Town & Country — and some perfume. I looked at the white and black box wrapped in clear cellophane and then placed the box on the bedside table.

"Don't you like this either?" Jenks asked.

"Oh yes," I said, but it was a lie. I've never liked Chanel. My first lover's wife used Chanel — Jason, the lover I had had years ago when I was in college, the one who had hurt me so much. I threw out the Chanel but became attached to the cow and now I have broken it, smashed it beyond repair. Still, that day I picked up all the pieces and put them in an envelope and stuck the envelope in a kitchen drawer in back of the stainless-steel-ware.

For the next two weeks, although I didn't hear from Cliff, friends of his or Alicia's kept us posted as to his whereabouts. One night, Sergeant Tagliaro of the Comstock police force called. They had Cliff — he'd been picked up sitting on the curb in front of the Grande Movie Theater at three A.M. with a bottle of applejack in his hand, drunk. I told them I didn't want him and hung up.

The next week Comstock General Hospital called. The nurse at the emergency room desk told me that he'd been hit by a car — he'd been walking down Route 22 at one A.M. doing a careful tightrope dance on the dotted white line between lanes of whizzing traffic. Some unknown joyrider had swerved to hit him. He wasn't really hurt, just bruised, and completely intoxicated — he'd spent the previous six hours at the Lion's Paw Pub.

A week later, Tracy Boyden called, a friend of Cliff's from the seventh grade. Things were just starting to go wrong then, in the seventh grade, but I kept hoping it was adolescence, and anyway, I didn't know what to do about it. Tracy, a nice kid, goes to a local college as a day student and works two nights a week as a volunteer on the rescue squad. She told me they'd picked Cliff up from the alley in back of Gino's Pizzeria. She said he'd been in a fight and his arms were all cut up and Gino was mad as hell because the fight had taken place in the washroom and there was blood all over the walls and the floor. I threw on some clothes — it was one A.M., Cliff's favorite hour — and drove down to the emergency room in the snarling Tank.

He was in a roomette across from the busy nurses' station, lying on an examining table, with his hands held up in the air, wrapped in wads of gauze pads and bandages. "You can put your hands down now, Cliff," a nurse in a pantsuit said. Looking at me, she said as if it were all my fault, "He's getting to be our best customer." Cliff's ruby satin shirt had a tear down one arm and there were splotches of blood on his faded jeans. The scuffed toes of his cowboy boots were a deep incarnadine brown.

I went around the side of the table and looked down at him. His gray eyes were open and he was staring at the ceiling. He smiled up at me wanly — his skin had a bluish color — and he dutifully whispered, "Look, Ma, I got my hair cut." He had, too, one of those 1920-ish cuts, shaved up high on the sides, full on top. He reminded me of someone — Franz Kafka?

A man in a brown velour jogging suit and white running shoes came into the room, went to the sink, rolled up his sleeves and started scrubbing. "Hi," he said, "I'm Dr. Moss." I wondered where he'd been running to at one A.M. He came over to the table and started unwinding the mess of bandages.

After a certain point I looked away. I looked at the walls — they were pumpkin colored. I looked at the white metal cabinets and the stainless-steel sinks and the shelves stocked with bandages.

Cliff said, "I'm sorry, Ma."

"Oh honey," I said, "it's okay. But what are we going to do with you?" and then I thought, I shouldn't have said that.

Cliff said, "I cut my hair and I tried to get a job."

"Oh that's *good*, Cliff," I said, the way I used to when I'd read his English compositions in junior high school. "That's very *good*."

"But what the hell, Ma, nobody wants me. Everything's against me now."

"Oh come on, that's just an idea in your head."

"See, I have too many problems, Ma, really I do."

I looked up at the dimpled squares in the acoustic ceiling. The jogging doc looked at me over his gold-rimmed half-glasses and then looked down and went on sewing. The other kid had gone in deep, slashing at Cliff's wrists with a knife. I said to the doctor, "I'm Mrs. Bigelow, Cliff's mother."

"I know," he said with his head bent. I felt that I should watch him — as a tribute to his skill perhaps — but I couldn't.

Instead, I looked at Cliff's face. He had closed his eyes and every once in a while an eyelid ticked. Then I looked up.

"You do?" I said. "Have we met somewhere?"

"I have a daughter at Barstow. She's been in your history classes. We had a discussion about her last year, you and I. No. Wait a minute . . ." He paused in his sewing and looked up squinting. "It was two years ago. Three? Sorry. Time flies." He went back to his task. I looked up at the ceiling again. He was a tall, nice-looking man, with brown hair parted on one side and a thin rosy face (perhaps he really had been jogging) and bright blue eyes. He looked about my age and I tried to think what kid he resembled: ruddy, black-braided Sherry Hayward, she of the laughing eyes and weightless mind? Susan Duffy, big and horsey and banal, or perhaps pale-browed Nora Frazer, small, round-shouldered and timid, whose moist little hand crept upward in class as if she were surrendering her virtue instead of knowledge. Moss, Moss, Moss. Who has a father named Moss? It's so hard to tell who belongs to whom these days.

"I give up," I said at last. "Who is it?"

"Althea," he said, not looking up, "Miller. Her mother, my ex-wife, married a Mr. Miller several years ago."

"Oh," I said, "sorry." Then thought, I shouldn't have said that.

"It's all right. Actually," he finished his work — he had sewed up Cliff's arms and wrists in several places and wound them all up with bandages and tape and he looked pleased with himself — "I think it must have been three years ago."

"Three years ago," I said. "Well, I guess that was one of my bad years because I don't remember. No 'trivial, fond records.' Of course, I taught her last year and this year, too."

"Ah," he said.

Cliff opened his eyes slightly and smiled and closed them again.

"A good job," Moss said and held Cliff's right arm as if it were a piece of display bone, a paleozoological prize from some museum, and then carefully placed the arm next to Cliff's side on the examining table.

"You or Cliff or me?" I asked.

"Me," he said. "My job is a lot neater than Cliff's and a lot easier than yours. I've called in Dr. Parker."

"Gordy? You have? Why?"

"Because he is the internist on hospital call tonight and he can admit Cliff to our new Chemical Dependency Unit. Cliff? Cliff, are you still with us? Nope, he's out. We gave him some pain medication. I'm an orthopedist and I can't admit patients to that ward. I gather he's a relative."

"You mean Gordy? He's my cousin's husband."

"Are you from this area?"

"When do you mean, now or before? I didn't grow up here."

"Neither did I."

"Where did you grow up?"

"Here and there, mostly there. My father was in the navy."

"Really? My father was in the army. He was an army doctor for about ten years after World War Two."

"And you moved a lot."

"Oh yes. A lot. I didn't like it. You know what I always wanted to have when I was a kid? A horse and wagon, like a gypsy's wagon. My own place — on wheels. I must have read about it in a book."

He smiled. "That's odd. I used to draw cars that looked like houses. Back then they didn't have RVs or even vans. I thought I'd invented something completely different."

Gordy's head poked in the door. "Hi, Steve," he said. " 'Lo, Barb. Bad night, eh?" He came in and stood where Moss had stood — Moss was now at the sink scrubbing again. Gordy looked down at Cliff and shook his head. "I don't know," he said. "How do they do it?" He looked dreadfully white and tired and his clothes were rumpled, as if he'd slept in them. He had on a brown plaid coat and a blue plaid shirt and a rust plaid tie. He stood looking down at Cliff with his hands in his pants pockets and I stood with my fists clenched in my rain-coat pockets.

"Damn kids," he said and shook his head. Yes. He knew all right. Some kids from Comstock had been skiing with them that year and told one of my kids, Alicia, that when they'd found Michael Parker his head had been split open — you could look inside at brains and blood. Then and for months after-ward, cruel rumors circulated around town — that Michael had been on dope, that he'd been suicidal and had wanted to hit that tree. They kept him alive for a week at the Burlington Hospital. He was a beautiful kid, a wonderful skier. I remem-ber seeing him race in a giant slalom when he was nine or ten. As they say, he had all the moves. He was a handsome boy, light blond the way Claire used to be and tall even then. Com-ing around those gates he made it look as easy and graceful as a dance. Cliff stirred slightly and turned his head but didn't wake up.

"I don't know," I said. "Gordon, I am at my wits' end." The water had stopped running in the sink and I looked up — Moss was drying his hands and looking over at me. Then he tossed the hospital towel into a plastic-bag-lined bin.

"I'll talk to you outside, Gordy," he said, nodded at me and went out the door.

Gordy raised his hand, meaning, See you in a minute, and said to me, "Are you all right? Do you want something to help you sleep?" His dark eyes looked so tired I thought perhaps he could have used pills himself.

"No thanks," I said, "never touch the stuff."

"You're going to have to stay in the room with Cliff overnight, I'm afraid."

"I am? Why is that?"

He hesitated and then said slowly, "No one saw the other kid. They're afraid this might have been self-inflicted."

I stared at him and then looked down at Cliff, so peacefully sleeping. All my life since I've had kids I have tried to keep them safe. But how do you keep a kid safe from himself? My hand lifted and dropped and I placed it on Cliff's head — his black shorn head. Gordy reached out and put his hand over mine — a warm hand — and then the nurse in the white pantsuit came to the door. She was holding a clipboard.

"Dr. Parker?" she said. "Telephone."

He turned away and went into the hall.

· · · 2 · · ·

This life I am leading now is full of disaster and pain, something my vast reading in literature has not adequately prepared me for. After I married Jenks, for a long time my life was like a Chekhov story: quietly boring, full of unanswerable yearnings and a rich sense of suspended melancholy, like a pale, greenish summer twilight observed from a veranda — fireflies appearing in the dusk, the sweet smell of raspberries ripening in the back garden and zeroing in out of a shadowy corner the menacing whine of an unseen mosquito. It is always too hot in hospital rooms.

The cot they gave me kept collapsing, so I shoved it out into the hall and slept on the mattress. No, not slept, passed the night.

The mattress was covered with a rubberized sack and then with a thin bluish hospital sheet and the mattress squished and squashed under me, whenever I moved a limb. Cliff groaned in his sleep and mumbled.

I should have taken a sleeping pill.

I was afraid that if I took a pill he would climb over my doped body to get to the window.

But the window is barred.

His life, too, is barred — or so he thinks.

But what is it barred by?

Himself.

He is standing in his own way and I can't help him. He, himself, is the maze and I can't help him find his way out.

And I, too, am imprisoned — by my love for him and my helplessness. If only I didn't care.

I was always so good at getting out.

I got myself out of Livia, New York.

I got myself out of living with Jenks.

But I can't get out of Motherhood, and I hate feeling stuck.

Then I thought of my mother, summer afternoons lying on the chaise in her bedroom, reading and smoking until my sister Dora and I, sitting on the hall floor outside the half-closed door (which we were on no account allowed to touch), chanted, "Mommy, we're hungry, Mommy, we're hungry."

She'd stagger out of her room in a long blue-and-white-striped seersucker robe smelling of cigarettes, looking blue under the eyes and as sated with reading as if she'd spent the afternoon with an athletic lover. Barefoot, still in the wrapper, she'd stumble down the stairs into the kitchen and blearily start throwing pots around. She said to me once that she could have been a writer but her emotional needs were too complex. She said, warning me, "Don't get stuck."

Sometimes I have a strange thought — that I should pick up all the kids and move back to Livia, New York. I know this isn't a move through space but back into time — I want it to be my childhood again, at least the three years we had in Livia before she left. My mother, I mean. She left when I was thirteen. She didn't mean to leave me. She'd told me to come straight home from school that day but I was at the saucy, head-tossing stage and, instead, I went downtown to Bill's Luncheonette next to the boarded-up Roxy Movie Theater for a cherry Coke, a quick cigarette and a flirt with Jack Zotti, star forward of the ninth-grade basketball team. He never showed, I went home dejected, and scuffing into the front hall in my beat-up loafers, realized at once that they were gone, everything had changed, nothing would be the same again.

I loved my mother very much.

I always felt that she loved me more than my sister, Dora, even though Dora looked like my mother and I looked like . . . nobody. Well, that's not true. I have my Grandfather Abner Ledyard's coloring. Abner Ledyard, the knit-underwear king. Great-grandfather Ledyard built our Livia house in 1888, kept a cook, two maids, a gardener and a stableman. They had their own carriage, two horses, a sleigh, gave card parties and a dance every New Year's Eve for which occasion the paneled double doors between the parlors were thrown open. Imagine a cold blue night with the gas lamps lit at the front door and snow flurries in the air, snow falling on the midnight-blue, velvet, ermine-trimmed cloak of a lady ascending the stairs, her hands in an ermine muff, she wears an ermine toque. Why can't I sleep? I'm thirsty, I can hardly breathe, my nose is stuffed full of small round rocks. It must be ninety-five degrees in here.

It seems unjust to me that I have cared so much for my kids and so much is wrong. Why is it that someone like Cliff, with so many talents, prefers to spend most of his life as a zombie? And Alicia seems lost to me, off the track in one way or another, another missing person. Is it because they lacked a father? I used to wish that Jenks were home and then I'd think, God, no. He'd just get drunk.

I don't know what I expected, anyhow. A home, I guess. You see, except for two years I had this unsettled childhood. For years when I was small we moved from army post to army post and all I thought I wanted was to light somewhere. I had a vision of living in my great-grandfather Ledyard's house with a porch, an attic, a backyard, shade trees out on the sidewalk, neighbors, friends, community ties. Small-town life. I kept saying it. "Why don't we have a home? Everybody else has a home. When kids ask me, 'Where are you from?' I don't know what to say. Why can't we have a real home?"

So we went back to Livia, New York, and my mother left.

And then I saw what it was — she was home.

I saw her after that, of course — during school vacations. She married again in the summer before my senior year at Vassar and went to live in London. They would come back to New York twice a year — spring, fall — and stay at the St. Regis. She died eight years ago. My sister Dora married an Englishman and lives on a farm in Devon. Also the flat in London, that kind of life. He sells classic cars and organizes rallies. They have three children. We sometimes write but we're not close. Early in my marriage to Jenks I had thought of having the nineteenth-century family all over again — babies, nephews, aunts, uncles, doddering great-grandparents all seated around a giant, candle-lit, damask-draped table with a holly-bedecked roast goose on a platter in the table's center. Standing at the sunroom window, watching Cliff run down the driveway, his ruby satin shirt gleaming and his feet (he had put on shoes) in Nikes, lifting and dropping, blue tops, yellow soles, I thought: wanting the classic family I had gotten — ha! — a sort of ironic version.

So now I dream of a life alone, a life in a New York apartment where no one can find me. When I get up in the morning I'll be all alone and I'll drink my coffee all alone and read the newspapers all alone. No one yammering at me for love, attention, money, help, love, and this terrible headache I have has gone away. Life is so serene. I don't even have a lover (anyway, they get to be just one more kid to worry about) and my life is outwardly undemanding. My God, what's happening?

In the next room, someone is screaming.

Nurses and orderlies come running, there is a great commotion and Cliff sleeps through it all. I get up and go to the door — good time to get a drink of water. I walk down the dim, rubber-tiled hall — what time is it? I never wear a watch, three A.M. says the wall clock in the glass-walled nurses' station. Some of the patients are up and sitting on their beds looking dazed. The patients here on the "chem" ward are mainly kids, some as young as twelve — druggies, alcoholics — we live in the age of the chemically addled. The woman's stopped screaming now and is sobbing instead, "Oh God, God help me, I want to die, I don't want to live anymore." They've wrestled her down on her bed — two orderlies in white and a security guard in a blue uniform. A nurse is giving her a shot. She's a huge fat woman in a pink nightie and her large pale limbs jerk outward reflexively like those of a starfish, and then softly succumb. She moans, relaxing. (The next morning she keeps wandering into the room to talk to Cliff. She coos at him and calls him "My lovey darling." Cliff says to me, "Will you tell her to get the hell out of here?" And turns on his side and puts his face to the wall. "You tell her," I say. I want him to see that it is his life. He doesn't understand.)

I lie down on the squashy mattress again and think about my mother. I wonder why? Because once when I was four and had chicken pox I slept on a mattress in my mother's room, next to her bed. I know she didn't mean to leave me, she thought she'd get custody, but the humpbacked judge, the one with the long nose, "awarded" me to my father, as if I were some sort of consolation prize. My father sat in the Montgomery County courthouse in his brown suit that needed pressing, with his arms folded and his long skinny legs crossed, looking up at the ceiling. He looked tired and pathetic. My mother looked too pretty and citified, I could tell the judge thought that right away. She had on a black suit with a little Persian lamb collar and a Persian lamb pillbox with a black veil. I was proud of her. She looked stylish and beautiful. Later, driving home, my father didn't look at me or talk to me, and

I kept twisting my handkerchief, trying not to cry, weaving it in and out of my grubby fingers. The next day I got my first period and I called my mother long distance to tell her. Two hundred and sixty-five miles away, at her Barbizon Hotel room in New York City, the telephone rang and rang and rang but no one answered and when I hung up I felt dull inside. Empty. Dead.

When I think of my mother I think of the "studio portrait" I have of her that sits on my bureau at home. It was taken by Gurney Photographic Studio at 182 East Main Street in Livia, New York. Her head is held up on her long neck and her chin is thrust out in defiance. She always hated having her picture taken and anyway, the marriage was wearing thin at the seams. She hadn't properly combed her hair and the crown of light curls is appallingly messy. She doesn't wear earrings — she never did — but at the base of her throat she wears the small necklace of real pearls my father gave her for her thirty-first birthday. I like her broad fair forehead and her long straight nose and the high slightly bruised-looking Slavic cast to her cheekbones above which (she always complained) her uptilted eyes were too small.

Her eyes were blue-green, her dazzling beauty modified by a drizzle of summertime freckles across her nose. She was tall, slender legged, broad shouldered, deep bosomed — I look nothing like her except through the eyes. And her laugh, my mother's clear rippling laugh, like a current it seemed to race musically along, taking you with it, dizzily bearing you up and along until, looking around, you saw, astonished, that you had arrived at quite a new place. Oh, her laughter, which like the trail of her perfume lingered here and there in the house after she left so that coming around an upstairs corner near her bedroom you were suddenly seized (at last, at long last) with the plain empty truth — that smell winding deliciously toward you was from a branch of flowering linden, and the chiming noise you had heard was only the dribble of a broken faucet falling upon the rust-stained sink.

Sometimes I believe my father hated her. You begin to hate someone you love so much — I had that feeling for Jason. It's because they have power over you, they can hurt you, they can leave you, they can destroy you. My mother always looked at my father as if he didn't exist and so, very gradually, he grew thinner, transparent, as if he were mere projected light. He fell into silence the last couple of years they were married and I knew he'd given up when he let her have her own checking account. For years he'd handled all the money. It was his way of keeping her back. Then when I turned twelve, he let her have driving lessons and I knew what he was saying: "I give up." He couldn't keep her anymore.

> He put her in a pumpkin shell
> And there he kept her very well . . .

No. Wrong. He couldn't.

When I was small, we lived for a time in postwar occupied Germany. Lace curtains, snake plants, rubble, the smell of cabbage cooking. Bad Kissingen, Darmstadt, Frankfurt. All the time we lived on army posts, my father would talk about home.

Oh Livia, New York! My childhood loved it there. At last we were going there — home. I remember getting out of the car — a new blue Plymouth my parents had bought when they got back to the States — and seeing it, my grandparents' house, the house of my imagination, set up on a long lawn, with a wooden tower, a tilted wrap-around porch, freshly painted steps and a carriage house in the back. I was ten years old. Our dog, Angus, a Scotch terrier, leaped out of the car and lifted his leg on the maple tree. My mother laughed. "Home is the nearest tree," she said, pointing.

Then she looked up at the house and her mouth curled and she opened her purse and took out a cigarette. "All right," she said in a low voice, talking to herself, "so this hick town is going to be my life."

My sister, Dora, who was five, was still in the car, kneeling on the seat, and with both fat hands on the window was licking the glass. Then she'd rub her fingers in it, smearing the spit around. I bent and rapped on the window. "Pig!" I yelled at her. "Stop that."

"Oh don't call her pig," my mother said gently. "It's not nice."

Often, lying in bed at night, I think about the years I spent in Livia, New York. My small-town childhood has become a deeply embedded memory, so richly, phantasmagorically American with its gray post–World War II atmosphere brightened by the gleam of Eisenhower's teeth, exposed in his Kewpie doll smile. In my grandmother's big Victorian house we lived as if on an island but the truth was that part of town — the "nice" part of town — was already showing signs of decay. The elms died of Dutch elm disease, the big back-yards became asphalt turn-arounds, the sidewalks buckled and heaved and cracked and the wide porches of the old wooden mansions with their towers and stained-glass windows began to sag and tip as if the very foundations of life were in up-heaval. The town spread farther up the hill and out. Everyone wanted a "split-level" with attached garage. No one wanted a porch — patios were the big thing, and barbecues. Anyway, there was no one to see from a porch — people didn't stroll anymore, they drove by. Even my mother finally learned to drive. Then, as my father used to say, sadly, humorously, at the dinner table, there was no holding her. First she drove to Schenectady, then she made a trial run to Albany, later she got as far as New Paltz, New York. One night she called collect from New York City and said she wouldn't be back. She'd taken Dora and my father got me. I lived with him until I was seventeen and then I got myself out.

That summer I went to New York to live with my mother. My great-grandparents had died in the winter and on the money they'd left, my mother sent me to Vassar. Summers, I lived and worked in New York. I was a salesgirl in Gimbel's; in a bookstore; in a small Madison Avenue lingerie shop. I worked as a waitress in a Mexican restaurant, where I had to wear sandals and an embroidered drawstring blouse. I worked in an art gallery and the summer after my second year at Vassar I worked in an antique shop in Greenwich Village. Evenings, I wrote a novel, sitting at Dora's desk (she was at camp) in her room in my mother's new Gramercy Park apartment. "Stick with the writing," my mother said and looked at herself critically in the triptych mirror of her dressing table. "I sold a story once, when I was nineteen." She leaned forward, her chin delicately laid on her folded fist, gazing at herself in the glass. "I could have been a writer, but my emotional needs were too complex."

I remember she had on a pale peach silk robe. Because of her grandparents' will, her wardrobe had improved. She sat straight up and with her fingers pulled taut the bluish skin under her eyes. "Ugh," she said to the mongoloid in the mirror, "you look like hell." She stuck her tongue out, at me, at herself, mocking us and beauty, as if we were both brats of ten. Then she sighed and began taking hairpins out of her chignon — she had long wavy gold and white hair. She said in a low voice that she was getting married in England at the end of the summer. "Better patch things up with your dad," she said, glancing at me in the mirror again. "Your stepmother's a nice person. She wants you home."

"That's not home," I said scornfully.

"Oh, what is?" she muttered, and looking down pinched up a pile of the hairpins with her thin fingers and put them into a lidless porcelain box.

"Why do I have to apologize? I didn't do anything wrong."

"I know," she said practically, "but it wouldn't hurt to be nice. You'll need a place to stay."

"I can always live on my own. What's Dora going to do?"

"Go to England. George enrolled her in a school in London. Who is it you're going out with now?"

"Why?"

"Myra Cross said she saw you walking down Eighth Street leaning all over some man."

"So?"

"Watch it. Fools rush in."

"You should know."

She laughed — one short hard laugh. She took a Kool from the half-empty pack lying on the cluttered glass top of the dressing table and lit it with a match from the packet that said "21." George had taken her there in April. She'd said the food was okay, the drinks excellent.

"Is there some reason you can't bring him home?" my mother asked, waving the match to extinguish it. She held the cigarette like a man between her thumb and fingers and watched me squint-eyed because of the smoke.

I said nothing. What was there to say? He's married and

besides, I want him all to myself. But most of all, he's married. Still, you know all about that, don't you? George was married when you first met him.

I smiled mysteriously and, instead, asked her if she loved George Bell. She smiled crookedly with her mouth closed and turned her head on her long neck and looked out of the bedroom window, where, through a scrim of cigarette smoke, a pink sky was settling with a Boucher-like *pouf* upon Gramercy Park. She was paying a fortune in rent for this apartment. I'd only met my great-grandparents once, ancient, frugal people with large gnarled hands who had worked a New Jersey farm their entire lives. The farm was soon to become a housing development. "No," she said, "but I like him. And I'm tired now. It'll be a good life."

"You hope," I said.

She laughed, not happily. I turned away feeling a deep triumphant satisfaction.

The owner of the antique shop I worked in was a needle-thin woman with a beehive of black lacquered hair named Mrs. Furnacz. She had a jumble of stuff in the shop — all sorts of tarnished bronze Mercurys and greenish cast-iron Dianas holding up yellow pleated lampshades; time-blackened candelabras, blue-speckled gold-framed mirrors; jewelry kept in mounds and heaps in cardboard shoe boxes under the counter; shawls and rugs over chairs; piles of dusty mold-smelling books and everywhere the cats — six of them. No one ever stayed in the store very long because the whole place smelled of cat, and the cats jumped everywhere, frightening the customers.

One day as I sat at the ormolu-trimmed desk near the front of the store, eating my lunch and listening to WNYC on my portable radio, I looked up (slowly chewing baloney and mustard on white bread) and saw a tall, pink-faced, brown-haired young man shielding his eyes with his hands and staring into the window glass. Was he staring at me or the stuff? Hard to tell. I looked away and then the door tinkled . . . *terring* . . . and there he was, in blue button-down shirt and sneakers, regarding me cheerfully. He had an odd way of standing, gangling and stiff, and immediately I said to myself, Uh-oh, the Tin Woodsman. But he smiled and seemed at first so bumbling and confused and clumsy and likable and shy that I was disarmed and then he flung out an arm — I'm not sure why — and an eighteenth-century shaving mirror flew to the floor. Head to head we squatted together to pick up the pieces and he inadvertently pressed his knee against mine. The looking-glass came out of my salary. He never offered to pay for it, I was too entranced to ask.

The Tin Man! Often I wish I'd never seen him. Surely my life would have been different. Surely right now I wouldn't be lying here in this hell-hot room where my son lies whimpering and the other occupants of hell, poor lost souls, moan and cry out for mercy. This place alone is enough to make you disbelieve in the dream of a merciful God. The sufferings of these innocents!

There is a kind of person — man or woman — who quite purposefully seeks your love and once you give it to them despises you for it. They batten on you, despising you, needing you. They feed upon your crushed heart and relentlessly suck at your broken soul and when at last there is nothing left of you but a shell, they blithely discard you — toss you away.

If I hadn't met Jason!

But I did.

And then there was Jenks.

And then there was Cliff.

But I can't bear to think about him.

· 103

· IV ·

Belle
View

· · · 1 · · ·

Of course in late June he called, profusely apologetic for not getting back to her sooner, but he'd lost her telephone number and he had no street address. What *was* her street address? He'd put it right on his Rolodex.

The second time he called (mid-July) Jason said that again he'd misplaced her address — did she believe that?

Claire thought, and then said: No.

He laughed, heartily. There ensued a long looping conversation full of brash charges forward, vague retreats, dips and curves, faint star glimmers and black holes. He was cautious but persistent, his tone as decorously pushy as an angled knee pressing against one's thigh beneath the prim starched folds of a restaurant's damask tablecloth. His questions were abrupt, demanding; his answers vague and dodgy. Mainly, she felt sweaty. From this primary conversation Claire understood that he had assigned her, the Writer, the role of Flora: she was to be all verbal abundance — directed abundance — while he, the Editor-Publisher, was to be all scrupulous wintery reticence and understatement. She knew, furthermore, that out of long coddled habit he would expect her (despite his verbal parsimony) to intuit his feelings. She was willing, for the sake of the novelty of it, to go along with this hackneyed male-female formula, although various professors of psychology and *Ms* magazine had recently campaigned against it. Still, why not at least try? she thought, amused.

In fact, (in a sweaty way) she enjoyed the conversation. It reminded her of the time in junior high school she'd snuck out of the house to go to a local carnival with a boy in her science class. They'd tried the bumper cars, Dutch treat, and while Claire sat, trying her best to steer the unwieldy little car around the track, Billy (such was the kid's name) made love to her by slamming his car into hers. Men. Who could resist such pure-hearted lack of technique?

He seemed to her odd, quirky, both (as they used to say in junior high school) funny-ha-ha and funny-peculiar. The next week he called on no pretext at all, said bluntly he just felt like calling. What was she doing?

Now? Right now? Nothing much.

Oh. Did she know Jack Welling, the novelist?

No.

Oh. Did she know Sally Richardson, the novelist?

No.

Well Jack liked little girls. His current mistress was twelve. Sally, on the other hand, liked young men. Her current boy-friend was twenty-five years younger than she. Remarkable, wasn't it?

Why?

Why? *Why?* What a question!

He seemed to know a lot of sexy gossip. He told her he had no children but fondly kept track of various nieces and nephews. He and his wife — well, that was a story for another time. By the way, he hadn't read her collection of stories yet, but he would, he would, and in the fall when Mimi got back . . .

Who was Mimi?

Why Mimi was his good right hand, his most trusted editor. She was in Europe this summer — part work, part pleasure — due back in September. When Mimi got back they'd confer; meanwhile, he should mention that although he'd only glanced at her work, dipped in here and there, he had seen at once that she was a wonderful writer.

Claire smiled one-sidedly. She recognized flattery when she heard it, although in the swampy depths of her writer's soul she hoped it was true.

And meanwhile (he said), before September, since it was summer and all the world was playing, perhaps she'd like to come into the city for lunch — not a working lunch, just a get-acquainted lunch, you know, at some nice cool air-conditioned quiet little place.

There was such hopefulness — and lubricity — in his voice (a deep, beautifully resonant voice) that Claire, standing there in her very own post-breakfast kitchen, with a stack of Todd's Y Camp T-shirts on the coffee-splotched countertop, next to a bowl one-eighth full of milk and limp Wheaties, felt herself blush, a strange blush that began at her waist, like a rosy fire enveloped her breasts, her sternum, her neck, her face, gave off such a roaring dry heat on this humid July morning that she almost heard the resultant hiss of sexual steam.

And then (coward!) she shivered, lost her voice. Some verbal abundance! She stuttered out, Oh! She couldn't! Whereupon, she heard, coming across the telephone wire, the kind of taunting male cynicism that masks male anger.

Oh, couldn't she now. Well, if she was too busy doing whatever it was she was doing, being a (sneer) housewife or mother . . .

Oh, it wasn't that, she explained nervously. They were going away.

Away? Where to?

The shore.

Ah. A nice (said with the slightest hint of scorn) family vacation.

She didn't reply.

Well, then, perhaps in the fall?

Yes, she said simply.

When did the family plan to return?

She gave him a date.

He would call in September, he said, in a low, somehow threatening voice. And then, like a cello string snapping, his voice broke and he said huskily, if not convincingly, September, then. Goodbye.

She hung up the telephone. Uh-oh, she thought. Like a light teasing fingertip she could feel a trickle of sweat slide down her chest and fall into the tiny median tunnel between skin and cotton bra.

"Ma?"

She jumped and reflexively laid her hand on her bosom. "Yikes, Todd. You scared me."

"Who was that you were talking to?"

She smiled, reached out a hand and ruffled her son's hair. "Nobody," she said, meanwhile relishing the thought that she'd just told a lie. Goody. Her first step on the road to ruin. Well. He was not at all nobody.

She drew the back of her hand across her damp forehead. Whew! What soggy weather. The main rooms of the old house all smelled of mildew. It would be good to get to the shore.

Or — on the other hand — would it?

· · · 2 · · ·

Every August, Gordy and Claire rented a house in Belle
View, New Jersey, from a Mrs. Depuy, an arthritic old lady
long confined to a wheelchair, who lived in Olympus, Florida.
The house was a wandering, drafty Victorian pile built on the
dunes in 1883, with a lopsided porch that shielded the vast
living room from the seaside sun, but allowed, through long,
quaint, Gothically arched windows, a resplendent view of the
North Atlantic. There was a stone fireplace and an angular
Gothic staircase that, after making two abrupt turns, disappeared into the misty light of an upstairs hall, and the hall
itself went vaguely off in three different directions, nodding at
many tiny bedrooms as it passed.

Claire had, at first, loved their summer life in Belle View.
She was fond of the sad, weather-beaten old house whose stained
brown shingles made it look as if it were crying. It was too
big a house to clean and the spare furnishings were mere de-
crepit relics — broken-legged tables, dumpy chairs — from Mrs.
Depuy's own sojourn there in the palmy, balmy earlier decades
of the century. Now sand sifted in through the loose window
jambs and between the shingles and sometimes, after a bad
storm, lay in delicate tracings on the scarred wood floors. No
one much cared. Mrs. Depuy's children were scattered, two
of them were dead, and an agent handled the house rental
for her.

But the old ladies of the resort town, who had known
"Connie" well, talked about her as if she were still present,
and sometimes, sitting around the yacht club porch on a black,

humid summer evening (slicks of yellow light wavering upon the black bay water), someone would tell the story of how her father's yacht, the *Dauntless,* had gone aground on the rocks near the Belle Bay light during a terrible storm in 1917. Belle View was a small, close community and its ghosts — living and dead — were preserved intact by these sighing, slow-paced, meditative conversations on the yacht club porch — which were always accompanied by the slap of the bay waters against the pilings and the slow creak of the wicker rockers and the tinkle of ice cubes in glasses and the harsh rasping breath of old Admiral Selkirk (USN, World Wars I and II) who should have died years ago from emphysema.

The second time Claire saw Gordon — their second date — she had just finished her junior year at Wellesley. He met her plane at Newark Airport and drove her straight down the Garden State Parkway to Belle View.

"We're going to swim and sail and play tennis," he said, "and just relax and hang around."

Most of Belle View's current families had summered there for three generations, and their tawny, towheaded children had sailed and swum together and would (everyone knew) marry each other and come back to Belle View to summer when they were grown. Thus, Mrs. Parker was somewhat disappointed in Claire — she had planned on having Gordy marry that pretty little Lisa Landis, the Landises were such good old friends and they lived only two blocks away.

But Ellen Parker was basically well-bred and accepted Claire with great stoicism and every outward show of good manners, propelling her through the proprieties of New Jersey high life, just as, at that very first cocktail party, she determinedly steered Claire through waves of navy-blue-blazered gentlemen and tanned, golden-haired, Lily-attired ladies — who all held bar glasses that flaunted a navy blue flag with a single white star:

"The, um, family ensign," Gorden said, turning slightly red and looking away in embarrassment.

Claire loved Gordy for this — he had an absolute belief in the integral worth of every human being and a total disinterest in the outward signs of rank, prestige or power. It was his mother who jealously guarded the Family Position, but under Ellen's rather frosty good manners, Claire sometimes espied a sad little girl — Ellen's parents had divorced before World War I and she had grown up mostly alone, on her maiden aunt's estate in Peapack. She once said to Claire that she hadn't had a friend her age until she went to boarding school, and then she briskly raised her lanky body out of the chair (she was tall and bony and elegant, with an oddly proportioned but beautiful face — a large nose sailed jib-like out of it and her shrewd dark blue eyes, surrounded by a halo of very white hair, were startling). She went on, humorously, that there was nothing like a childhood lived mostly alone to prepare one for life with a doctor — Gordy's father was a physician, too.

In the many years of her marriage, this was the closest Claire had come to an intimate conversation with her mother-in-law. The formal curtain was never again raised, and indeed, in the Parker family, the manners were so good, and the family rituals so precise that anger or sadness or fear appeared only indirectly, as silence, or music: all of the Parkers were musical. Claire sometimes wondered how a woman like Ellen, who was always perfectly dressed and always in control, managed to take off her clothes and get into bed with someone — and that someone, a good head shorter than she.

So Claire's first feelings about Gordon were intertwined with her memories of that first sunny weekend at Belle View. Her own childhood, Claire felt, had been straitened, isolated, unhappy and full of pretenses; her own mother had been intent on making them all think they were happy despite everything — despite her father, despite their foreignness — and she had given them an odd, perhaps European upbringing. Until adolescence broke in, they lived at home as if in an enchanted castle full of books and art and each other. Gordy's world looked to Claire like heaven — easy, full of family and old friendships and old houses, boats and tennis and cocktail par- - ties, people and things that had known each other forever: "Why, my grandfather was Ellen Parker's mother's first beau!" It had seemed to Claire a world of webbed, shimmering ties, transparent but unbreakable, infinitely safe, infinitely secure, and she had gazed upon it with the wistful longing of the true outsider.

On the Thursday before Labor Day weekend, in the sum- mer Claire met Jason Conover, she saw Jenks Bigelow coming out of the Grand Union in Belle View, New Jersey. In stained T-shirt and faded jeans, carrying a single brown paper bag of groceries, Jenks looked like a scarecrow. His shoulder-length brown hair fell from a balding pink dome and blew about his shoulders in the brisk ocean breeze. He stumbled once, then pulled himself up and went off along the sidewalk in his knee- jerk alcoholic's gait. His face was red and raw — it looked pitted and eroded as if by sand and wind and spray. She knew he lived in a boardinghouse room in Duvernoy and that he lived with a woman, a big fusty-looking dyed redhead who worked as a barmaid and drank on and off the job.

Dear God, she thought, and adjusted her sunglasses and prepared her face in a smile. He didn't recognize her, despite the welcoming grimace on his face, and he passed her in a sweetish near-combustible cloud of alcohol vapors. When he shifted the bag in his skinny arms, she heard a trio of clinks.

Every Labor Day weekend, Gordy and Claire asked "the sibs

and their spouses" down to Belle View for a family reunion. In her rambling, rented house, in the comfortable but anti-quated kitchen with the walk-in pantry that smelled of vinegar on rainy days, Claire spent the early afternoon putting away groceries — fourteen bags, good heavens — and mentally planning the weekend's menus. Saturday night they would eat at the yacht club ("Plain food at outrageous prices," Gordy always muttered as he signed the chit) and Sunday and Mon-day they would barbecue. Tomorrow, Friday, she'd have some kind of pasta, something that would keep in case Charlie and Midge were late in arriving. Since Claire's brother Edward lived in Paris and Nikki, Claire's sister, lived in California, the re-union meant Gordy's family — his older brother, Charlie, and Charlie's second wife, Midge, and Gordy's younger sister, Muffy, and her live-in, Carl. Well, what to have? Lasagna. She'd make two big dishes. The kids would eat leftover lasagna cold right out of the refrigerator.

Claire sighed and looked out the window at the beach. It was a heavenly day with a playful green ocean rising and falling under a drift of white feather-flocked sky. The many suntan-oiled bodies that lay on the sand were not visible from her kitchen because the grass-speckled dunes first climbed, then dipped, hiding them. No one else was home. Penny, the golden retriever, lay asleep in a square of sunlight, Todd was sailing, Leslie was playing tennis; Gordon was working.

Claire seldom sunbathed but the thought of the weekend suddenly made her feel tired — all the beds to be changed, bathrooms to be scrubbed, meals to be gotten in what always seemed like twenty-minute intervals. She put on an old white bathing suit and climbed the dunes, looking for a private spot to spread the beach towel. She covered herself with a tanning lotion (it smelled of coconut) and then lay down under the sun. Not too long, she reminded herself, knowing that in just an hour she would look parboiled. As soon as she closed her eyes, she thought of Jenks. The encounter had been sad and startling. With what high hopes and great expectations they had all started out together twenty years before . . .

The sun's strong rays printed an afterimage on her eyelids — orange discs whirled in a thick blackness. She thought of Gordy and wished, suddenly, that he would come home early. This summer, with one of his partners sick, he had taken only a week's vacation. Perhaps he would come home early and they would sit on the porch and she would say, "I saw Jenks today," and Gordy would say, "Oh God, poor Jenks."

She turned over on her stomach and dug her toes into the hot silky sifting sand. Oh surely there was a way, some way to get over this cycle of anger and depression the marriage seemed stuck in. After all, they had Leslie and Todd, and for her, Claire, there were strong, intricate ties to Gordy's family — she had indeed married all of them, his mother and father, his brother and sister, too. Despite some quibbles these were enjoyable ties, a fabric of family life knit together over many years. Yes, tonight they would sit on the porch and have a drink and she would say, "Gordy, listen, I'm frightened. I met a man I'm terribly attracted to."

And Gordy would laugh and tease her and later on they would make love and it would all be the way it was before. Once upon a time they'd been a lucky family (Gordon had often said it) and they'd felt themselves, each one, to be vastly loved.

After all, Claire got sunburned and when Gordy came home — early, as it turned out — she was in their bedroom coating her face and neck with aloe lotion. Still, when she heard the back door slam and Gordy hollered his cheerful

"Hello!" she was filled with tenderness for him. When she came downstairs he was making himself a drink and he said to her in his careful, ironic way, "How are you? How was today? Survive another day in the old barn?"

He went past her into the library and closed the door.

In a moment she heard music — a Scott Joplin piano rag from the stereo — but the tinkling gaiety of the prancing piece seemed calculatedly distracting. She knocked at the door. He didn't answer. She tried the door handle. The door was locked. She called his name. He didn't answer. The Scott Joplin rag began again.

He didn't appear for dinner. "Oh now what?" she thought angrily. No doubt he'd fallen asleep, still . . . still . . . At eleven, feeling lonely, angry and shut out she climbed the stairs to bed.

· · · 3 · · ·

When Muffy and Carl arrived the next afternoon, Claire was mixing cake batter in the dowdy old kitchen. "Go right on up," she told them. "Same room as last year but use the blue bathroom, the yellow's got a leak. Do you like spice cake, Carl?" Carl, a man of few words, beamed and Muffy smiled at him so tenderly Claire longed for a moment to brain her — she was still angry at Gordy. He had gone off to work that morning as if nothing had happened, which was exactly the trouble — nothing had happened. When Muffy and Carl reappeared, bumping down the narrow back stairs together, Claire noted wistfully that some part of their bodies — hands, hips, elbows — always lightly touched. Together (they were almost never apart) they seemed totally in touch with each other and out of touch with the rest of the world, a trancelike state of interior completeness that Claire remembered from the early years of her marriage.

Muffy was tall and very thin, as straight as a blade, with a pinched white face, long chapped hands, black hair that hung in hanks and tufts, and beautiful dark blue eyes behind small black-framed glasses. She had survived a terrible marriage and, once divorced, she'd begun remaking her life. She took courses in crafts, learned how to dye fabrics and did so (to Claire's astonishment — Muffy herself dressed drably in navy or black) wondrously.

Muffy's lover was a potter. Carl Petersen was not long from North Dakota, a tall, shy, red-faced, blond-but-balding, near-sighted man with big, delicate-looking hands and a wide silent smile. Carl and Muffy were perfectly happy together, had no friends, had no pets, and seemed to need only each other. They had turned up this Labor Day weekend in jeans and black T-shirts that said in white letters: Craft Lovers. Ha ha, thought Claire. Muffy's black hair was tied back with a piece of fat red wool but cut-off hunks of it bristled over her ears.

"How's my mom doing?" she asked, while Carl went out to lock up their Toyota wagon.

"Oh beautifully," Claire said. "She looks wonderful and the lens implants seem to work." (Ellen Parker had had a cataract operation three weeks before.) "If you're just going to stand there next to the stove, Muff, you might grease those cake pans — give 'em a little shake of flour, too. You look so happy! We haven't seen you in ages, Easter Sunday, wasn't it? Life seems to be going by faster and faster. I hardly get over the Fourth of July when it's September and the Christmas catalogues start coming in the mail."

"I'm really looking forward to Christmas this year," Muffy said shyly. "We're going to North Dakota. I've never met any of Carl's family before."

"This is getting really serious, isn't it?" Claire said and laughed. Carl and Muffy had lived together for two years.

"And also," Muffy said, putting her cake pan down on the counter, adjusting her eyeglasses upward and facing Claire, her dark blue eyes shining in her thin face, "we're having a baby."

In her surprise, Claire stopped beating the cake batter. She set down the old yellow mixing bowl on the wooden counter and stared and then she went to the other woman and put her arms around her. "Oh, Muff, that's wonderful. Have you told people yet? When is it due?"

"Late March. No, we haven't told anyone, only you." Muffy smiled and dropped her head and said (in the tone of a little girl who has finally gotten a good report card), "I can't wait to tell . . . my mother."

Then Carl came in, silently gliding up behind Muffy. He put his big red arms crosswise around her and she glanced up at him over her shoulder and smiled. Claire finished beating the batter. She poured it into three worn tin cake pans and as she did so she felt a strange rush of emotions — happiness for Muffy, who had been unhappy for so long, but a sad wistfulness, too. How happy she had been waiting for Michael to be born.

"What's wrong?" Muffy asked Claire. "Are you okay?"

Claire turned her head away. "It's the nutmeg," she said. "It always makes me sneeze."

Charlie and Midge arrived at six, just as the sun was beginning to set and they were all sitting out on the front porch having a drink.

The wicker chairs on the porch were old, splintered, creaky, and when Charlie, who was six-four and weighed two hundred and forty pounds, lowered himself into a rocker, Todd, who was lying on his stomach on the porch floor reading a paperback copy of *Lord of the Rings,* plugged his ears with his forefingers and said, "Watch out, everybody, there goes another chair!" The chair creaked and groaned but bore up: several people clapped, Gordy said, "Wonders have not ceased," Charlie grimaced at Todd and said, "Naah to you, nephew!"

Claire smiled and went on knitting. She was fond of her brother-in-law. He could be pompous but there was also something sweetly engaging about him — his shaggy-dog rumpledness, the way his graying brown hair stood up in peaks and his ties always hung askew and his excellently tailored suits would immediately conform themselves to his heavy rounded shoulders, giving off a general air of comfortable sag.

When his first wife, Anne, had left home (taking the children), Claire felt torn apart for him. He sat in a large rumpled tweed heap in her living room, weeping and mopping at his tears with a large white handkerchief. Without his glasses, his big, big-eyed face had looked nakedly innocent.

Midge was ten years younger than Anne, a brisk, orderly, precise person who ran Charlie's life with the regularity of a metronome. She was always immaculately, fashionably dressed and her blond curls were so well placed Claire thought she must wear a wig. However, Midge was tone-deaf and when Charlie sang — he had a tawny, gold-edged baritone — Midge would sit with a look of panicky paralysis on her features, as if her entire face had been dipped in a clear waxy liquid. She reminded Claire then of the head of a Roman matron: one of those sightless staring stone busts in the Roman collection at the Metropolitan Museum.

In a way, music had brought Claire and Gordy together. In June, after her junior year at Wellesley, Claire had gone to spend a few days on Cape Cod with a college friend named Nancy Graves.

When the girls came in through the kitchen door with their bags, the boys (Nancy's brother and friends — they were men, really, juniors in medical school) were sitting at the round kitchen table drinking beer and playing poker. Claire remembered, later, how as she glanced at them, Gordy (she did not then know his name) had flashed a wide white grin around the table and spread out a row of winning cards with a spring-jointed thumb.

"Dammit, Gordo," one of the young men said, "not another full house. This is disgusting. I wanna check your pockets."

Gordy laughed — his square handsome white face showed deep dimples and his dark eyes were illuminated by the smile. His dark hair curled up around his ears and at the base of his neck and even in the kitchen lamplight showed reddish glints. (Later Claire would laugh at and love the rakish side of Gordy that was a gambler — the zest he brought to a day at the track, carefully picking his horses from a tout sheet, getting to the window just before it closed, standing pressed against the wire fence urging his horse on and — most of the time — winning, like the day just before Michael was born when, unspeakably broke, they had hocked a silver cigarette box and gone to Aqueduct on the subway. That was the day Gordy had won [in the eighth race, no less] the trifecta. "Yahoo!" he had roared and picked up top-heavy Claire and spun her around, and then they'd collected four hundred and ninety-nine dollars at the window and gone to the Four Seasons for dinner.) But that first night, he had raised his eyes up from the table and when he saw Claire something on his face changed: the smile held but trembled slightly, like a photographic print that is briefly, waveringly, dipped back into its solution. Then the smile faded, and a long slow serious blush began at the neck of his gray sweatshirt. He never dropped his eyes, Claire frowned and turned away and Nancy's brother stood up and offered to let Gordon ("clearly he's comatose") carry everyone's bags upstairs.

On Sunday night, they all went to bed late but Claire couldn't sleep. Moonlight fell in through the eyelet-trimmed curtains at the windows and through the window screens she could hear the bay gently lap at the stony little beach. Then, in the still house, the music began. Downstairs, someone was playing the clarinet and the notes, first richly somber, then higher, more plaintive and piercing, chilled her heart. He was playing sad, slow, yearning jazz which wandered into the first bars of the Mozart clarinet quintet.

Claire put on her robe and went down the stairs to the living room where Gordy, in his sweatshirt and old pants, was playing in the moonlight. He stood sideways to the window and the moon lit up his serious white profile and the silver keys of his clarinet. He heard her come up to him, but only slightly lifted his brows and went on playing. She thought he looked odd, enchanted, not a faun with a pipe — he was too tall to be faunlike — but someone sad and mythical. He stopped playing, wiped out the clarinet with a rag and put the instrument away in its red-satin-lined case. Years later Gordy told her, "I was playing for you."

They sat in the moonlit dark. He had a beer, she had a Coke, and they talked until almost dawn. He was from Short Hills, New Jersey, and his father was a doctor there, a cardiologist. His sister was a freshman at Smith. His brother was a lawyer and lived in a Washington suburb.

Her brother (she told him) had graduated from Harvard and was in Geneva in a bank training program and her sister had just gotten married and lived outside of Los Angeles. All the small facts they revealed to each other seemed magical illuminations; they seemed as moving and mysterious to each other as ships gliding on a dark sea.

He had gone to Princeton and had always liked science, math, music, ice hockey, sailing and gambling. He sometimes read poetry. Poetry, he said to her, was like music, whereas stories were not.

"Oh that's not true at all," she said, and laughed.

She was at Wellesley and was good at music, art, literature and history. She detested sports. Sometimes, she disliked herself. "I think I'm too serious, too conscientious," she said suddenly, and without knowing why, added that her parents were unhappily married. There was a moment of sustained quiet. The Graveses' summer house was furnished with simple early-American pieces and on the sofa where they sat someone had placed an old-fashioned afghan made of crocheted squares. She took up the afghan and wrapped it shawl-like around her shoulders. She said, "Do you think your parents are faithful to each other?"

He put his head back and laughed and she watched his Adam's apple bob in his wide neck. Oh God, he said, he couldn't imagine his mother with anyone else. Not that she wasn't attractive — she'd been beautiful when she was younger — but he somehow couldn't imagine it. Claire said, "What about your father?"

"Oh Lord," Gordy said, laughing and shaking his head. He pulled a cigarette from the pack of Kents on the table. "I doubt he's ever so much as looked at another woman."

She said she'd like a cigarette too, please, and he lit one for her and passed it to her. She said, after a while, that her father was unfaithful, not just occasionally, but continuously. It was awful for her mother. Her mother wasn't an American, she was German. Her father, too, had been born in Germany but had gone to college in this country and then, afterward, he'd gone on a trip to Germany and through friends had met her mother. He married her and brought her back to the States. "He makes her so miserable and she's got no money of her own and nowhere to go. It's like keeping someone in a cage and torturing them. All the time I was growing up girls would say to me, 'Oh your father's so handsome,' and I'd just smile. He's handsome but he's destructive. For a while he was an actor. You know something? He's always acting, always. I used to ask myself, 'Why?' My mother loves him and does every-

· 124

thing for him but it's never enough. Why does he need so many others? Why is he like that?"

Gordy had said nothing. He told her later he wanted to reach for her hand, but in anger, shaking, she'd drawn herself up into a corner of the sofa, hands clenched about her knees.

"Well," Gordy said carefully, "you know, it's funny. Sometimes people fool around a lot — have affairs — and they still do love the person they married."

"I don't believe that," Claire said sharply. "And it won't be that way for me." She laid her head upon her knee. "I want the whole thing," she said in a muffled voice. "I want it all together — something real."

Gordy said nothing in reply to this; she tipped her head and studied him. She thought to herself, I bet girls go after him all the time. I wonder if he's slept with a lot of girls.

Gordy said quietly, "Phil Graves used to go out with your sister Nikki. He was in love with her."

Claire said stiffly, "Nikki and I are opposites in every way." Then she unpeeled the afghan and stood up. She said she was getting cold. She walked by him — he was lying back on the sofa with his head on the cushion, watching her from under half-closed eyes — and she stopped in front of him, bent forward and, leaning over him, kissed him on the forehead.

"Nice," he said softly, and caught at her wrist, and attempted to tug her down beside him. She smilingly shook her head and pried his fingers away.

" 'Night," she said and went off, smiling at him over her shoulder.

" 'Night," he said, turning his head to watch her go.

Upstairs, she thought before she went to sleep that he was too handsome; she didn't trust handsome men. In fact, she didn't easily trust anyone, and so it was a long time, months,

· 125

in fact, before she admitted to herself that she loved Gordon Parker.

"We dropped by to see Mom and Dad," Charlie said. "Mom's doing really well, don't you think so, Gordon?" No one in Gordy's immediate family called him Gordy — his mother had never allowed it.

"Very well indeed," Gordy said. He had on a white knit shirt open at the throat but looked tired and pale around the eyes. He did not tan well.

Carl and Muffy were sitting side by side, looking out at the darkening purple sea, smiling and occasionally glancing sideways at each other, with their arms placed in identical positions on the wicker chair arms. All around them on the porch the air had turned a dusky shade of lavender.

"Let's see," Gordy said, rising, "who needs a refill?"

"Oh, look, Ma!" Leslie said to Claire. She was sitting on the porch steps with her back against a post, laying out a game of solitaire with the ancient dog-eared playing cards they kept at the shore. "There goes Trudy Mitchell with her new baby!" Leslie jumped up and ran, slip-slapping in her flip-flops, her long freckled legs flying across the boardwalk to the dunes where the young woman, a neighbor's daughter, walked with the baby held up against her shoulder.

"It's a boy!" Leslie cried, running back, her legs flying out at the sides. "It's six weeks old and its name is Teddy — not for Edward, for Theodore. It's got one blond curl under his bonnet!"

"Oh God," Charlie groaned, "how dull! How boring! How I hate talking about babies! Gordon," he bellowed toward the screen door, "hurry up and bring me my drink! Thank God," he went on in a calmer tone, "that I've done my all for posterity."

Claire glanced at Midge, who was staring straight ahead with her wax-mask look. I wonder why she doesn't like children, Claire thought. Too messy? Then, glancing at her sister-in-law again, she saw that under the mask, Midge's skin had turned the lightest shade of red and Claire blinked and looked away. So that's the way it is, Claire thought. They're trying. She cast a look at Muffy, who caught it and smiled briefly and dipped her head and pushed up her black-framed glasses. Across the ten inches of space that separated their wicker chairs, Carl reached for Muffy's knobby white hand. He cleared his throat. His big lips smiled.

Oh, here it comes, Claire thought, the Big Announcement. Muffy turned her head to look at Carl and shook her head: No.

Nope, not yet, Claire thought. What are they waiting for, a star in the east?

"Listen everybody," Claire said, "we're eating at home tonight and at the club tomorrow night. I made two huge dishes of lasagna and I hope that's going to suit everyone."

Midge said, lifting her small chin that was pink and shiny and shaped like a *U*, "Charlie can't eat lasagna."

"What?" Claire said. "Well why not? I've never heard that one before. Are you allergic to lasagna, Charlie?"

"It's the cholesterol," Midge said stubbornly, looking at the air above Claire's head. "Hasn't Gordon told you about Charlie's angina?"

There was a long taut silence, as if someone were stretching a thin elastic band, and then the sound of footsteps and the tinkle of ice in glasses — Gordy approached the screen door with his tray.

"I guess Gordon didn't want to worry you," Charlie said to Claire, apologizing for Gordy.

"About what?" Gordy asked, coming through the door that Carl held open for him.

"Charlie's not being able to eat lasagna," Claire said. "Honestly, Gordy, you could have told me earlier he was on some kind of diet."

"Well, no problem," Charlie said easily. "Despite what my warden says I don't think one small helping will hurt."

Claire stuffed the knitting into her work bag and stood up. "Gordon, I don't understand how you can be so . . ."

"Oh, Mom," Leslie said.

"It's not the end of the world, Claire," Gordy said, looking at her over his shoulder as he held out the tray to Midge.

"That's not the point," Claire said. "I could easily have fixed something else if you'd told me. You never bother to tell me anything. Never." She stepped through the screen door and into the house, thinking how unredeemable it all was — their timing was hopelessly off. When she reached out, he clammed up and this silence of his — this constant depressed, depressing silence — she found infuriating. Turning now to close the screen door (it had a loose hinge), she saw Steve Moss standing in the gloaming, in white shirt and white pants, standing just in front of the porch steps with his thick brows tilted up in a quizzical look. His hands were in his pants pockets and he looked pained.

"Hello, Steve!" Gordon boomed. "Come on up here and have a drink. Where've you been hiding all summer?"

Claire called through the screen door (with only a small grinding of gears shifting into her hostess role), "Hello, Steve, we're all going to have lasagna in a minute, and there's tons of it. Won't you stay and have some with us?"

In his low humorous voice, Steve Moss pleasantly called out that he would be delighted.

Despite the lasagna fiasco, the mood at dinner was casual and festive. Claire kept no good linens at the shore and so the diners at the long table ate from two kinds of plastic place mats. The napkins were paper (Kleenex extra-large), the glasses were plastic from the Walgreens on Main Street in Duvernoy and the plates were Mrs. Depuy's Fiesta-ware from the 1950s.

Charlie was pouting over his portion of lasagna. "Now that's underdoing it," he said, staring down at the minute square on his yellow plate.

Everyone laughed. Gordy said, "Pass the salad to Charles, please." And Midge said defensively, looking around the table, as if for an ally, "You see, he's got to lose forty pounds."

"Forty!" Claire said. "That's an awful lot. Charlie, why don't you ask Steve his secret? I've never seen anyone else eat so much and stay so thin."

"What is your secret, Steve?" Charlie asked, leaning forward seriously.

"I do my own cooking," Steve answered.

"Carl cooks a lot," Muffy said, glancing sideways at her love. Carl blushed and smiled beatifically down at his plate.

"What do you cook, Carl?" Claire asked, anxious to get Carl to do what Ellen Parker would have called "contribute."

Carl only smiled and Muffy said, "On Friday nights he cooks marvelous things in a big black frying pan, sort of inventions with onions and peppers and hamburger and Spaghetti-O's."

"Good Lord!" Steve Moss said, looking up in horror with his lasagna-laden fork in midair.

"And on Sundays," Muffy went on . . .

"Oh, heavens, Muff, do let Carl say something!" Claire said, laughing, then looked, puzzled, at her sister-in-law. Carl and Muffy, who were sitting side by side, had lifted their heads and were synchronistically staring through the uncurtained windows on the dining room's outside wall. Claire turned her head. A bizarre grinning face appeared in the first window, a face so raw and eroded it looked at first glance as if it were made of ground beef. And then the face turned sideways and the figure — in white T-shirt and faded jeans — appeared in the end window and then the screen door squawked as it opened. Oh no, Claire thought.

"It's Jenks," Gordon announced, somewhat grimly.

At once Gordon changed his countenance and rose up and walked toward Jenks Bigelow, who stood in the dining room's arched doorway, a grinning scarecrow figure, scourged and flayed by time and the seaside sun and so thin that even his narrow blue jeans hung slack upon his hips. "My God, Jenks! How are you?" Gordy was saying, shaking Jenks's hand and with his other arm around the man's shoulders propelled him toward the table. "Come right in and sit down. Claire? It's Jenks."

I know, I know, she thought.

And of course, Gordon led Jenks to the space between Leslie and Todd. Leslie shut her eyes and shuddered while Gordon gave her a slit-eyed look and Todd laughed, then stuck a nervous forkful of pasta into his mouth.

"How about some dinner, Jenks?" Claire asked. "There's plenty and I made it myself."

Jenks did eat something, not very much, but it seemed that he needed to speak to Gordon in private and so the two men, Jenks with his grimace and his high-stepping walk ("peripheral neuropathy," Gordy would have said) and Gordon solicitously touching the man's red bony arm, went off by themselves to a corner of the living room while Leslie and Todd cleared the table. He wants money, Claire thought, despondently. Claire could hear the murmur of the men's voices in the other room and then Jenks's high uneasy laugh and then the screen door squawked again and Jenks's face went by the dining-room windows in ragged, grinning profile.

After dinner, while Claire was upstairs using the bathroom, she heard a rising clamor, shouts and cries interspersed by repeated slams of the front door. When she came out of the bathroom, Todd ran past her in the hall, calling over his shoulder, "Oh hi Mom we're all going to Grandma's she just called." He thudded down the stairs but at the front door stopped stock still and, like the good soldier he was, said, "Oh gee, Ma, do you want me to stay and help with the dishes?"

She smiled at him. "No, but I have another request."

"Yeah?" he asked worriedly.

"How about a hug and a kiss?"

"Oh, gee!"

"Come on, be a good sport, just brace yourself, okay?"

She planted a kiss on the sunburned, squinched-up face he offered. He squirmed away, grinning, and bounded out the door (slam!) and called out, "I'll help you when I get back, okay?"

In the kitchen, dirty plates were carelessly stacked everywhere. Cold strands of mozzarella had cemented the dishes together. Claire felt exhausted. She tied on an apron and began running hot tap water over the plates, but wanted (really!) to crack each one like an egg on the edge of the porcelain sink.

*   *   *

Claire and Gordon lay on their twin beds in the dark bedroom listening to the ocean boom and fall away, watching the thin curtains move in the mild, salt-laden breeze.

Gordon tried to apologize but his voice seemed to Claire as distantly faint as if it had come from under the sea by transatlantic cable. "Thanks for doing dinner. . . . I should have told you about Charlie, I guess."

Oh why bother telling me? Claire thought. He's your brother. I'm just the housekeeper around here anyway.

The sea rose and fell and they were quiet and then Gordon said wearily, "Claire . . ."

The word, her name, stood out in the dark with painful emphasis, like one plaintive note of music, but Claire was unable to reply. She lay in the dark feeling utterly tired, thinking how useless this was, this so-called marriage. A marriage of what? Not minds and not bodies, certainly. Of memories, perhaps, but so many of their memories were painful and therefore repressed. The Parker family sense of tact. All evening long, no one had mentioned Michael or Evan.

And it was awful, this silence, like consigning her children, her babies, to oblivion, as if they had been . . . nothing . . . when at four and three (how clearly she could hear their voices), lying in their bunk beds at night, they would have intense treble-pitched conversations in the half dark and she would stand in the kitchenette, her hands in soapy dishwater, and lift her head and listen, amused, to the little dialogue. Evan's voice had been somehow stockier, as if he'd been born more at home in the world, and his questions were tough and persistent whereas Michael's answering voice had been graver, sweeter, philosophical. What did they mean, these people, by their ghastly grinning silence? As if the series of prints and imprints the boys had left upon her life would be wiped away like words chalked on a blackboard, or ever effaced by the blows of time's hammer upon her ancient, chalky, fossil-rich heart?

Gordon sighed and his bed creaked as he turned over in the dark.

Claire turned the other way, toward the windows, and watched the thin curtains blow about. The waves slapped the sand and withdrew, rose up again, fell. How endless it all was!

These memories, she thought dully. It's no use. We are stuck . . . mired in unhappiness.

· V ·

Mother's
Night Out

· · · 1 · · ·

"Nesta!"

Where are you, monster, ogre, wretch, half-formed girl-bitch-beast, you've left your smears (peanut butter, strawberry jam) all over the kitchen counter again.

Oh the mess, the mess, I can't deal with the mess anymore, the mess of my life, the mess in my head, the mess all around me. This sly awful house seems to exert a rude eruptive force, seething and bubbling, a cauldron coughing up dust, dirty clothes, cheese rinds, crumbs and paper litter every time I turn around. Nesta's not home today, it must be Alicia.

"Alicia! Alicia Bigelow! Where are you? Come forth villainess, hideous teenage slob!"

I wish I had some place else to stay, some cool, quiet anonymous hotel room with venetian blinds and a thrumming air conditioner. I could take off my shoes and sit on the bed and watch inane game shows on the inane tube. I love it when some blond booby wins and jumps up and down clapping her hands and screaming "Eeeeeeee!"

Or maybe a quiet clean guest room in Claire's house. The room I like best has in it an antique maple bed with a carved headboard and heavy turned posts. The bed is covered with an old quilt of red, white and green, sewn in the Rose of Sharon pattern; there is a small wooden trunk at the foot of the bed; there is a pine dresser and a lady's desk and a straight chair with a caned seat.

It's funny how after all the years I've been in *this* house I still feel like the major domo — none of it belongs to me. I never really liked the house although at first I was hopeful about it. I thought, We'll paint here, and wallpaper there. We'll cut back the scraggly woods and have a garden. Never got around to it. Every day, just getting by took all my time. Weekends, Jenks was mainly stuporous. He'd snarl, Don't ask me to rake leaves, I have work to do. Mostly, the work consisted of polishing off whatever happened to be left in the liquor cabinet.

Back in August I saw Gordy downtown. He was sitting in a booth at Norma's Whole Life Café having a hamburger and cole slaw. I was surprised that he was in town — he's usually at the shore then. I went in and sat down across from him. I ordered a cup of coffee and a whole-wheat blueberry muffin. "Hey, Barb," he said, "how's it going?" He looked as he always does lately — sad, tired, depressed. One of his partners has had a heart attack so this summer he only took one week's vacation.

We talked about Cliff, we talked about Jenks. When he said, "Claire," his face had such a grim, set look I felt my heart go thump-a-thump. So, I thought, they're not getting along. Plus, since she's been back from the shore she hasn't called me. Is she avoiding me?

Whatever could it mean?

Oh I have such naughty thoughts! For instance, if Claire goes off with Jason, that leaves poor Gordy all alone!

Despite his depression, there's a lot about Gordy that I like. First of all, just to be truly crass, he makes a good living which is something yours truly hasn't had the benefit of for many eons. Believe it or not, that isn't even all — there's something about him that reminds me of someone, some man from one of my other lives. When I look at Gordon I feel a strong inexplicable pull, as if, in my gut, just below my last rib, there's a band of elastic and this band is being tugged by an unseen hand. TWANG! It's not love exactly, but what a great beginning.

Of course he's also kind, sensitive, thoughtful. He has a steadiness that (after Jenks) just knocks me out. When I think of Gordon I think of warm, comforting things — blankets, wood fires, wine, good food. I think of music and laughter and sex, and from the constricted look on his face I'll bet he hasn't gotten much of that latter lately.

Susan's head pokes into the kitchen doorway. "For heaven's sakes, Mother, whatever was it you were bawling about? Alicia's not here, she's down at the Y working out in the weight room."

You see? Every time I have a reverie it's interrupted. "How come," I roar at poor Susie, "every time I step into this kitchen it looks as if the Visigoths have just left? Oh I can't deal with this anymore, I can't do it. Can not. The old engine's just wearing down, you people are wearing me out. Where is the Brute anyway?" Meaning Nesta.

"Where would she be?" Susie asks scornfully, while the wall phone commences to ding-a-ling. "She's at County Hospital of course, stroking Cliff." She reaches out a slender gold-downed arm and lifts the telephone to her ear. "Hello?" she says, in her most melodious contralto. "Who?" she says, bored and abrupt, so I can tell it isn't for her. "Oh, just a sec, here she is. It's for you," she announces in disgust. "Some man."

"Hello?" I shout, not yet having readjusted my modulation, and hoping it's Gordon. "Oh! Hi!"

"Who is it?" she hisses, standing eagle-eyed at my shoulder.

"Go away," I tell her and then to Steve Moss in my sweet soprano, "Oh no, not you, sorry, Dr. Moss, I live in Bedlam, someone's always cracking up. How are you? Thanks ever so much for what you did for Cliff — he's doing better. He's in County, now, in the alcohol rehab program. Uh-huh. Uh-huh.

Oh! Well that would be . . . very nice. I, um . . . pardon? Oh, I'd like that very much, that sounds like fun. . . . Why? Where are we going, Alaska? Not around here, no. How about New York? I mean, if we're going to go out . . ." ("Mother," Susie whispers, "will you stop pushing?") "we might as well . . . (shut up!) . . . go to the city, don't you think? Sure! Fine! Great! See you then!" I hang up. Susie, sitting at the kitchen table with her head leaning on a forefinger as if it were a pistol pointed at her brain, slowly, ironically, shakes her head.

She says, "You're out of practice."

"You! Do I butt into your *intime* conversations? No, I do not. Who do you think you are?"

"Who was that, anyhow?"

"What do you care? He's too old for you. Besides, do I give you the third degree on every phone call? . . . He's the doctor who sewed up Cliff's hand."

"Oh boy," she says, "how every cloud around here hath a silver lining. By the way, what ever happened to Fred the Gardener?"

"I weeded him out. Dr. Moss told me to wear pants. Why, do you suppose? Do you think we're going bowling? Susie, is there anything in your closet . . . ?"

He arrived half an hour late on a damp Saturday night wearing (strange!) a black nylon jacket with many silver zippers. I had flung open the front door smiling and looking past him for what I hoped would be a superb form of deluxe transportation, but off in the darkness there was only a coughing rumble.

"Oh, hi, Steve. Gee, are we walking?" He looked at me wryly and handed me a black helmet with a black Plexiglas viewing panel. It looked like a bowling ball and weighed about the same.

"What's this?" I asked, stunned. I had on Susie's black silk pants, high-heeled black satin sandals, a white silk blouse. Silk pants, he said, were not exactly what he'd had in mind, and I'd better go get my running shoes just for the trip. Did I have a rain jacket? It might rain.

So! Reclothed for the great New Jersey out-of-doors, I climbed aboard his quivering Kawasaki 800, put my arms around his nylon jacket and we roared through the black September night with the leaves a-rustle about us, shining green and gold where the street lamps beamed down, and the lights in far-off houses as cheerful-looking as the lanterns lit by gnomes in an endless fairy tale forest. Down Route 78 (east) a broad swath of a six-lane highway that spills like a cornucopia toward the External City and where, past the cluck of the ticket machines at the New Jersey Turnpike entrance (tickets popping out as naughtily as kids' tongues), we fly, skimming the road, lofting into the mild black sooty night and then, just past Exit 14 (Bayonne) as the turnpike stretches yearningly upward, see all of New York City spread out in a semicircle before us, a display of yellow diamonds on smoky velvet with the tall buildings to the north looking two dimensional, as if made of cardboard, with pinholes pricked out and a simple candle set in back, the way, when we were kids in grammar school, we made little Christmas scenes in art class to take home. Newark Bay is to the right, a black shining puddle, and Liberty, with her back turned, is holding up her torch. We zoom (surprisingly) through the Holland Tunnel and bounce down potholed Hudson Street, coming to rest at a tiny corner restaurant in Greenwich Village. I stagger off my steed. My bones have turned to jelly and the humming sensation in my crotch is not due to glands. In twenty minutes or so my teeth will stop chattering.

"Hope this place is all right," he says, once we are inside and seated. He twists his head nervously on his long neck. "Friend recommended it. My usual at home on weekends is Friendly's with Roger or for really big nights we go to Albino's

Spaghetti Palace." I suspect this hick-bit is an act — he likes to yep and nope a lot. There is something shrewd about his dark blue eyes that I like — shrewd and humorous. I like humorous men. He picks out wines for dinner, murmuring to the attentive waiter, and I notice he knows one wine from the other — a slicker in hick's clothing? I have stopped shaking and attempt a sentence: "Don't you own a car?" Heads turn. In the quiet restaurant, I have shouted over the noise of the Kawasaki engine still roaring in my skull.

He grins. "Roger has it."

A whisper: "Roger is . . . ?"

"My son. Freshman at Georgetown. Comes home a lot 'cause there's some girl in Comstock he likes. Patty Pendleton. Know 'er?"

Ugh, what bad luck, this is Horrible Hal's sister, plus Mrs. Pendleton thinks I'm eccentric. I tell him this, head bent to menu.

He looks blank for a moment, then laughs. "Waal, that's good," he says. "Eccentric, eh? Some of us wonder about Mrs. Pendleton. Know that party she gives every Christmas Eve? Three thousand people for wassail and dinky bites of ham?"

I nod, shortly. I am never invited.

"Last year, under the mistletoe, she squeezed some of my most private possessions. I near went through the roof."

Good God! I say, "Why, how unfair. You could hardly protect yourself, since she weighs more than you do."

He says modestly, "I told myself it wasn't all that bad. She was drunk as a skunk and I wouldn't remember a thing in the morning. At least that's what I told myself. This Christmas Eve I plan to keep different company."

We smile at each other, the kind of modest hopeful smile two people exchange that involves no contractual obligations. Under the black nylon Windbreaker he has on a white shirt with faint brown stripes, a light blue jacket, a plaid tie. He looks nice, the way I think a man ought to look, clean and ruddy and tailored. His cheeks are still rosy from the ride — they have a long, slightly chipmunk look; his eyebrows are brown, thick, straight, his eyes are biggish and dark blue. He has a long dent in his chin. His brown hair is very straight and combed straight back and needs to be cut — it hangs down in funny hunks in back of his earlobes. Like me, he has grown up all over the place: in Boston, Washington, D.C., Buffalo, New York, Pittsburgh, Minneapolis, Short Hills, New Jersey. His father is dead, his mother lives with her boyfriend in Delray Beach, Florida. She is eighty-one, the boyfriend is seventy-nine. What is it they do down there? Afternoons, they play bridge for money and on Friday nights they fox-trot at the club. Steve's ex-wife (I know this, of course) lives at the other end of Short Hills in Mr. Miller's house. Mr. John Miller and Mrs. Gertie Miller used to own the Big House in front of his (Steve's) place but Mrs. Miller went off with Greg Partridge to East End Avenue in New York City and so Sandy (Steve's ex-wife) took John and moved across town. That left him. The cheese stands alone. Well, that wasn't so bad. Sandy'd been pickin' away at him for quite some while, telling him he was boring. Well, it was true. I had better know it now. He looks up. "I am boring," he says patiently. "I know it. I never was entertaining to other people. I've always lived off by myself a lot. All I could ever do was entertain myself. I don't play bridge and I don't do card tricks. I can't tell a good story and I can't sing. I like to dance. Do you like to dance?"

"Love it," I say. "Do you like to read?"

He looks uncomfortable. "Well, no, actually I don't. Basically, I like to do things. Mechanical things. Motors, cars, things like that."

I say, "If you like to dance you must like music."

His eyes light up. "Yes, I do like music. I like Mantovani."

I stifle a sob. A long pause commences and I think to myself, Uh-huh, this is it, we've run out of conversation already. I knew we wouldn't have anything in common, although (I tell myself) who cares, I don't want things in common, I don't want all that other love stuff anyway, it's too complicated. All I am hoping is that he doesn't have any kind of male problem and this is not a real waste of time. Basically, Dr. Moss, what I am looking for is a good solid non-neurotic male with no organic problems who would like to take me to bed on Saturday night. And (seeing how things go) maybe on Sunday night too. Maybe we could even have a midweek break.

"You're married still, aren't you?" He fastens me with his dark blue eyes. "I met your husband."

I shudder. There must be a draft in the little restaurant. I feel a candle gutter in my soul. "You did?"

"Sure. Jenks Bigelow, lives in Duvernoy. He stopped by the Parkers' house one night when I was there not too long ago."

"I see." My face, I know, is bright red. "He stopped by and Gordy gave him a few dollars, I bet."

"Something like that."

The little white-haired, white-coated waiter arrives nervously smiling and serves us old-fashioned style, sliding the plates down the length of his arm onto the white tablecloth. "Bon appétit, monsieur, madame," he calls out. "You have made a wonderful choice. The goat cheese soufflé is . . ." He kisses his fingertips, winks, disappears.

I say to Steve, "I'm starved. The ride in was so exhilarating! But if we talk about my husband I'll lose my appetite."

"Okay," he says cheerfully stabbing a pinkish piece of pâté with his fork. "We can always talk about my ex-wife."

"Let's just eat," I say, thinking: Please, please spare me the memories. It's Saturday night. I don't want to rummage around in your old emotions. I don't want to share a thing except a meal, a mattress and, if pressed, a towel sometime early to-morrow morning.

"I saw you once down at Belle View, on the beach. You were with a man. Then, I've seen you a lot in Comstock, out running when I drive to the hospital in the morning. White shorts, navy blue shirt? I haven't seen you out this fall. Still running?"

"I never stop. I have to run at night now because I coach tennis in the morning. I hate tennis."

"Never caught on to tennis. I'm left-handed and I seem to swing at the ball all wrong. My grip worked all right for base-ball, I don't understand it."

It occurs to me that since Steve had been down to the shore I might get out of him a little basic information.

"By the way," I say, "how was Claire when you saw her? Was she all right? I kept hoping she might ask me down, just for a weekend."

He looks at me as if he sees right through me, a keen, dark blue gaze. "Claire was all right," he says. "She had a lot of company."

"And Gordy? How was Gordy?"

"Gordy was tired. Here comes the soup. You know, I deeply admire a woman who can order cream of cauliflower."

We eat a lot and slowly, enjoying it. I have salmon with cucumber dill sauce, he has cassoulet. The table for two next to us is vacated and refilled, this time by what I call a Typical New York Couple — he is sixty-two and scrawny but well-dressed, she is twenty-three and cheaply but glitteringly clad. Her conversation has more diphthongs than a nanny-goat's but she doesn't talk much, preferring to spend the dinner hour twisting her head this way and that to catch pouting glimpses of herself in the mirrored wall. He is being enormously witty to impress her, only she doesn't get half his jokes. Over my dessert I catch her glancing at us hostilely, or maybe it is wistfully. I imagine she envies us, a nice couple the same age who have been married for twenty years and know each other so well that they can spend almost an entire dinner together and say hardly a word.

Glancing at her, Steve says to me in a low voice, "Do you think that's her dad?"

"No."

"I don't think so either. If that were her dad he'd be chewing her out for not combing her hair. But then I thought, say, maybe it is her dad because she's got this real sullen look on her face."

"It's not her dad."

"Did you ever go out with a man who was younger?"

"Not seriously."

"How come?"

"Because I have three kids of my own. I don't need another one."

"Uh huh. I feel the same way. And besides that, I know my daughter Althea is very messed up. See, we had a little girl who died when she was four." He gives what at first I think is a ghastly grin, and then I see it's a grimace. His hand on the table has so tightened around the stem of his wineglass that I expect any second I'll hear the glass snap. "I don't think my ex-wife ever got over it. Maybe none of us did. Maybe you never get over something like that, it just gets merely bearable. Anyhow, I think that's why Sandy — my ex-wife — left. It was all too sad. Say. I shouldn't have told you that." He puts his crumpled napkin on the table and stands up.

The tables are well spaced but the restaurant is so small

that everyone looks startled as Steve stalks the three paces to the back of the place. I turn my head and the scrawny guy at the next table gives me a look that is gray-eyed and transfixed with terror. Meanwhile, his pretty friend pouts and tosses her long rhinestone earrings in the dark mirror and makes kissing lips at herself. Looking at her I think: What a dope. She knows nothing. And then I think: Maybe that is why. He knows that; he enjoys her not knowing. That age, we all think we can get by. At *this* age, you know that when you draw your first breath, no matter what, silver spoon or not, life has its hooks in you and will not leave you alone.

Steve comes back and sits down. I say, looking up at him, "Life hasn't let any of us alone."

He looks pale, as if he'd just vomited. He picks up his napkin and spreads it neatly upon his lap. "Oh, I know," he says ruefully to me. "I've met your son."

But we don't speak of our troubles again that night. Holding hands, we walk the streets of Greenwich Village, stroll up Hudson to West 12th. We stop to admire an old building with Mansard roof and fancy wrought-iron trim.

"It's so Parisian looking," I say, thinking something here clicks — some bit of intuition sticks on this pile of crumbling painted brick, as if it wanted to tell me something. In his youth, Steve says, he had lived in a building like this one in Paris. In his youth he had wanted to be a sculptor. Then one day the elderly concierge of his building fell down the stairs carrying her bird cage and his future career was revealed to him. Plus, orthopedic surgery paid better and he had just met Sandy, an expensive-looking young lady who was on her Junior Year Abroad.

We continue to wander the sleazily exotic neon-lit bazaar

that is Seventh Avenue South, where the shops sell rhine-stones, Bibles, pizza, sushi, hookahs, whips, smut and self-help books in True-False question form. It turns out that both of our mothers had gone to Vassar. We both like old movies, both voted for Thomas Kean of New Jersey. Amazing how we have so much in common. In fact, Dr. Moss reminds me of Billy Erskine, the boy I was in love with my senior year in high school. A nicer kid you couldn't hope to meet, despite his jail record. Steve, too, is funny, gentle and kind, and I almost wish we weren't going to bed together tonight. Like an adolescent I long to savor the denser, more ambiguous folds of his personality . . . some part of me craves courting, flowers, romance and mystery. But alas, men are beasts, he'll no doubt force his way into my home and sweep me up the stairs in his arms and I will have to (heh, heh) succumb.

On the ride back it begins to rain, not hard but enough so that when we roar up my steep bumpy driveway, I am soaked and shivering and I know for sure that next day I am going to 'ave zee 'ead cold. I get off the Kawasaki feeling all bits and pieces, a Halloween skeleton strung together with staples and string. He kisses me on the forehead and says, " 'Night now."

I am cold and tired and am having more moods than a fifteen-year-old, and had, after all, been looking forward to a little carnal comfort, so I think, Now what does this mean, he thinks I'm ugly? Thus deprived I stomp inside in a petulant rage, letting the door wham behind me. Another one! Does he have a problem or what? To make it worse, the air of my living room is heavy with desire, darkness and breathing, and out of sheer spite I stamp my foot. The breathing stops. Alicia's voice cautiously calls out, "Mother?" In the dark I hear the slow shift of body weight on pneumatic leather cushions.

"Yesss," I hiss, mad as a witch casting spells, "it's me." I stomp past the L.R., not looking so I don't have to see anything obscene taking place in my very own home. I creep up the stairs. In my bedroom, utterly depressed, I peel off wet clothes and fling them about on the floor so that they look headless and gutless, desiccated cadavers left lying about in some prison yard. Well, this is a prison, isn't it, and I am the Countess of Monte Cristo trying to tunnel out of here with my fingernails. I begin to 'ave zee 'eadache. What's wrong with me, I feel awful, am I getting the curse? I pull on my nightgown and crawl into bed and cry out loud, "I can't! I can't!" I surprise myself, this comes out so hard and fast, as if it were the expulsion of some kind of demon. What is it I mean?

I flop down under the blankets and curl up but something is happening to me — the beginning of panic, that terrible feeling of an immense internal landslide, as if I were crumbling away. I can't! I can't! Can't *what,* for God's sake? Care! Can't care! I lie there with my teeth clenched, shaking, until it is over and I can fall asleep.

When I wake up in the morning the panic is gone, I don't care and I am in control again.

· · · 2 · · ·

Something strange is happening to Nesta. She is bathing daily, washes her hair, uses deodorant and has stopped porking-out in the pantry. It seems that all along, under her fat, she was pretty. Her dark eyes have a glow now and her creamy face is oval and lovely, cheeks lightly touched with pink. Now she and Susie fight all the time, mainly over the use of the second-floor bathroom. As Nesta becomes more recognizably human I find myself softening toward her, while Susan, who used to ignore her, is often sharp with her.

"Oh leave her alone, for God's sake," I say wearily. "Come on, what's the matter with you? She's trying hard, so let her be. She's even been picking up after herself."

"Not in the bathroom she hasn't! She leaves her darn bloody Tampax tubes right there on the windowsill."

"Rome wasn't built in a day! She looks a heck of a lot better, doesn't she? And she smells better, too. It's almost bearable to be in the same room with her."

"She's a pig! I hate her! Why the hell doesn't she get out of here and leave us alone?"

"Because," I say, "she has no place to go."

I am in the kitchen with the usual mealtime mess on the round table. There are ketchup spots on top of a stack of papers I am correcting ("The Byzantine Empire"), peas and carrots bubble in a pan on the stove, meat loaf à la ketchup bakes in the oven, baked potatoes in aluminum foil sit next to the meat loaf, and as in a mosaic, Empress Theodora's goiterous glittering eyes shatter in my head as the telephone rings.

" 'Lo?" I yell into it.

" 'Lo," says Steve in his low voice. "How's your cold?"

"Who told you?"

"Althea. She just called to say that she'd gotten a B-plus on a history quiz. Look, you didn't have to go that far, I was planning to call you again, anyhow."

"She totally deserved her B-plus, and this is a very old cold, thank you, I got it back in *September* on a *dinner date*. I've had going on six weeks of nasal congestion, so it couldn't possibly be all your fault, I guess I am just run down. However, I am sending you the cleaning bill for my black silk pants, the white silk blouse and the angora sweater. Also, do you happen to remember seeing a pair of black satin sandals? I think I left them under the table at the restaurant."

"No, I have them." He says this with such imperturbable patience I imagine he was married to the kind of charming scatterbrain who left gloves, hats, scarves, shawls and shoes wherever she went so that he became resigned to making a general sweep of the area after any outing. "I thought maybe you'd need 'em again sometime. If you don't need 'em before Saturday maybe we could try dinner."

"Oh, that would be lovely, in fact I was thinking of asking you here only I've been so busy and things are kind of a mess here and anyway . . ."

"Then why don't you come here? I have fewer kids. We could sit by the fire and play Parcheesi."

"Are you going to cook?"

"Sort of."

"Shall I bring the wine?"

"No, that's all right, I'll take care of the wine. Just bring the cleaners' bill."

"Fine. I'll bring my prescription for erythromycin, too."

"Pardon?"

"For my cold. I might need a refill."

"No dice. I don't do ENT. Come at eight. I'll mail you a map so you won't get lost on the way."

I suppose that mostly I hoped his house would be neat. I understand how strange this must sound coming from me but I knew what I wanted not to find — a masculine mess (this has happened to me once or twice) with a sink full of crusted-over dishes, a dusty, stale-smelling living room, a bed with gray sheets and a lipstick-smeared pillow case and the smiling, help-less, hapless host hoping you will simply whip on an apron and service the house after you've serviced him.

Steve's house was on Primhouse Lane (ye gods) and he had sent me a tiny map done in ink on a prescription blank. Up the hill past the Playhouse, turn left at the orange blinker and just after the Nature Preserve follow the first driveway on the right to the huge lit-up Stanford White domicile (the Big House) that gleams out like a pleasure ship docked at some dark, glistening jungle-river-town harbor, continue all the way down the gravel drive to the Little House. Park at the turn-around, Roger is going to be home after all. I felt at this scribbled admonition a keen admixture of relief and disappointment.

The Little House was at one time a carriage house but three tall Palladian windows had been inserted into the space where carriage doors had previously hung. I could see the cottage interior as I came down the drive and a peaceful beaming glow came from it — lamps lit, a fire in the white-brick fireplace. Steve came out to meet me as I pulled up.

"Made it, eh? Sorry about Roger. There's some sort of Hal-loween party in Comstock he and his girlfriend are going to. Come in!"

"Oh! Everything's so clean!"

He looked puzzled. "Well, I have a cleaning service."

He had set up a round table in front of the fireplace and after we'd had a drink, he commenced to bring in a number of steaming aluminum foil containers on a tray. He set the tray on a serving table and proceeded to dish out from these containers a number of things that seemed to me mainly unrecognizable — bits of brown string in brown sauce and vegetables all covered over with a shiny, lumpy, translucent gray coverlet. I recognized the handiwork of "Mary and Jane," Comstock's leading catering service, a business put together by two Comstock women whose husbands, a divorce lawyer and a commodities broker, apparently stinted on the pin money. The stuff was called boeuf bourguignon, potato soufflé and veggies royale. It tasted worse than it looked but we were drinking lots of a soft beautiful Burgundy and talking about Halloween. One Halloween I had been a gypsy, my favorite costume. My mother made my earrings out of curtain rings and taped them onto my ears with Band-aids but all night long they kept falling off. While the other kids ran from doorway to doorway collecting candy, I crawled around on my hands and knees under a streetlamp looking for these brass rings, the story of my life.

"My favorite costume was Lord Nelson," Steve said, smiling fondly at the image of his eight-year-old self in tricorn, sword and brass buttons.

"Did you even know who Lord Nelson was?"

"Certainly. My father, remember, was in the navy. So was his father, and so was my great-grandfather, which is as far back as we go in this country. Before that there were Mosses in the British navy. My father was the last of the naval Mosses." The fire crackled, as if applauding. "It's a sad thing," he said, "to be the last of a line. Now, of course, no one cares. No one cares about the past and no one wants to think about the future. What we have now is the concept of happiness *right now*." He gave me a neutral look. "Do you want to say something? This is just a theory. I am making conversation."

"No, you go on," I said dreamily, and swirled the wine in my glass.

"You see, I've never completely understood the concept of happiness. It seems to me that it often resides in such little things. I was, ah, happy with you the other night."

"That wasn't so little. The bill was enormous."

"I had a *fine* time. It seems to me people often go to a lot of time and trouble to make themselves happy, and then, anyhow, they're wretched."

"Some people want more than others. . . . Do you think that's true of yourself?"

He sat up straight and looked at the ceiling. "No. Sandy said I didn't want enough."

"What did she mean? That you weren't ambitious?"

"Mainly."

"Do you think she was right?"

"Mainly. Most of all, I like doing a good job at something I'm good at."

"Mmm. But when I was young I wanted a lot of different things. I was ambitious — I was terribly ambitious. I wanted to write novels and have great love affairs. I wanted a fabulous place to live and interesting friends and enough money so that I could travel. Now? I think a hot bath is luxury beyond words, and if I get through the month without going deeper into debt I treat us all to a steak. I don't care about much anymore. I care about my kids. I think, Oh, if only I can get them grown up. The problem is, grown up now means forty. Will I last that long?"

Steve laughed abruptly and turned his head to the fire. He

rose up out of the chair and bent to the pile of logs carefully stacked on a canvas carrier.

"That's called survival," he said, kneeling and looking over his shoulder at me. "I believe I want a little more than that."

Roger had left toward the end of the entree. ("Oh, hi, Mrs. Bigelow, how are you, remember me? I used to see you down at the Lion's Paw. Still hangin' out down there? No? Well, see you guys later.") We were eating chocolate mousse (watery) when the front door slammed and he stalked past us, home again.

"Hmmm," Steve said and looked down at his chocolate-streaked dessert plate. "Lover's quarrel, I guess." From down the hall, Led Zeppelin started up full blast. Silently, we both stood and began carrying plates into the kitchen. Steve rinsed, I put the dishes into the dishwasher. The telephone rang; Led Zeppelin ceased. Moments later a car horn honked; the front door slammed; a car went hurtling out of the drive.

Steve said, looking sideways at me, "When I saw you down at the shore there was a fella with you, a big guy with curly gray hair and twenty-four gold chains around his neck."

"One! He only wore one! That was Ted, we're just friends. We go out to dinner and hold hands. I feel sorry for him, his wife just left him. He screwed around for years and his wife didn't say a word but the minute he had a heart attack she was out the door. This shows that we all have varying priorities. Hers, I guess, was good health."

He looked at me benignly. "You sure kid a lot."

"If you had my life . . ."

"You don't have someone then?"

"Have? How do you mean, have?"

"Maybe you could do your routine another night."

I narrowed my eyes at him. "All right. *I don't.*"

Steve took the dishtowel out of my hands, folded it in half and hung it over the towel rack. He took my hand and we wandered back to the living room together but shyly settled into opposite corners of the long beige tweed sofa. He said, calmly, "I haven't had anyone special at all. I've gone out some — there seems to be a dearth of men in these parts — but I'd kind of like to know what your interests are. The truth is, Ms. Bigelow, your reputation has preceded you."

He was sitting with his long legs stretched out and his hands knit in back of his neck. I saw that he had sneakers on. What was it he wanted me to say? He went on, "Well, I suppose what I'm asking is, would it be worthwhile for me to go ahead and learn more about you?"

I childishly bit a hangnail on my right thumb. I said, "How'm I supposed to answer that? Isn't that called hedging your bets? Everything in life is a gamble, no?"

He was silent a moment. "I couldn't stand it if . . ." And then he sat up straight and said, accusingly, "You're still married. Why is that, anyway?"

"Why . . ." I, too, sat up straight. "Well, I don't know. It seemed just as easy to stay married."

"Easier in some ways. But you haven't lived together for a long time?"

"Not for seven years."

"Do you see each other?"

"As little as possible."

"Doesn't make sense to me."

"I can't really explain it."

"Some sort of guilt?"

"I don't *know,* so let's just skip it."

"Waal, now, the thing is . . . you can see how really cautious I am . . . if we started seeing each other and we got really interested, what would happen then?"

"It hasn't happened yet, so why worry about it?"

"But it could happen. It might very well happen. Or don't you think so?"

"Oh," I burst out, "this is absurd. All these maybes and what-ifs, for heaven's sake. We don't know each other at all."

"You could come a little closer."

But now I felt surly and I said in a muttering voice, "It seems such a long way."

He stood up in a graceful swoop and pulled me up by the hand. I felt as clumsy as a twelve-year-old and couldn't remember where to put my arms, so he had to arrange them for me, around his neck. We kissed each other standing up. The first kiss was soft and warm and I could feel his heart beating through his sea-green shetland sweater. He had his hands placed gently upon my hip bones and he stepped back a bit and looked down at me. His long face was rosy and his eyes seemed so blue and guileless. We kissed again, this time opening our mouths to let each other in, and I felt a terrible rushing pain in my head. Something black and crushing careered through my brain, I remember saying, "I can't!" and then I fell to the floor.

When I opened my eyes, Steve was kneeling next to me with a pink washcloth in his hand. As I looked at it, he clamped it to my forehead. I screamed: "Ow!" It was cold and wet and I tugged it away.

"Some kiss!" he said, sitting back on his haunches.

I tried to hoist myself up on an elbow, but the elbow hurt. I must have fallen on it. "What happened? I don't know what happened."

"You fainted."

"I did? Really? Wow, I've never fainted before. Think of that, a Victorian interlude."

I stopped trying to sit up and lay back flat and looked at the ceiling. All the beams and rafters were painted white. "I don't know what to do."

"Neither do I," he said. "Sure you're not prone to this? Had a checkup lately?"

"Whatever could it be? My blood pressure's on the low side." I raised myself up again and managed to sit with my back propped against the sofa. He sat down next to me, same position. He folded his arms, I knit my hands around my knees.

He said, "We could play Parcheesi. That's real genteel."

"I'm sorry," I said. "I really don't know what went wrong."

"Maybe our feeling isn't mutual." He stared ahead into the fire.

"Oh I like you very much!"

He reached for my hand. "I like you, too, Barbara."

"But, I . . ."

"But what?"

"I think maybe I should go home. I might be getting the flu or maybe I'm having an allergic reaction to erythromycin. I do have this crashing headache."

"Uh huh."

"I'm really sorry."

"Oh, shucks, it's all right. It's just that . . ." He lifted my hand and kissed it. "I really wanted to make love to you awfully much."

A wave of pain laced through my brain again and I pressed my free hand against my forehead.

"All right?"

"No. Could you drive me home? One of my kids can pick up my car tomorrow."

On the way home, we came up the hill into Comstock and passed Claire's house. It was totally dark.

"Parkers are out, I guess," I said, conversationally.

"Claire's not home," Steve said.

I let that sit for a moment, then turned my head. "What do you mean?"

"Claire's gone away somewhere," Steve said. "She just up and left. I saw Gordy this morning. You're not to tell anyone."

"Oh no!" I said, shocked.

"Poor Gordy," he said.

Thoughts tumbled about in my head but the feeling that remained and became persistent was my gleefully paranoid certainty of her whereabouts: she was with Jason.

My face felt flushed, my heart pounded. The wine I had drunk raced around in my veins. If there had been a full moon I would have exposed my throat and started howling. Steve looked at me peculiarly, and I realized that I was smiling. My headache had disappeared.

· · · 3 · · ·

All night long, Steve Moss in his sneakers and sea-green shetland sweater moved in and out of my dreams, smiling encouragingly, nodding, understanding.

He is me — or some part of me — and he is watching while Gordon and I make love. We make love on a bare parquet floor in front of a fireplace; we make love in the sand dunes (ouch); we make love on a bed in the Parkers' house. Steve keeps on smiling. I think in my dream, It's nice he's so tolerant.

As is the case with dreams, no action is ever completed, so I wake up cross, mean and raunchy: if King Kong walked through my bedroom door, I'd soon have him screaming for mercy.

Besides this, it is leaf-raking day. Outside the windows, black branches sway and whole troops of gold leaves go streaming by — they seem to be flying backward, reminding me of little figures out of some animated film, Wald Disney leaves with squeezed up eyes and stick legs, holding on to their hats as puff-cheeked Mr. Northwind drives them away. Steam knocks in the pipes. How cold is it outside? Hard to tell. I put on a heavy brown turtleneck sweater, old tweed pants, wool socks, yellow work boots.

Downstairs in the kitchen Susan is in her wine-colored velour bathrobe drinking orange juice out of a Dixie cup and looking dreamily out of the kitchen window. Two glimmers of sunlight wobble on her veloured hips — her beam is gently broadening. Alicia comes in. She has her blond hair screwed up in a bun so tight her scrubbed rosy skin looks taut — a smile would tear it. She, too, has on a heavy turtleneck — black under a denim jumpsuit that has the name DAN embroidered in white over the pocket.

"What's up?" I ask. "Where'd you get the new outfit?"

"It's not mine," she says, "it's only a loan for a couple of days until mine comes in. I've got a new job." She busily pokes up a straggling hair.

"Oh yeah?" I say. "What's the new job?"

She grins and says, "Pumping gas. You know the Sunoco Station on Maxwell Avenue? Well, there."

"How come you switched jobs, I thought you liked being a waitress."

She says sullenly, "The boss made a pass at me." She drops two slices of extra-thin Pepperidge Farm whole-wheat bread in the toaster and socks the toaster lever with her fist.

"So you had to quit?"

"Yeah, Mom, I had to quit, Mom. I didn't want to sleep with the old fart."

"Don't get riled, I didn't say you had to go to bed with him, I'm just wondering if there wasn't some other way to handle it?"

"No!"

"Okay, okay! Who got you this new job?"

"*I* got it, Mom. There are a couple of things in life I can do all for myself."

"Holy smokes, Alicia, what's eating you?"

"I'm sick of the way you hike on me."

"I wasn't hiking, I was just being curious. I thought maybe Bear with his vast army of potential contacts . . ."

"Ha, ha, ha. It's okay, Mom. You can be snide about Bear now if you want, we've broken up."

"Oh yeah?"

"Yeah, as of last night. So relax, I am between men. Just like you."

Susie turns from the window and says lazily to Alicia, "Mom's got a new boyfriend."

The toast pops up, hurtling itself into the air, and Alicia, well practiced, snags it out of its descending arc. "Say, congrats," she says, "who's the lucky new dude? It's not that jerk Fred, the flower fancier?"

"No, it's not," I say. "Actually, there is no new dude. He was a mere two-date fling."

"Gee, tough," Alicia says, blue eyes wide. She bites into the charred toast — ka--rrunch.

"Is that right?" Susan asks worriedly. "I thought you really liked him."

What's she so worried about? Maybe she's afraid she'll get stuck with me in my old age.

"I did like him, I do like him, it was just, ah, just . . ."

"He didn't like you?" Alicia interjects, coldly.

"He did too like me," I say, as hot as a fourth-grader. "That wasn't the problem."

"Then what was the problem?" Alicia asks.

"Alicia," Susie says calmly, "obviously, she can't define it."

"Your love life is so complex," Alicia says cruelly.

"Yours has always been too easy," I snap back, wanting to hurt her. And I do. Her rose skin floods red and her blue eyes enlarge and flash. She gives me a look of pure poison, and dusts the toast crumbs from her fingers onto her denim thighs. "When I have the money got together, I am leaving this dump."

"Swell," I say, "when can we plan the going-away party?"

"A couple of weeks."

"I can hardly wait."

She turns and leaves the room. Like me she has a high, well-rounded derriere, and her buttocks move — one, two! one, two! — under the tight denim of her gas station jumpsuit. She won't be long at a loss for a male, but I wish to God she had better taste. Well, let her leave. When I left home — such as home was — I took some clothes, my paperback collection of F. Scott Fitzgerald and all my young girl hopes. *He* sat at the kitchen table drinking tea and eating cinnamon toast, his face all shiny and wet. I said, "Dad? I'm going now." Silence. He was good at that — silence.

But what was I supposed to do?

· VI ·

The
Missing
Person

· · · **1** · · ·

Dear Edward, (Claire wrote)

I've done the strangest thing. I have left the house (odd, she thought, that I said "the house" not "Gordy") and am living in a place in New York, an apartment that had been, for at least the last eight years, our father's apartment. I know, I know. It sounds incredible. That he would go to so much trouble to get away from . . . us. On the other hand, why not? He was good at drama, scenarios. He was always something that he was not. Here was the perfect opportunity for another dramatic exit, and then on to the new role, the new life — and one without alimony.

The apartment is on the second floor of an old Parisian-looking building on West 12th Street. The building is circa 1860, very Second Empire, with a steep, tiled mansard roof and, decorating the roof, a finely wrought iron railing. The apartment walls are cracked, the plaster is crumbling but there is a fireplace in the front room and it is sunny and pleasant. The little kitchen gets some light from a steep-walled courtyard, and a number of plants — houseplants — are down there left over from the summer. There's been a frost so they look close to death. Perhaps their owner moved away or is ill or is as dead as Father — perhaps — who knows? — they are Father's plants and now no one knows what to do with them.

But who is this "no one"? Although there are names over the mail slots in the tiled entrance hall, I never hear a soul. The building is thick walled, true, and the ceilings are high, but shouldn't one hear doors slamming, TV blaring, dogs barking, telephones ringing, children crying, people shouting, door buzzers buzzing? Maybe the building has been abandoned or maybe it's a Flying Dutchman of a building and all of its silent tenants are dead or this place is one I have dreamed or imagined and perhaps someday it will disappear. One day in the future, some fine spring day, I'll walk down West 12th Street and look up and there will be a gap like a broken tooth where this building stood; or I will look up and see that another building, quite a different building, has slipped in to take its place.

Still, the heat is on; the utilities work.

The whole story is strange, isn't it?

And why not? Father was strange and we were a strange family. At least that's what I grew up believing. Now I know better: all families are strange in their own ways. There is no norm. Perhaps families merely project certain myths about themselves, myths which do not need to be told out loud but are sustained by unconscious and silent mutual assent.

You see, Gordy and I . . . we always maintained the myth that we were not just a happy family but superior in some ways: more intelligent, gifted, happier, luckier. Michael's death proved us wrong. We weren't anything better. We were subject to death just like anyone else, only worse, because in our family a child had died and in this country, at this time, children don't die, why even old people are not allowed to die, no one dies except on TV and we all know that's not true. Death is an affront to the sensibilities so that if a child dies people tell you how sorry they are but you know there is something seriously wrong with you, you have failed at the most important thing, you couldn't keep your child alive and a subtle shame, like a secret coat of perspiration, covers you all over and you feel uneasy when you are with someone as if, very faintly, you can discern your own bad smell, yet you stand there, foolishly smiling, and sweating, and knowing that what you have on you is a whiff of death.

And then there is Evan. In my dreams, I tell Evan over and over not to get into a stranger's car. But he was almost sixteen years old and what does getting into a stranger's car have to do with it anyway? I couldn't keep him safe — that is the point. You see, in my own grief for Michael, I didn't see what was happening to Evan — his introspection, his bad dreams, his depression. I ascribed these things to adolescence because Michael had been like that, too, at that same age. I didn't *see*.

We never got a gravestone for Michael, did I tell you that? I never thought I'd want a gravestone. We were the sort of family that smiles at gravestones and thinks cemeteries are quaintly lurid but now there is nothing, he has been dispersed into the elements and since no one will talk about him, it's as if he never existed. I raised a child to the age of thirteen — now he has been erased. That's why I work so hard at believing Evan is still alive.

I feel that I, too, have been close to death, am dead or dying. No, that's not accurate, I exist but I don't feel alive. Now and part of the reason I have come here is that I have set out to find or regain the living part of me.

This is my first morning here in the city, a November Sunday. Sitting here in the flat's sunny, overheated front parlor, at the small, rolltop desk, I am aware of the sizzling radiator just at my side and the cyclical nature of the heating system. First there is a faint, then louder clang in the pipes and then a steady hiss and slowly the room's geographic location shifts from Arctic to tropical and then, very gradually, the hissing dies away and the warmth dies with it, and we slowly return to polar conditions which begin with a faint feeling of loss and then a slight enveloping sense of chill and then the final frosty moments, when you begin openly shivering and wonder if you will survive, or who will find your frozen body, until, far away downstairs, you hear the clang of the furnace beginning again. Is this, do you suppose, a metaphor for life?

I started my new life this morning by getting up and going around the corner to Lanciani's for croissants, and then down the street to Gristede's for apples and coffee, enough to see me through until dinner. I plan to eat out alone tonight.

It's strange to live here. The notice is still on the door, "This Apartment Is Sealed" so I am living here illegally — an illegitimate life, a life out of context. Whatever it is now, it feels better. I had reached the point where the context of my life, like the coils of a boa constrictor, had wound around my neck and were tightening so that I could no longer breathe. I don't know exactly what I will do here. Write (I hope), sleep, eat, read, walk, go through Father's things, see a man I hope to fall in love with. As hopeful as an adolescent, I am hoping that love will cure me. Not that "he" will cure me but that love might, the process of love, of giving love will restore me. Is this too much to ask, do you think? How we all depend on love to resurrect us! Do you think God is Love, Edward? I don't. Even if I believed in God I would say that He is a spiteful God, jealous and cruel, who has turned His face away from us in our hour of peril. On the other hand, I see us humans as fools, all the bad, gullible kids setting off in crowded wagons pulled by braying donkeys — off to the Isle of Pleasure!

The man I may be in love with is a publisher, a very strange, odd, hurt, needy person who (it seems to me) suffers a great deal. He was Barbara's lover years ago. Of course her version and his vary a great deal and I haven't yet decided whose version I believe. I suppose it depends on my own feelings about him.

In any case, you know, I'm sure, how desperate I am. I'm not a brave person. These last few years I've lived so internally — my friendships have dwindled away to acquaintanceships. People have tried to be kind but I am tired of kindness. I don't want any more kindness or civility from people, I just want to be a living, feeling person again. And with Gordon, too — this friendship, too, seems dead.

No one knows I'm here. I've told no one about the apartment and Father. I won't tell Mama or Nikki or even Gordon.

On Saturday morning I woke up and thought, Why, today is Father's birthday. I told the kids I was going away for a while, that I had some business in the city but I'd be back soon, though of that I'm not certain at all.

Then I packed my bag and took the train for New York.

$$\cdots \; 2 \; \cdots$$

At two o'clock on Monday, on the second day of her new life, Claire got up from her desk to stretch, and then wandered listlessly around the apartment pulling out books from the shelves, putting them back. Not one of the books seemed to be anything her father would have had — they in no way reflected his taste. Perhaps he had rented the place with the books and furnishings intact, taking over, as it were, the furniture of another life.

Saturday when she'd arrived, she had dusted and swept, all with the blinds down and as quietly as possible. No one must know I am here. My secret life. Why does my real life have to be a secret?

She went out for a walk. The Village streets were strange to her, some prettily tree-lined, with small old houses, crooked windows, shutters, window boxes. On Christopher Street, she found a clothing store that sold cheap, impromptu clothing and she surprised herself by buying black cord pants and a baggy purple sweatshirt. The salesgirl had on a shirt hand-painted in Day-Glo orange and green; she wore safety pins in her ears. Her spikey hair was half pink, half magenta; her fingernails were painted black. She'd said to Claire, "You're not from the city, right?"

"Right," Claire said firmly.

"I thought you looked different," the girl said.

Back in the apartment Claire listlessly paced and then sat down at the desk. At three-thirty, she had a drink of water in the kitchen — a small brown roach scuttled out from under the drainboard, saw her, paused, scuttled back. She went into the living room. A truck roared by on the street below and the windowpanes shook. So. Now what? She didn't know what to do with herself. Usually at this hour she'd be shopping for groceries and planning the evening meal while she wandered up and down the cool, sanitized, fruit-smelling aisles of the giant gourmet supermarket that had opened on Route 24 a year ago. The place to go if you were lonely or bored. Maybe at the back of the store, next to the fresh fish laid out on chopped ice, and the lobsters swimming in their mini-Jacuzzi, they should install a café. You could sit there and drink cappuccino and observe what everyone was taking home in their carts, find out what secret cheapskates bought the label-less brands. She did. She thought their ketchup perfectly good.

The digital clock on the living-room mantel nervously pulsed. I ought to go home, she thought. What am I doing here? Answered herself, I am waiting. Right on time, precisely at four — he was never late — the telephone rang and Jason's cello-voice rang out — deep, resinous, confidential. He would see her tomorrow for a brief lunch and then (he laughed — shakily, she thought) Wednesday for dinner. Wednesday they'd have some time together. Wednesday was a good night, a very good night. He gave each word a separate, clear emphasis.

Since September, she'd seen him five or six times for drinks or lunch, until one windy day in October, like two homeless kids, they'd stood kissing in a flutter of paper scraps in a Union Square discount department store doorway. Then he'd taken her hand and, tugging, led her to the sidewalk's curb, hailed a cab. They drove around and around Union Square, breathlessly kissing, meter ticking, hearts pounding, for forty-five minutes. Disembarked, paying the cab driver, red-faced Jason dropped wadded bills and silver coins, as seemingly shaken as if he'd been buffeted by an orchard breeze. She'd stood there laughing at him.

"Oh God," he'd said to her, "you are . . . ," then slowly backed away from her, solemnly waving, pink-faced, glassy-eyed, a kid loath to go back to school. He'd backed up, then, against a blind man, with dangling sign, black glasses, cane, cup, dog, and the cup shot upward, spinning coins flashed in the sun, spangled the sidewalk. The blind man had torn off his glasses, howled, cursed them and muttered complaints as the three of them knelt (Claire laughing all the while) to pry up the coins while the patient dog, a German shepherd, sat, pink tongue lolling, looking off toward Wall Street. Getting up, flustered Jason had stuffed two bills into the tin cup. Telling him goodbye — again, again — Claire had put both hands on his tweed-covered arm, stood on tiptoe to kiss his cold ear. Dear Jason. He'd loped off into the dim building, turned again to wave, collided with a messenger in headphones.

"Say, man, what yo trouble? Can't yo see nuffin'? I'se standin' here plain as day!"

Jason poor Jason was blind as a bat. Horribly nearsighted, he never wore glasses and only when truly desperate pulled out a smeared little wire-framed pair he kept in his shirt pocket.

He was so big! So awkward! So like an adolescent! All knees, blunders, wrists, elbows, pokes, gropes, wanting. She laughed at him and felt he was amusing, touching, and wanted to love him and go to bed with him. He had never mentioned it.

"Pardon me," she'd whispered into his long pink ear as the cab crawled east on 14th Street for the third time while the black driver chewed gum and steered with two fingers, tactfully pretending not to notice, "are we never going to, oh . . ."

Immediately, Jason had sat straight up looking scared. "Oh God, oh God," he'd whimpered in a low terrified voice.

· 174

"What's the matter?" she'd asked, alarmed, sitting up herself, in a swish of tweed skirt, taffeta slip. "Wouldn't you like to?"

For answer, he had taken her hand and placed it upon his well-tailored gray flannel fly where a tumid struggle seemed to be taking place. She laughed at him teasingly, tried to remove her hand, but he firmly kept hold of her wrist. "The driver!" she hissed at him, pretending shock.

She always laughed at him and he blushed and glowered but although he played the charming bumpkin, she couldn't quite believe it, then told herself, scolding, that her disbelief was all her father's fault: he'd taught her, by sheer weight of bad example, how to be cynical, why to be cynical.

But New York City is full of women and why would he take me up if he weren't more than attracted? Isn't love still possible? You can get simple sex anywhere these days and lengthy seductions are as passé as high collars and whalebone stays. It's not exactly the thrill of the chase, either, since his method seems to be to chase until I stop and then run past me. Is this a game that's too subtle for me? Am I naïve or only cynical?

Still, with Jason she felt she was someone completely different (wasn't that the point?), another person entirely, someone younger with a lightness of heart she hadn't had for years. Walking up and down New York streets arm in arm — those shadowy lurking Union Square streets, West 15th, West 16th — she felt almost happy. He told her anecdotes about the authors he'd published. He published two or three well-known novelists who were also good writers but he made his money on nonfiction: self-help books, diet books, cookbooks, travel books. His best-seller last year was a book on how to housebreak dogs. Did she have a dog?

Of course she had a dog, she said, and her children . . . she stopped, thinking, appalled, that she'd nearly forgotten she

· 175

had children. Then she thought briefly, sadly, of Gordon, her children's father, and then said lightly to Jason, "Oh, I ought to write a book on how not to raise children. It might make me rich."

"Nonsense," he said, and jovially squeezed her arm. "Stick with fiction. You're a wonderful writer."

"So," she said, squinting her eyes up at him as they walked, "you've finally read my manuscript?"

"No," he said, "Mimi told me that." Mimi Garr, Jason's senior editor, was a stout, gray-haired woman with thick glasses and a chain-smoker's cough. Her clothes were always vaguely spotted, her literary taste impeccable. Claire thought she was in love with Jason. Why else would anyone work for so little pay?

"Well," Claire asked, tilting her head up at him, "are you going to publish it or is my seeing you a mere waste of time?" He blinked, his long face quivered and Claire said, "Oh Jason, that was a joke!" but he wheeled around, away from her. They were passing a fruit stand and Jason stood under the orange-and-green-striped awning looking at the dark, shiny Ribier grapes, bananas, Macintosh apples. He said, irrelevantly, "For a while, when I was a boy, we owned an old farm in Washington County." Then he took an apple from its purple tissue-paper nest, polished it on his coat sleeve, offered Claire a bite. The fruit store owner, a small Korean, delicately coughed.

Claire thought to herself, Why do I tease him and put him off?

Because, she answered herself, I'm afraid of him.

She bit into the apple and wondered what possible relation the farm had to her?

"Tut, tut," Jason said mockingly, "you've got apple on your face."

· · · 3 · · ·

On Tuesday, in a crimson wool jacket and matching cap, Claire went to meet Jason for lunch at a bistro on West 4th Street. The place was Spanish — red leather and black grill-work, Picasso bull-fighter etchings hung on cracked stucco walls and a cigarette smoke and seafood smell that lingered in the dingy red café curtains. For the first fifteen minutes he was cool and ironic — she had been ten minutes late and he was punishing her. They sat in a patched red leather booth; he drummed his fingers, consulted his watch, looked bored and asked her where she'd gotten "those clothes."

"Down here, a few blocks away. Why?"

"They don't suit you," he said. "They look ..." He turned to look at the wall where a sketchy picador was lancing his bull. "... too young."

"It's an outward expression of my inward state," she said, smiling relentlessly at him.

He grunted.

When the check came, she paid. Absentminded Jason had forgotten his wallet.

"The woman always pays," Claire said practically, shaking out all the coins in her wallet for the tip.

"Yes," Jason said, but once outside in the bright November sunshine, he smiled and took her arm. "This is a new suit," he said modestly and she beamed at him, gave him her lavish approval, told him how wonderful he looked and he bashfully reddened.

In the bright autumnal sunshine, they walked uptown toward Jason's office, past assorted Village stores, fancy or tawdry antique shops, health food stores, small cafés. They passed a shop that sold "vintage toys," not antiques but artifacts out of Claire's own childhood, playthings of the forties and fifties, paper-doll books of Elizabeth Taylor and Debbie Reynolds, *Treasure Island* illustrated by N. C. Wyeth. They pressed their noses against the window glass, Jason staring at a set of toy soldiers on parade. The soldiers were hideously pink-faced and wore the shakos and gray uniforms of West Point cadets.

"Look at that!" Jason said. "I can't believe it!" and he steered her quickly inside.

Here the air of Claire's childhood was thickly palpable. There were rubber-skinned baby dolls that wet, Lincoln Log sets, a toy kitchen made of white painted metal — the dainty-footed big-bellied stove had a little red hex sign painted on its oven door and even a tiny muffin pan inside. The young clerk who sat behind the cash register seemed purposefully incongruous. He should have been a gnome, Claire thought, with a beard, a twinkle in his eye and a pointed red cap, but instead he had close-cropped black hair as smooth as cut velvet and he wore a large yellow Gay Rights button pinned to the shoulder of his Eisenhower battle jacket. He was knitting. Jason asked to see the soldiers in the window. He looked at each one eagerly.

"What are you knitting?" Claire asked the clerk while Jason pondered, frowning.

"Oh it's just a scarf," he said. "You see I'm terribly nervous and my therapist suggested handwork and I do so love scarves. I have a whole collection but I don't have anything in this khaki color. I think it's going to be awfully attractive."

Jason began a crisp exchange with the clerk on the prices of the soldiers and the clerk, who seemed reluctant to bargain, said in a tremulous, high-pitched, nasal voice that he'd have to check with the owner. Jason cheerfully persisted. While they negotiated, Claire moved away, down the length of the lit-up glass display case, childishly trailing her hand along the cool metal strip at the top of the case, the way she'd done on Saturday afternoons in a dim little corner grocery when she was a kid in Wickham. She used to spend her entire weekly allowance, a dime, on penny candy. Listening to their voices — Jason's was deep and insistent — Claire thought how Gordy never bargained. Getting a deal meant nothing to him and whenever they bought anything, a car, a house, an antique table, Gordy would say with a shrug, "Well, if you want something, you have to pay for it." Consequently, they often paid too much for anything they acquired. Gordy was a giver — he gave his time away as well: to patients who couldn't afford to pay for it, to people at cocktail parties who badgered him for free medical advice. Now Claire felt that the time Gordy spent, the time he "gave away," had come out of her time, the kids' time. He'd become adept at avoiding them.

"Tell you what," Jason said loudly at the front of the store, briskly finagling, "I'll give you twenty for the entire lot." The clerk looked distraught, Claire ducked her head and stared into the display case. The end of the case featured four little "miniature scenes" representing the four seasons, each scene on a plywood plinth. The scenery was clumsily done, the figures made of pipe cleaners. "Winter" was a bluish mirrored pond dusted with glistening snowflakes, a church steeple painted into the make-believe distance, and a steep cardboard hill covered with white glitter upon which a skier hung, motionless, knees bent, pipe-cleaner hands looped about tiny perpetually outflung ski poles. He wore a navy blue ski suit — baggy panted, like the ski clothes of the 1940s.

That day, I came all the way down the top of the mountain on the Expert trail and it was terribly icy, I heard the bright whisk of snow under my skis, the skis were running faster and faster and I thought, I am out of control. It wasn't just the ice, ugly and yellow, that lay in treacherous patches on the steep run, but a streaming fog had drifted across the mountain and I couldn't see, there was no warning gleam or glare, you had to be keenly alert to the faintest change of texture under the running skis. There was a shout in back of me and a whistling sound and two members of the ski patrol, their red jackets muted by fog, flew past trailing a bumping litter that had upon it a green metal box decorated with a large red cross. They turned off to the right, a closed trail, and dropped over an icy crest. I went on, over the dangerous hump of the mountain, and did not fall and coming out of the fog at last felt triumphantly safe and schussed straight down toward the line that snaked around the chair lift. Stopping short in a blaze of wet snow I felt ecstatically happy and then there was a crackle as the loudspeaker came on, and I heard a name, my name, ringing out through the moist cold air over goggled, helmeted, uplifted faces. Someone must have crossed his path and forced him off to the right — he was too good a skier. Why? Why? Michael!

The cash register rang out its shrill *ter-ring* and Jason appeared next to her looking elated. He steered her outside, past the clerk who kept his downcast face turned away, into the bright November afternoon. Trucks barreled down Bleecker Street as if heading for a holiday, the street was filled with plangent music from an open upstairs window, a couple in sweat clothes and headphones trotted past them side by side, plugged into each other's sets, and the day was so bright, so blue and gold, cool blue air, pools of liquid sunlight, that life seemed to have no purpose at all except to celebrate itself — sun, sky, and at the end of the street, a small city park whose mottle-trunked trees wore crowns sparsely studded with bits of gold.

"By God!" Jason said, laughing, exultant, "I've never done so well on a deal. I happen to know . . ." He reached down, took her arm, tucked it around his own. ". . . these are rare pieces, made in Germany around nineteen hundred of something called elastacon. I paid thirty dollars. Thirty dollars! They're easily worth three hundred the set."

She smiled sadly up at him — happiness made him look boyishly handsome — but there was an ache at the back of her throat she had to suppress.

"What's wrong?" Jason asked her sharply. They were at the park and he pulled her down next to him on the bench and pressed his knee against her thigh. She shook her head, smiling at him, not wanting to spoil his pleasure and her own. It was such an amazing day, and that morning, leaving the apartment, she'd felt certain she would be happy. Jason studied her. With his fingers he clumsily tucked into her cap the fine wisps of hair that blew about her eyes.

"You look sad," he said, accusingly.

She glanced away. In the play area, two toddlers fought for possession of a large yellow plastic Snoopy dog big enough to straddle and ride. She said slowly, "Something made me think of my son Michael. That day — the day we were all skiing and he hit the tree — that's the last day I can remember being perfectly happy."

Against her side, Jason's arm was as thin and tensile as a spring. He suddenly moved it away, leaving a cold space, and he said, ironically, "Thanks very much."

She looked up at him — his face was hard. He hated it when she mentioned her children. And why should he not? When she was with him she wanted to be free of these burdensome memories. With him she'd hoped to feel free at last, as free as she'd felt when she was young and in love for the first time. She said softly, "Jason, I'm trying."

A sly look came over his face and he said, "Anyway, isn't that what therapists call magical thinking? Your happiness didn't produce your son's accident. Perhaps you're punishing yourself — refusing to accept happiness."

She nodded and then said, "Were you in therapy?"

He said with some satisfaction, "No, I have that from a friend of mine, quite a close friend. Laura was in therapy for many years."

At once Claire felt a chill pass through her as if a long shaft of icy air had pierced her marrow. He constantly alluded to other women. She told herself it was his insecurity, but what about hers? The act of falling in love, so revivifying, so rejuvenating, exposed under the calloused layers of wisdom and experience tender new places in herself, as if love had peeled away tough lamination to reach living but vulnerable heartwood.

Abruptly, he stood up. "Well, if I can't make you happy I'd better go back to work. I've got a three o'clock appointment."

She walked a few blocks with him. On University Place he pulled her into a doorway and kissed her, pressing his long bony hands through the wool of her jacket into her ribs. His lips were cool. "I can't see you for dinner tomorrow night," he said. "I've got an important meeting I must go to. However, I'm free on Friday."

She pulled her face into a teasing smile. "Are you sure it'll be convenient?"

He laughed and squeezed her ribs. "Very convenient," he said. "Now don't spend your time being sad. Forget the kids and think about us. It's *now* that's important, isn't it?" He turned away and when he looked back at her once, over his shoulder, she felt a pang of amused affection for him — he was so like a kid himself — and then he strode away, into the path of a pretzel vendor who, in the instant before collision, adroitly shifted the heavy cart.

Oh God, Claire thought, laughing as the pretzel vendor hurled manic curses after fleeing Jason, it's a wonder he's survived this long. And she stood looking after him as he crossed 14th

Street, loping and weaving around trucks, cars, and taxis, charging straight ahead at the change of the light — he had blindly crossed on the DONT WALK sign.

Days and days with nothing to do. At home she spent so much of her time doing caretaking chores that here in the apartment, with no one to take care of, her days seemed endless, her nights forever. She missed the children, missed the dog, thought of going home, saw herself sitting in the low-branched maple tree at night under a full autumn-orange moon secretly spying in on her family from the back yard, looking wistfully into her own lit-up kitchen. There, at the round table, Gordy and Barbara sat holding hands, looking at each other yearningly. She missed Gordy, too — it was lonely sleeping alone, but then she'd been lonely at home sleeping with him. No, whatever she'd set out to find, she hadn't found yet. Whatever it was.

One day she walked uptown to the Guggenheim, trudging in running shoes, the next day she walked to the Metropolitan. She avoided the Modern Museum because there, in the Sculpture Garden, next to a giant pin-headed nude, Gordy had asked her to marry him.

Evenings, her father's ironic presence stood challengingly in the dim corners of the apartment. She battled him with books, hiding behind book covers just as she'd done when she was a girl. Nothing had ever satisfied him. A sneering perfectionist, he had baited her into studious solitude, then laughed at her for being studious. When she'd won awards, prizes, scholarships, one after the other, he was secretly pleased and her glory reflected as if from the flash of his smile. But later, after yet another humid June parent-student reception, he would take a lock of her fine blond hair between his fingers. Rubbing it, he would mockingly recommend a trip to the hairdresser. "You don't have to *look* like a little grind."

Meaning, of course, that she was.

Her armor was silence, stoicism, withdrawal, her mother's love. She was amazed when, at college, girls told her she was pretty — she'd grown up thinking herself big, dull, dumb. She remembered once when she was fifteen, still at the lumpy jeans-and-moccasin stage of adolescence, her father had announced at dinner that he was concerned about her, Claire. The way she dressed and behaved, he said, was "generally sexless."

Claire had looked up stunned. "Yes, my dear," he said, "I am talking about you." He smiled sardonically down the table at her, taking a sip of red wine. "You are a very convincing neuter." Claire had felt such scorn for him, this preposterous person, this imposter-father, and at the same time she'd felt a bolt of pain, like a massive, iron-gloved blow to the chest. She had wanted to cry out, but hadn't. Nikki had giggled and Edward had stared straight ahead, paler than ever.

But why remember this now?

Later her mother had said, "Oh you mustn't take him so seriously. He's trying to do *Hedda Gabler* and it's going badly. You know what a perfectionist he is. And after all, you could, perhaps, dress more neatly. Is it necessary to wear these wretched clothes?"

Her mother always protected him. Sometimes Claire thought there were four siblings instead of three, and of the four, *he* needed the most to succeed, and so, as if he were the indulged child, a charming child, who, after all, was only cruel to his family, they let him.

One day on Madison Avenue near the Whitney Museum, she passed a small shop that sold toy soldiers and she stared into the window, thinking of Jason. Something stung her, some little bit of memory, and she remembered that she had paid cash for lunch but he had paid cash for the soldiers. It troubled her. What was it he was saying, that she would pay? She felt a shiver of real fear. All of her life she'd been careful with men, protecting herself with a coat of surface coolness. What if now . . . ?

Now what? she asked herself crossly, and turned away from the window. She disliked this in herself — this timidity, this cowardice. Jason was forgetful and had told her more than once, gloomily, that he had a bad memory.

"Bad memory or bad memories?" she had asked him, teasing.

"No," he had said stubbornly, confusingly, his face flooding a dull red.

No what?

He wouldn't say.

Nothing ventured, nothing gained, she said firmly to herself, and opening her umbrella (it had started to rain), walked down the street to a delicatessen. There, amid the warm seductive odors of expensive pâtés and cheese, she bought Brie and crackers and a little tin of caviar to give herself courage for the oncoming festive evening.

· VII ·

Gains
and
Losses

· · · 1 · · ·

"Now hear this, now hear this. It's Big B, your mother talking. All hands are expected to hit the grass at two o'clock today for a little leaf-raking session."

All afternoon in the scudding, ruffle-edged wind, under the glancing silver sky, we rake and bag leaves until, looking at the bottom of our steep driveway, I can see, in the late afternoon glimmer of sun, a mound of plastic sacks, shiny pillows of black, neatly placed in rows at the curb to wait for the sanitation men — there must be thirty bags, a good day's work.

At five, red-cheeked, good-humored, with blistered palms, I make a new pot of coffee and set out a plateful of doughnuts. I am feeling comfortable and domestic, congratulating myself on the felicitous warmth of hearth and home. I lay a fire in the living room and I think sentimentally to myself, It will be like old times when the kids were small, we'll pop some corn, we'll eat apples and crack nuts and gossip, and I say brightly to Susan, "Shall we have supper in the living room, by the fire?"

She says, "I won't be here for supper, I'm going to Maggie's." Alicia is working, Cliff is living in a halfway house two towns away, Nesta has a date or at least so she claims; she is going to meet him at the railroad station and they're going to . . . "Elope?" I ask hopefully. No, go to New York to see Ice-O-Rama at Madison Square Garden. Oh well. Another night home alone.

Now I ask you: is this a home? is this a family?

And then: inspiration! and I am revving up the Tank and

we, the Tank and I, are bouncing happily down our driveway and across the leaf-strewn streets of the town, under the black, mostly bare branches tangled overhead and illuminated here and there by the gold lights from the town's chic-antique iron streetlamps. Up the ridge, across Chestnut Street with its row of stately maples and then, at the crest of the hill, behind the circular driveway, the Parkers' big white house. It glooms up unlit, with black holes where beaming windows should be, but wait: there's a gleam behind the foliage of the north wing — the kitchen. Somebody's home and eating supper.

I creep quietly up the back steps and, shielding my eyes Indian-scout style, look through the uncurtained window. Gordy is sitting at the round kitchen table with his gold-framed reading glasses on and a section of the Sunday paper folded in front of him. He has on middle-aged clothes — a tan cardigan such as my dad used to wear, buttoned with one button over his white shirt. He is eating cold baked beans out of the jar and he has, as well, a steaming mug of something or other. I knock lightly on the glass. He starts and looks up frowning, then removes his glasses and comes to the door.

"Why, Barbara," he says.

"May I join you for supper?" I ask.

"Oh," he begins, confused.

"Just kidding!" I say. "I see it's only a simple meal."

"Yes . . . Would you like some tea?"

"Fine!"

He puts the kettle on the burner and I sit down nervous but smiling, rubbing my cold-reddened fingertips together. I have come, I tell myself, to talk to Gordy about my affair of the heart and get a little kind advice regarding Stephen Moss.

Steve is, after all, Gordon's friend. Maybe Gordy could tell me what to do.

"Listen, Gordy," I begin, as he puts a mug of tea in front of me. "I have this problem. There is this man I like very much. I like him more than I've liked anyone for years."

"Why, Barbara," he says, sitting down and showing his dimples — long lines at the sides of his bluish square jaw, "that's wonderful. Who's the lucky fellow? Anyone we know?"

"Let's leave it hypothetical for a while, okay? Because I need your disinterested and objective opinion."

"Shoot!"

"Well, it's like this — I have this block."

"Block?"

"Yes. You see, I like him so much but I can't go to bed with him."

"Oh. You're not attracted?"

"Oh no, I'm very attracted. That's the problem. Sometimes, with some men, you know, I'm attracted but not interested, but with this man I am both. I like him so much! Too much. Do you follow?"

Hands in pants pockets, Gordon leans back in his chair and looks up at the ceiling. "I think so. It's a little pathological, Barbara." He is smiling sadly, his dark eyes gleaming. I think it is odd of me to sit here and confide my love problems when his own wife is missing. I know she is missing but he doesn't know that I know and it is getting harder by the minute to fool myself. Why are you here, Barbara? Because she is gone and I like *him*.

Gordon blinks, looks down at the table, broods. I look up past his head at the kitchen wallpaper. It is yellow, patterned with a bamboo lattice. The kitchen cabinets are birch, a light, elegant, well-grained wood. The countertops match in color the bright yellow walls. It comes to me suddenly that Jenks, too, disappeared once, for ten days in the middle of the worst winter the Northeast had had for ten years. I knew he was off somewhere drinking but still I was worried and the worry made me angry. A man down the street (we lived in Brooklyn Heights then) came to help me shovel my walk and I started an affair with him. His name was Bill Travis. They had no children. His wife (who looked the picture of blooming health) had made a career of chronic (albeit mysterious) invalidism. She spent her entire day taking pills, napping and reading health books by crackpot authors. If any conversation deviated for ten seconds from her "condition," out came her cough, straight from *La Bohème,* and with the rat-a-tat-tat of a tommy gun she annihilated the poor conversational insurgents. The apartment smelled of brewer's yeast; they had no friends. Neither did we — a perfect match. When Jenks finally staggered in our front door I'd been with Bill that afternoon and couldn't bear to have him touch me. The bedroom, I remember, smelled of wet wool and apples. We had lain in bed, Bill and I, eating apples and watching snowflakes in the window and telling stories to each other like a couple of grade-school kids.

Gordy has considered for a long time, staring down at the kitchen table. The table has a large wooden salad bowl on it that contains a shriveled orange, a brown-spotted banana and two skittering fruit flies. Gordy's cardigan reminds me so much of my father's, down to the transparent thinness of the wool at the elbows. No matter what he had on my father looked dowdy — as if even his clothes had given up on him and agreed among themselves: "He's a failure." My father was tall and lean but he never exercised, his shoulders were bent, he had a potbelly. I believe my mother had a physical aversion to my father. Toward the end of the marriage they slept in separate rooms. Did she ever love him, I wonder, and how did it all go wrong?

"Because," Gordon says suddenly, raising his dark eyes and allowing the tilted chair to fall forward, "I guess, Barb, you must be scared. Does that sound right?" He goes on, "Maybe you're scared you'll love somebody again."

"Huh!" I say. "Even were that true — I'm not saying it is, I'm just playing with your hypothesis — then what could I do about it?"

He gives me a piercing look — hey, Barb, come on — and says, "You don't know why you're scared? Well, heck, who isn't, it's a scary business."

"No, I don't know . . . well, not exactly. Maybe because of someone I loved once, before I loved Jenks, when I was at Vassar."

He looks away sadly. I notice how his black hair curls about his ears. It has delicate silver streaks in it, like the expensive pelt of an exotic animal. "There's something I've always wondered about, Barbara. Did you love Jenks when you got married?"

I feel crushed by this question. How can I explain? I did not *not* love Jenks. That is all I can think of to say, so I say it. He nods and looks down at the floor. We sit together quietly, sipping tea. The refrigerator's sudden hum is startling. I don't smoke anymore but I long for a cigarette. I say because it needs to be said, "Steve Moss told me about Claire. Is there some way I can help?"

He looks up at the ceiling. "Why no, I don't think so. She seems to be all right."

"Did you talk to her?"

"She left me a note."

"But you don't know where she is?"

"No. Do you?"

"Me? No, I don't know. . . . Are you worried? I guess you are worried, I guess that's a silly question."

"Well, I'm not really worried." He looks down at the fruit bowl, picks up the dried orange, squeezes it hard, puts it down again. "I was angry at first, of course, but now I feel . . . uh . . . it's just that I wonder if, uh, oh what is the point? There used to be a point. Then after Michael . . . Michael and then Evan . . . we somehow, you see, lost the habit of happiness. It's strange how much I miss being happy. I would like," he says wistfully, "to be happy again."

We decide to have more tea and sit silently, companionably drinking.

I say, "Well, this is really nice. It's pleasant. You see, I was home all alone."

He says, turning his head to look out of the kitchen window in which we are both reflected — he in his cardigan, me in my turtleneck — "Yes, so was I."

I say, or blurt: "Gordy, I was so lonely!"

Without looking at each other we let our hands creep across the round table and our fingertips touch and entwine. We sit holding hands for a moment under the fluorescent ceiling light, like two people lost on an island after a nuclear blast — that's how it feels, so lonely it is like the silent end of the earth, there is an oily dark purple sea swirling around us, and a great fuming acrid cloud coming closer and I foresee that we will cling to each other, just for a while. He looks at me with dark, sad eyes. I know what he is thinking but I know he won't ask and so I stand up, still holding tight onto his warm hand, and come around the table and I say, looking down at him, standing in front of him with his hand clasped in both of mine, "Would it be so awful if we went to bed?"

He looks up at me in some kind of pain. And then, very

slowly, he stands and we put our arms around each other and hold each other. We are like an old broken-down couple whose friends are long gone, whose children are dead. We hobble out through the kitchen, totter together through the dining room to the front hall. He goes up the staircase first and then gently, as if we were ascending lofty Everest, helps me up the final step. Arms around each other, hips bumping, we pause at their bedroom door and then look the other way, into the guest room, a pretty room with a high old-fashioned fourposter bed. On the bed is a quilt, appliquéd in red and green in the Rose of Sharon pattern. Outside the black branches swaying in the wind seem to be shoving each other to look in the windows and I primly pull down all the shades as far as they'll go.

· · · 2 · · ·

Gourd, gored, Gordy. Someday, when I write my memoirs, I'll let you know what a lovely man I think you are, how with a smile or a glance you say more than many a verbal profligate does in ten chapters.

I had, later, no special guilt about it — I had only done something I'd wanted to do for a long time.

It was soothing, comforting, sad.

The cold, black room with its hushed windows and myself burning from the inside out so that the clothes fell away from my skin like thin sheets of melting Saran Wrap.

Gordon, sad and meticulous, hung his pants over the back of a chair.

We hurried the first time, my hips lifting toward him almost before my head found the pillow, and we both came right away, together, he with a gasp and then a groan.

I lay back and folded my arms around him. He lay there flat on top of me until I pried him upward, indicating that I couldn't breathe. I sat up and pulled the quilt back and we climbed underneath like two tykes playing house. The sheets were cold.

We slept a bit and later woke up and tried again, making love slowly, pleasurably. Nice, but with a sadness to it. Well. Of course I knew he was having a bad time, still I guess I'd been hoping for a little more zest and eagerness — hoping that we would both get into the spirit of the moment or that a little love would turn the tide of depression into a slightly more giddy froth. It wasn't bad — no, not at all. He is dexterous in a silent, somewhat repressed way; the good thing about doctors is this: usually they know where everything is.

Afterward, nobody talked. We lay there and felt warm and relaxed while the wind sniffed and circled the house. I thought it was pleasant and friendly that we could just rest there skin to skin without having the burden of postcoital cleverness upon us. At last he rolled over on his back, put his hands behind his head and sighed.

"What's next?" I said. "Sit ups?"

"Huh?" he said.

"You look like you're ready to do crunches."

"Well that's apt," he said. In the dim light of the bedroom I could see the gleam of his teeth — he was faintly smiling. "Sometimes I feel crunched. You know, Claire . . ." He paused and then went resolutely on: ". . . Claire was right to leave."

"Why do you say that?"

"I don't really know."

I propped myself up on an elbow and leaned over him, peering closely into his shadowed face. His skin smelled of lemon after-shave. I said wickedly, "Maybe it was a noble gesture. Maybe she left so we could get together."

He laughed, harshly.

"You don't think so?"

"She's not that noble."

"God, I hope not. Still, she knows I've been slouching around after you."

"She thinks you do that to annoy her."

"Oh no she doesn't. She doesn't think that at all. Tell me something. What do *you* think?" I let my free hand now dribble slowly down his chest, through his soft curly chest hair to his navel. There I paused and stroked lightly, lightly.

He grabbed my wrist. "Ah-ah-ah. Mustn't touch."

"Why not?"

"Because I say so." He held his wrist up in front of his eyes and the luminous green dial of his watch said 8:05.

"Is that a hint?"

"Nope. Just checking. Todd's away overnight, visiting his Aunt Muffy. Leslie's gone into New York for a Rangers game." He added proudly, "It's a date. Her first official date."

I smiled and stretched comfortably, pointing my toes under the quilt and looking up at the dark ceiling. Outside the wind rattled the tree branches and then howled and flung itself against the house. Something groaned deeply, the groan and creak of timbers and stays on a sailing vessel. There was a hapless repetitive banging — a shutter at the back of the house had come unfastened.

I thought what a fine thing it was on such a cold, windy night to be in bed with a man like Gordy. I thought for a warm sleepy moment that I was Claire and this house was like an anchored ship — we had sailed round the Horn in it and we had survived and now we were in port before setting sail again.

Gordon squeezed my hand. "I've always liked you, Barbara," he said.

"I like you, too, Gordon," I said, "or I wouldn't be here!"

This made him chuckle — ah, we were gaining, gaining. "Is Steve Moss the man you were talking about?"

"Not telling! He's a sweet man, this Mister X, he has a nice sense of humor. But when I think of love something gets in the way."

"Strange," he said in a thick voice.

"Something," I said, "or *someone.*"

There was a fuzzy silence. He didn't seem to take my meaning. He said, "Maybe you're scared of yourself."

"Myself?"

He yawned. "Your other self."

This made no sense to me. I sat up, pulled on my sweater and emerged, struggling, through the turtleneck. I pulled on my pants and zipped the fly. I shook out my hair, stamped into my work boots, leaned over Gordon and kissed him on the forehead.

"Sleep tight," I whispered.

"Yes," he said, drifting off, eyes closed. I covered his bare shoulder with the quilt and stood up straight. He opened his eyes. "You ought to tell her to go away."

"Who?" I said, startled.

He smiled and closed his eyes again. "Your other self. Your father . . ." My father? My father what? I waited for more but nothing came. He was asleep. My father?

I went down to the kitchen, turned off the light and left. Driving home, I remembered that Claire had said she'd always liked my father. What she'd always wanted in place of her own — an amiable American dad. Oh yeah. She didn't understand. These weak ones like my father, they drive you nuts. They give you nothing but hang on, hang on, with their terrible curved claws, digging into your skin, draining you with little pecks until you are eaten up and bleeding to death. You have to leave to save yourself. Then everyone says, as they did about my mother, "Wasn't she awful to leave him like that?"

Only which self did he mean?

My good loving self always got me into things and my bad angry self got me out of things.

All at once I saw what the trouble was: that I feared both of them.

Straight from Gordy's guest bed, I went barreling down the night-shadowed streets full of amazement and alarm — so that was it! I was just as afraid of hurting as I was of getting hurt.

A car swerved at me and away, a lime-green Volkswagen Rabbit of the same dusty vintage that Jenks's girlfriend drove, and the face at the wheel, revealed in the quick wash of my headlights, reminded me, in its colossal erosion, of Jenks. I shuddered and jerked the Tank's wheel straight and decided practically that it couldn't be, Jenks was safely down at the shore miles away, I was just experiencing some sort of primordial guilt and as punishment had resurrected in my mind the scarred visage of my drunken husband.

On shot springs I bumped up our steep rutted drive and noticed, puzzled, that every light in the house was on although everyone should have been out for the evening. The house shone forth from behind bare tree branches and stripped shrubbery like a lantern of pierced tin or a bulging tinderbox about to explode. I parked, leaped through the front door and stood bewildered for a long moment in the front hall — looking down the hall into the living room (right) and then into the dining room (left) — chaos, everywhere chaos. The house had been ransacked, perhaps by a gang out of some grade-B sado-mas horror movie, a bunch of juvenile thugs with features distorted by panty-hose masks who were looking not just for plunder but thrills. Everywhere, things were overturned, chair cushions up-ended, dumped, tables swept clear of plants (a long philodendron lay groaning in its shattered clay pot in the living room) as if by a giant menacing hand. In the dining room, the top of the carved Italianate nineteenth-century sideboard, a gift from Jenks's grandmother, had been picked clean, nothing upon it but dust and fingerprints. Not a candlestick, not a silver tray, no silver service and all of the little silver objêts in the downstairs rooms had been kidnapped as well. The house had been raped. Thank God no one had been at home. Thank God Susan hadn't been at home. And then I heard a dullish thud upstairs and my heart felt pinched —

someone was coming down the stairs. I stood still in back of the dining-room doorway not breathing, until a shadow in a wine-colored bathrobe glided by a few inches away and stopped.

"Susan!" I said. "Oh, Susie, are you all right?"

Slowly, she turned a sad dull face. I reached out for her — she looked at me dumbly. I thought, She's in shock, she's been raped, she's been hurt. I held her at arm's length examining her critically. Her pale face was tearstained and she looked tired around the eyes and she whispered, "That hurts, Mom," and pulled her arm away. I saw that her shoulder stuck out at a funny angle. "Oh, Ma," she said, "I was tired and I had all this homework to do so I came home early. He was robbing the house. I couldn't believe it and when I tried to stop him he yanked at my arm."

"I'll kill him!" I said. "Who was it? It wasn't the Jones kid, was it? They got him on a B and E last year. Did you get a good look at his face? Was he wearing a mask?"

She shook her head from side to side. "It was Daddy."

"What?"

"It was Daddy. I came in and he had all the lights on and he was stuffing things into big plastic leaf bags. I asked him what he was doing and he didn't answer and when I tried to stop him he just yanked at my arm — I can't even move it."

"Bastard!" I yelled. "Louse! Rat! Wretch!" I howled like someone howling at heaven and then I took Susan to the emergency room of the hospital. ("What? You again?" the nurse said. "We ought to give discount coupons.") At 11:35 P.M. I called the police. Officer Serio and Officer Slavin came to the house. "I see, ma'am," they said as I told them the story. What he had taken was most of all silver — the flatware was gone and all the little silver knickknacks — porringers we had gotten as baby presents and silver cigarette boxes, and silver candy dishes, two Revere bowls and the silver vegetable dishes still in their discrete flannel jackets, and the tea service, a wedding present from my mother and George Bell, her second husband, and the four candlesticks, a wedding present from my father and his second wife, Leora.

I was surprised at how bad I felt about these things. My life had been so non-middle-class that I was looking forward to giving my children "family silver" to make up for the more-or-less bohemian times we'd all had growing up together. I wanted my kids to have a few bourgeois trappings. I wanted them, each one, to have a few pieces of real sterling that they could point to, saying, "It was in the family."

But what would they do with those things anyhow? They might be married to Mister or Ms. X a year or two and then one night (so insubstantial are modern marital bonds) spouse and silver would disappear together. That's it, Barbara, I tell myself, keep looking at the bright side, or as Susan would say, rolling her eyes, "How every cloud doth have a silver lining."

But damn him anyway! What right does he have coming into this house? He hasn't lived here for years. Susie said he looked like hell, as if he had some sort of skin cancer on one side of his face, and I thought, *He* is the cancer. He's been eating us up for years.

I took a tepid bath and, most disheartened, crept into bed. Alicia had come home, looked around shamefacedly, silently gone off to her room. She was ashamed of her father. None of my kids talked about him anymore — he might just as well have lived in Anchorage, Alaska. My nice kids! I thought sadly how, in a year or two, they'd be mostly gone. Well, I'd be free then, wouldn't I, free as a bird. I could buy a camper and tour the country, find a job out west in Utah or maybe Montana. I've never been out west, always wanted to go. I think of myself as a Free Spirit who's been tied down too long. Who needs silver, anyhow? Where I'm going it would only be a burden. Can you imagine a camper with sterling candlesticks and a tea set from Tiffany's? There are many places I'd like to go and things I'd like to see. I've always been an adventurous sort, but lack of opportunity and money, plus obligations unduly onerous, have kept me nailed down.

Next year I'll be mostly free of family ties — what a thought. I've had responsibilities since I was thirteen. You see, I always felt *I* was taking care of *him* — my father, I mean. We weren't much of a family, we were two people in dire straits living together — washed up together, you might say.

After we were married, Jenks and I used to do "the upstate run," visit his family outside of Syracuse and then, on the way back, drop off the Thruway to visit my father and Leora. Leora really worked at "bringing the family back together." I liked her. She had a long plain sweet face. Then he had a stroke and all the things he had (maybe) been saving to tell me, about my mother and what happened between them, were gone forever. He never learned how to talk again, there were only his wild brown eyes starting out of his head. He had waited too long to tell, I had waited too long to ask. He died two days before Cliff was born.

So, maybe because of my parents and their split, I had this romantic Dickensian notion of family life. I thought it would be a bunch of fun people who would hang out together. Well! Here we are! Barb and her Fun Family! I have loved my kids but I've probably done lots wrong. Still, I never left, so score one for me. Like my father, I stuck it out. Say. I guess that is one for his side. He never left either. It wasn't much but maybe more wasn't in him.

Where I think I have really failed is in my love life. What Gordy said to me sounds true — I am scared! I am scared! I don't want to be hurt again — kicked out or abandoned. Lying alone in the dark of my crumbling bedroom, I think again of Gordon. That night I dream of him. We are making love under a thin wool blanket in the cabin of a dark, anchored boat. The boat rocks and rocks, water slaps against its sides. We are making love slowly and I feel comforted, happy and safe.

· · · 3 · · ·

This November morning I have a free period between American History I (1492 through the Spanish American War) and American History II (everything else) and I am sitting at my desk trying to think of a thought-provoking question for next week's midterm exam: "Compare and contrast the Spanish-American War with the war in Vietnam, giving particular attention to the popular ideologies that promoted our entrance into both wars."

Good.

I am feeling cross this morning because I need one more chapter — a pivotal chapter — for my novel and right now all I have in my head is light: different kinds of light — gray city light and November country sunlight, sunlight that is the same thin color and consistency as the mild light that this morning falls through my tall classroom windows. Still, what a joy to have an entire evening free to work without quizzes to correct or classroom preparations. I will dive into my other life as into a cool clear pool with the added satisfaction — ha! ha! — of knowing that her life is even worse than mine. Shall the lost be found? Yes indeedy, all of life is a search, but for most of us the goals have shifted inward. However, I do have a few crass exterior goals like paying my giant electric bill.

Thanksgiving is tomorrow and school ends at twelve noon today after my American History II class. The problem is, I don't get paid until next week and what fun is there in shopping on Thanksgiving Eve when you're overdrawn at the bank? I might have called up Steve Moss and asked him to Turkey

Day Dinner but I haven't paid his bill yet either and besides, I'm not sure I want to see him — I still don't think I can go to bed with him. I called Gordy last night just to check in. He said Claire had written a postcard saying she was trying to lose herself or find herself, something like that. I think this self business is mainly a problem of modern times. I imagine in the old days folks were so busy keeping the wolf from the door that they never worried too much about who they were — it was more like: will I last until dawn? My Uncle Henry used to say that nothing firmed up a boy's character as much as a pregnant girlfriend, but that was in the good old days of shotguns and outraged fathers, when nobody at all worried about what firmed up girls except of course pregnancy. This brings to mind Jenks, the father of my children, and the fact that this year, on my Thanksgiving Day table, aside from glass bowls of walnuts and glass dishes of celery and fruit, we'll be using stainless-steel utensils from the kitchen drawer — four different patterns that I have gotten over the years with books of supermarket green stamps. When I finish my novel and make some money I will get a divorce.

Then suddenly I have an idea. I don't know where it comes from, but a thought so pure in inspiration seizes me that I know just how Jonathan Edwards felt when he had his revelation in Northampton, Massachusetts. Very clearly, as if a whirlwind had arisen and brought me the words in newsprint form, I see this message: SELL THY HOUSE.

What a hot idea! Where did it come from and why hadn't I thought of it before? If I sell the house I could buy a smaller house and maybe live for a while on the difference. Oh! Oh! Oh! Instantly, I throw down my Papermate pen and grab my handbag and make a dash for the pay phone outside of the teachers' lounge. I call the first name I come to under Real Estate in the Yellow Pages. I stab the number with a broken nail, excitedly dial. Someone named Tooky Twill, who claims she used to know me, says she'll come over and look at the house this afternoon.

Driving home, I remember Tooky Twill. She used to drive in Cliff's nursery-school car pool. Her son Bruce had a brain tumor removed when he was seven. I used to see Bruce on the school playground, a little kid with no hair playing by himself. I haven't heard anything of Bruce in years. I hope he's all right. I know this is magical thinking (oh what's wrong with a little soothing magic now and then?), but maybe if Bruce can be all right my son Cliff can be all right, too. Oh, well, it's not a thought, it's just a wish.

As if there had been a small Kansas tornado, kids are lying all over the house when I get home, looking as if the windstorm had picked them up and flung them about in various broken attitudes. Susan is on the leather sofa in the living room with her moccasined feet up on the sofa's back and her head (in a headband made of twisted leather, my Indian princess) awkwardly propped on the sofa's arm. She needs deerskin pants and a tunic but instead has on denim overalls over an orange sweatshirt. She is reading a paperback — air terminal trash! I pluck the book out of her hands, toss it over my shoulder. "Greetings, my sweet. It's the day before Thanksgiving and guess who has a chore for you?"

She rolls her eyes and says in a bored voice, "Who could it be? Can't you take it easy, Mother? I just got home a half hour ago and I'm suffering from student burnout. This is supposed to be a holiday weekend, remember?"

"Tomorrow the holiday, today we work. Which would you rather, dust or vacuum?"

I hear a noise behind me and turn my head in time to see

· 207

Nesta (who is sitting in the wing chair with both legs over an arm) gently slide over said chair and disappear into the voluminous folds of her black skirt like a mermaid sucked into the mire of a bottomless sea.

"Ha! I see you, Nesta! Peek-a-boo! Just think how lucky you are, you get to work off some calories lugging the Hoover around. Get up, get up, this has to be done by two o'clock."

Groans. "Two o'clock! Why?"

"Because someone is coming to see the house at two."

Susan laughs: yuk, yuk, yuk. Who would want to see this house?

"Mrs. Twill is coming to see the house, my dear. She's a Realtor. She sells houses for Better Homes, Inc. and she sold over two million dollars' worth of property last year. Her picture was in the paper."

"Wait a minute," Nesta the Lorelei says, slowly rising up from the seafoam. "You are going to sell *this house?*"

"Maybe."

"You can't do that!"

"Why not?"

"This is our *home.*"

I am touched by this. Poor Nesta! If only she hadn't reminded me so much of myself at her age I might have liked her better.

"So?" I say. "We'll get us another one."

"*I* think it's a great idea," Susan says, all hoity-toity, lifting her chin and batting her lashes. She asked me the other day if I didn't think she resembled either Kit Cornell, Gertrude Lawrence or Margaret Sullavan. "I hate this falling down dump. Someday," (she says, looking off dreamily into her future) "I am going to have a little house all my own up on Cape Cod. It's going to have gray shingles and black shutters and the windows will have white trim. I'm going to have a white picket fence around the flower garden and I'll have daisies and roses and phlox and those tall blue flowers. Mom? Remember when we all had that vacation on Cape Cod? When was that anyway? I was terribly small." She pronounces this "tellibly," like Gertrude Lawrence.

"It was ages ago," I say briskly, not falling into her bathos. "Get up, dusting time."

"But Ma." Her eyes widen. "What about all my stuff in the attic, like the dollhouse Daddy made for Little Letitia and Baby Doris."

"Susan, grow up. Everything's going to get sold."

"Oh *no*. Well then I think you should wait until I go to college."

"What for? Maybe you won't get in, ever thought of that?"

"I'll get in," she says grimly, rising and leaving the room. "If it's the last thing I do, I'll get in."

"Better get a scholarship!" I yell after her. There is nothing like a harrowing home life to provide kids with academic incentive.

"Oh, *this* place," Tooky Twill says, whipping off her sunglasses. Sure, now I remember her clearly, only I haven't seen her in fourteen years. Her black hair is striped with gray but she looks otherwise the same. "I'd completely forgotten this place existed, it's so buried in shrubbery."

"I like the privacy."

"Uh huh. The Plumleys used to live here, didn't they? They were darling people, at least she was. Marvelous tennis player. She ran off, you know," Tooky says, unwrapping her red plaid scarf, "with the golf pro from Claremont Country Club, but . . ." (she's unbuttoning her camel-hair coat) "she and her lover were killed on the Jersey Turnpike that very same day.

Some people said it was fate. Otis, of course, was thirty years older than she was. He's remarried. So! This is the hall. Uh *huh!*" She glances upward, observing the lace-doily effect where paint has fallen from the ceiling. "You've had it for . . . ?"

"Sixteen years. Of course it wasn't in terrific shape when we bought it."

"Well, Prissy was . . ." I know, I know. In love.

"And," I hurry on, "due to circumstances beyond my control, I haven't done much to it since. The stain up in that corner? It was there."

"Aha! And this is the living room! A good-sized room, what is that in the . . . oh, beer cans. Clever, very clever. Some sort of interesting radiant heat device? Or . . ."

"No, it's just the kids fooling around, they —"

"Oh, I thought maybe the cans collected heat and —"

"Exploded?"

"Exploded? No, I . . . well, let's go on. This is the dining room, I see, a nice-sized room, too, but I would say, however, to be blunt, that it does need to be, oh, decorated."

". . . uh . . ."

(Firmly) "Painted . . . And here we have — my, this could be pretty, couldn't it? — a sunroom. I love these sunrooms in these old houses, although of course this one, with the shrubs all around it is, um . . ."

"Pretty shady."

"Well, yes, but nice and cool in the summer, I'll bet. Now. The kitchen is . . . ?"

"Right through that swinging door, just —"

CRASH.

"Ow!!"

Tooky gets socked in the jaw as Nesta slams through the door looking as of old, pale and glum, with snarled snakey hair and a dinner plate with a four-layer peanut butter and jelly sandwich stacked upon it, and an airmail letter clenched in her other hand. She attempts to sail by, while Tooky stands there dazed, rubbing her jaw.

"Nesta, you just ran down Mrs. Twill. Mrs. Twill, this is Nesta, a *young lady* who lives with us."

" 'Lo," says Nesta, not so much as raising an eyelid. I notice her black lashes are glued up with dewdrops, her pale cheeks show glistening snailtrails of tears.

"Nesta, is everything . . . ?"

"Nnn," says Nesta, now such a full-fledged member of the household that she speaks in the family code — slurs and grunts.

"Is that a letter from . . . ?"

"Mmm." Nesta starts to snuffle and then, reverting completely to her self of yore, turns over the hand that holds the airmail letter and wipes her nose on its blue-veined wrist. "Gago," she mumbles (got to go) and flounces off while I apologize to Tooky, who is delicately pressing the side of her jaw with three fingers.

"I'm sure it's all right," Tooky says bravely, "although it does feel just a little swollen. I don't think she got any teeth, though." She laughs, shakily, and I pat her arm — stout heart! — and push open the swinging door. "Oh!" she says brightly, "a Primitive. I haven't seen one of these in ages. Some people love them, you know. As a matter of fact, there are two kinds of house-buyers who love them. Those who like to gut houses and start over and those with an interest in antique cooking equipment. For example, I sold a house just last week and the big draw was a wood cooking stove, the real thing. It was a second stove, of course, but still . . ."

"This one's gas."

"Yes."

More of the same goes on upstairs. Oohs and aahs over our antique plumbing and our cute little ol' tubs with their cute claw feet. By the time we venture into the basement, I am geared up to give her the house if only she'll take it off my hands and I have to remind myself that Realtors Think Low, so add on ten thou to whatever she comes up with. Still, I am beginning to wonder if I will get back what we paid for it, way back when. At the time we bought it, the general reaction was hoots of laughter that meant, "You were had." Everyone then thought fifty thousand dollars an enormous sum.

In the front hall again, Tooky sighs, winds the plaid scarf around her neck, flattening out the ends crosswise upon her bosom. I politely hold her coat. All this time I have wanted to ask about Bruce but didn't dare. She buttons up, puts on her sunglasses. I stand with my back to the front door so she can't make a run for it before I ask the crucial question, which is: "How much?"

Her eyes drop. My heart plummets. She says, in a low voice, with her chin tucked into her scarf, "Barbara, you understand the house needs a lot of work. It needs, well, everything. It is, basically, a roomy, interesting . . . er . . . shell."

"Uh huh. Would you say, um . . ."

Her head drops lower — even her forehead is sinking fast. She whispers. What? Pardon me? Three. I am stunned. Three thousand dollars? It's got to be worth more than that. I try to say something but my lips won't move, my mouth feels full of novocaine. "Maybe," she whispers, "if you painted a little . . . three twenty."

I put my hand to my forehead — it feels cold and sweaty: wait a minute.

"I'm sorry it's so low," she says, "but that's just an estimate. You can put it on the market for whatever you want, but I'd say three thirty tops."

"Three hundred and thirty thousand dollars?"

"In that area, somewhere."

"Sold!" I say.

"What?" she says.

"It's a deal," I say. "Let's put it on for . . . three twenty and see what happens." I grin, open the front door for her.

"Do you think," she asks over her shoulder, "you could have it *cleaned?*"

Magnanimously, I promise. Why not?

She waves her gloved hand. "Must rush." And then her thin face expands into a wide white smile. "I don't know if you remember my son Bruce?" I nod. I remember, yes, I remember. "He's coming home from college today."

"Oh that's terrific. Where does he go?"

"M.I.T."

I smile and close the door after her and think, humming, of my son Cliff. My son Cliff is coming home, too. I wrote him a letter inviting him for Thanksgiving and he wrote back accepting.

Thinking I'm about to be rich, I fly down to the supermarket on Route 24, buy the world's biggest turkey, cranberry sauce, pecans, wild rice, sausage, mushrooms and condiments of all kinds, write out a stunning check at the checkout counter with nerveless aplomb. Outside, the November wind has picked up, the air is a four o'clock old-rose color, the parking lot lights twinkle on, a gaseous green, and one lone green star blinks on in the deepening plum-colored sky. All around me there is the cheerful clink of shopping carts slamming into each other and the wind sings and whistles to the happy holiday spenders. I don't know what the wind is saying to the rest of the world, but it murmurs soothingly into my ears as follows: rrrrich, rrrrich, rrrrich. What a grrreat rrrreassuring song!

· · · 4 · · ·

"Guess what?" Susan gloomily quizzes Alicia at the dinner table in our primitive kitchen that night. We are having our Thanksgiving Eve primitive usual — hot dogs, baked beans, sauerkraut, mustard, ketchup and chili sauce.

"You're not really going to eat all that!" Alicia says to Susan, wrinkling her nose in disgust. "Mother, can't you say something to her? This is revolting. She's obviously having some sort of infantile regression. Anyway, it's bad for her skin."

"Oh, kindly shut up," Susan says. "Nobody ahsked you to comment. One cahn't even eat in peace around here."

Alicia is not having hot dogs à la mode. She is having a dish of skim-milk yogurt with slices of apple, raisins, walnuts, co-conut, a sprinkle of granola and a side dish of tofu. Nesta, very down in the mouth, is having what Susan is having only more of it. I don't know what Cliff is having tonight but tomorrow — my heart zings! — he'll be home. Cliff is coming home! My son is coming home!

"I ahsked you a question, Alicia, and you still have not responded," Susan says.

"Cripes," Alicia complains, "do you have to talk like *thaht?* Okay, okay, what is it?" Alicia looks pretty tonight. With her earnings at the gas station she bought herself a dress of soft blue corduroy which she wears with her new caramel-colored Frye cowgirl boots.

"*She's* selling the house," Susan says, pointing the end of the dripping frankfurter at me, as if it were a loaded revolver.

"You are?" Alicia asks, turning her head gracefully, and arching her plucked penciled brows. I can't figure out who she thinks she is tonight — Joan Blondell?

"Yes," I say, "I am. We're going to get a smaller, more manageable house."

"Ha!" Alicia says. "The house is manageable, it's the people in it who aren't. Why are you selling?"

"We need the money. I'm sick of being broke."

There is a silence. In it, Nesta slurps her cocoa. She hunches over her mug like a second-grader, her dark eyes looking at me reproachfully over the thick white rim. Susan says grandly, "Money isn't everything."

"Just what is it you have against money?" I ask her. "It never did anything to you."

"It's not money," she says, "it's my room. I spent hours getting just the right shade of purple for my walls and now you want me to abandon everything just like that. And what about all my things? I'm very attached to my old dolls and stuff. I was saving everything for my children."

"I thought you weren't going to get married, ever."

"I'm not. That doesn't mean I can't have children. I believe . . ." She raises her head and her eyes look high-minded and loony at the same time. ". . . in the concept of planned generation."

"Yeah? So did Hitler and look what happened to him. Listen, Susie, wouldn't it be nice to have a nicer house with a better room? I mean, it might be a bit smaller but it would be clean and airy and warm. Don't forget how cold your room is, come January. In another house we could have a better furnace and a hot-water heater that works."

"Mother," Alicia says, "is there really going to be some money?"

"God, I hope so."

She looks at me then lowers her blue-shadowed eyelids. "Do you think there'd be enough . . ."

"What?" Okay, what's it going to be? Her own car? A trip to Paris? A Yamaha 600?

". . . for me to go back to school? I'd really like to go back to college."

"You would? How come?"

"I don't know, I guess pumping gas isn't for me. Besides, I've wanted to go back for a while but, see, there hasn't been any money at all."

I look at her hopefully, thinking how great it would be if she actually finished college. I don't know, I guess I am just stuck with these old-fashioned aspirations for my kids like education and marital happiness, that latter of course being the daydream of all time. Of course Alicia is not one bit like Susan who is dopey, dreamy, talented, romantic — Alicia is a whiz at math and science and problem-solving of the detached, logical kind. I see her sitting in some light, spacious office, at a drafting board perhaps, yellow pencils stuck into her chignon, while beautifully rendered drawings of complicated structures rise up from under her swiftly moving hand and handsome young male engineers admire her from afar.

Susan sighs and noisily rises. "If it's all right, I think I'll run down to Maureen's to watch a little HBO. Will we get cable TV if we sell the house?"

"Anything to make you happy in the new home, but here in the old . . . unhappiness prevails as usual. In other words, no, you can't run down to Maureen's because I am counting on you for the pecan pie."

Suddenly, Nesta begins to cry. All this while she has been quietly stuffing her face, and now, with half a hot dog in her hand, she is chewing and bawling, dribbling chili all down her chin and onto her dirty pink sweater.

"My father . . . ," she says, while a wad of orange food tumbles around behind her teeth. Her father! Oh how nice it would be to see her father again. Pete was one of my all-time favorite lovers, had a great sense of humor and *joie de vivre* to spare, was, in bed, as elegant a craftsman as ever I'll come across. I think now maybe I might have loved him. Yes, definitely I might have loved him.

"My father's coming home," Nesta wails, puts down her hot dog, wipes her mouth and eyes with a paper napkin, blows her nose — honk! honk! — in it.

My heart leaps. Down, dog. No, Barbara — I remonstrate with myself — forget him and concentrate on the man at hand, since lately you have made a little progress. "Why that's wonderful, Nesta," I say. "Aren't you happy? You missed him a lot."

"He got married again! He's bringing home this person and she's French and I've never met her. And that's not all!"

What else could there be?

"She's nineteen years old! That's only three years older than me and she's going to be my stepmother. Is he kidding or what? I mean, what is he, some kind of imbecile-pervert?"

All of us exchange uncomfortable looks.

"Well, goodness," Susan says consolingly, "maybe it won't be as bad as you think. I mean, what do you want to bet it doesn't last? Once she's over here she'll probably run off with someone her age."

"I don't even speak French!" Nesta cries. "I hate him! I hate him! Who does he think he is? All he's ever done is louse up everyone's life. All he's ever thought of is himself. He never gave one shit about me, never. It's all his fault they got divorced, he was such a selfish jerk, always being the great creative genius and mooching off my mother. Having *affairs* in the afternoon while my mother was at work and he didn't . . . he didn't even have much talent, everyone said so."

We stare at her in fascination. So. All this time, all this impacted crud has been lodged in Nesta's brain.

I clear my throat. "Nesta," I say, "you're welcome to stay with us as long as you like." Susan gives me a sharp look — Nesta catches it, squares her shoulders.

"Huh! Stay here with this bunch of bizarre creeps? Never!" She gets up from the table, shoves in her chair. "Besides," she says, looking at me maliciously, "as soon as Cliff gets a good job we're getting married."

Silence. Then Susan laughs. "Baloney!" she says scornfully. "Cliff would never marry you."

"Oh no?" Nesta cries. She digs a hand under the neck of her dingy sweater and comes up with a gold lump on a gold chain. My God, and all this time I thought she had a small tumor growing on her upper chest. Instead, this is Cliff's Comstock High School class ring. "We're engaged," she says triumphantly.

I am trying to ignore this silly person. I say, very calmly, "Alicia, do you think I might try a teeny bit of tofu, I've never had any."

"Why of course, Mother," Alicia says graciously, pushing her plate toward mine.

"What is it you'd like me to do, Mother?" Susan asks, standing almost at attention next to her chair, her thumbs pressed to her sides. "Are you sure you want pecan pie? Is there anything else I can do?"

"Wasn't that Cliff's pie?" Alicia asks Susan. "Cliff always did pecan, didn't he?"

"No," Susan says, "he did mince, Mom did apple, I did pecan, you did pumpkin."

"Luckily," I say, "this year we don't have to polish the silver." We all laugh. Nesta stands looking around the table at us warily, sensing that we have joined forces against her. Why not? We had offered her the hand of friendship but instead she seduced our son and brother while he was in an emotionally vulnerable condition. On the other hand, maybe marriage might be good for Cliff, especially if Nesta could find a paying job.

Nesta slinks off toward the kitchen door and I feel a brief wave of compassion for her. I call out to her, "Nesta, is there something you'd like to make for tomorrow?"

She looks at me from the doorway. "Go to hell," she says.

Nice talk for a would-be daughter-in-law!

"It was you, too," she says, looking spitefully in my direction. "I remember that time I came home early from *E.T.* because I threw up in the theater from too much popcorn and when I got home my father was asleep in bed and the bathroom door was locked and who came out of the bathroom? You! So I had to throw up in the hall!"

What a memory this kid has! She plunges out of the kitchen and I yell toward her back, "That was afterward!" but she is gone. My children are silent, looking at me appalled. "It was," I say to them, "it was ages after her mother left, not before, and I don't want to hear any more about it."

Alicia and Susan start clearing the table but so baleful is their silence, so heavy with reproachful import and adulterous implication, that I fling myself wrapless out through the back door yelling over my shoulder that I am going to run down to the 7-Eleven to buy some cream of tartar and cinnamon and whipping cream and ARSENIC.

"What a showoff," Susan mutters to Alicia, shaking her head.

"It's okay, Mother," Alicia calls from the sink where she is scraping a plate. "We all know his divorce couldn't possibly have been your fault."

I feel heartened by Alicia's remark but getting into the car — who left these beer cans on the front seat? — suddenly see the truth.

A back-handed compliment if ever there was one.

Crackle, crunch. There is nothing like a crisp black autumn night to clear one's sinuses and purge a heart occluded with sorrow. Pete the fink. So be it. I'll bet this French kid has a long Gallic nose, a small mouth, bad teeth, and tiny black moles all over her body. We didn't get along that well anyhow. He was good in bed, but self-centered? Uh huh!

Pete did these strange sculptural collages — he'd use rivets to weld together pieces of hunks of scrap metal, broken-toothed saw blades, rotted boards all a-bristle with bent rusty nails. I never could make a whole lot of sense out of these pieces. Once I asked him jokingly what he planned to call this series, "Tetanus II"? They did give you a painful "after the air raid" feeling, as if, emerging from the basement of your smoking ruin, you stood peering at a pile of charred debris from which (you hoped) no bloodied head, hand or unshod foot would suddenly appear, twitching. I wonder why it is he got custody of Nesta? Before this, I always thought she'd picked him.

And darn it, I hate to have my kids think that of me. Besides, this time it isn't true. Ernestine was long gone — at least by a couple of weeks — when I met Pete down at the Lion's Paw. I was with someone that night (who? I don't remember) and Pete came over, said, "Hi, how's the History Department?" pulled up a chair, ordered a beer, started to cry — he seemed devastated by his wife's departure. That was just before Thanksgiving five years ago, so I invited them — Pete and Nesta — for T. Day. It was a flop — Nesta whined and sniveled throughout the feast and the next week we all whined and sniveled — she'd given the entire family Asian flu.

Other Thanksgivings I have known — let's see: the Thanksgiving after my mother left and my father took all of us, Aunt Min, Aunt Betty, Uncle Henry and several cousins to the country club for dinner and Aunt Betty got crocked and socked the waitress so that olives, celery, carrot sticks and three drinks including her margarita flew up into the air and landed all over the next damascened table where Mayor Caspar Tweedy and his wife, Minerva, were dining with "a large party of friends" as it was reported the next afternoon in the *Livia Messenger*. I remember Mayor Tweedy rising up from his chair, wrathfully brushing off the sleeves of his tweed suit, his eyeglasses coated with tequila, which gave him a ghastly, ghostly, blindly Oedipal look.

Or the next Thanksgiving, which we spent home, alone.

Or the Thanksgiving Cliff, aged thirteen, got meningitis and I spent it in the hospital waiting room. We had dinner (the kids and I) in the hospital snack bar and for three days after that I couldn't locate Jenks. ("Why bother?" I screamed at him when at last he arrived — drunk — at our door. "Why the hell don't you just get out?" and a couple of days later he — Thank God — did.)

Back from the 7-Eleven I march through the front door and, glancing into the living room on my way to the kitchen, see something that makes me clutch my little sack of groceries close to my sweatered bosom — a man in a dark three-piece suit is sitting on the brown leather sofa. He is tall and scarecrow thin, his legs are crossed above scabby red shins showing slumped black socks, and the hand holding a lit cigarette is shaking so badly that the cigarette smoke appears to be wobbling off into brown air in a series of dots and dashes like a Morse code: H E L P. Oh God! That riddled death head, the small eyes ablaze and atwitch, the pate with a large patch of fresh adhesive upon it, and the smile — small, uncertain but snide.

" 'Lo, Barb," Jenks says in a thick voice.

Help! "Get out!"

"Now, Barb . . ." He doesn't stand, no doubt he can't. "I'm here to explain and apologize."

"Don't want to hear it. Just get out. I don't want to see you again. Ever!"

"I'm sober, Barb."

"What?"

"Sober. And I'm going to stay that way."

"Ha ha. Do dogs fly? Do birds swim? Will you please get out? You're not just a thief, you're a brute. You dislocated Susan's shoulder."

"I didn't mean to. It was an accident."

"Get out!"

"I have every intention of returning the money."

"Sure!"

"No, honestly. I've been in Ocean County Rehabilitation Center for ten days and tomorrow I'm off to Minnesota for the long haul — real rehabilitation this time, and this time it's going to work."

"Yeah? Why?"

"Because this time I want it to work. Anyway, just to explain, that's what I needed the silver for. I had to pay in advance for the program. When I come back I'll be a new man."

"Oh yeah, like 'On the Third Day He Rose Again from the Dead.' "

"And I'd like you to think about something while I'm gone."

"What?"

"Us. Our getting together again."

I stare down at Jenks Bigelow, still my legal spouse — his red, ruined face, his tiny red-rimmed eyes, the sparse gray-brown hair hanging down over his ears, his trembling hand holding the cigarette. "What happened to that woman you were living with?"

He says carefully, "She died. Cirrhosis." Any pity I may want to feel is instantly negated by what he does next — he flicks his cigarette ash onto the rug. Somehow, the simple presumption of this gesture enrages me and confirms me in my vast repulsion. No. This is not possible. I say, pointing, "See that thing? It's an ashtray."

He glances sideways at the table. "Oh," he says, "sorry. I'm a little nervous." He gives me a tight little smile.

"About what?"

"About being here, Barb. This is a hard thing for me to do, coming to you like this. What do you say, will you think it over? We had some good times."

He weighs, all of him, about one thirty-five. I study him coolly (the groceries still clutched to my chest) and say coolly, "Jenks, I would like you to leave now."

"Barbara?" he says. "Couldn't you have faith in me? I am trying so hard for us."

"No. Don't say 'us.' Do it for yourself, not us. There is no chance for us at all. I am now going to leave the room. I hope that in ten minutes or less you'll be gone."

Half an hour later, when I come back to check the living room, he is gone. I didn't hear a car outside, I guess he walked. No car, no woman, no job, no money, no friends, no family, no life. On our honeymoon we rented a cottage in Maine and it rained every day and we walked everywhere in ponchos, holding hands. The cottage smelled of mildew, pine needles, woodsmoke — the damp sheets smelled of sex. He was strapping then and had a marvelous white-toothed smile and the truth was that for many years after we were married, whenever he touched me, I glowed. I guess I did love him once but . . . Help!

At once, I run to the telephone and dial Gordon's number. Help!

Somebody tell me what to do!

The telephone rings and rings, I clutch the receiver so hard I feel it gasping for breath. I am sending Gordon all my ESP — answer it!

Nobody home. I hang up clumsily and the receiver tumbles downward off the hook, and helplessly jerks and pitches about at the end of its cord. Dope! I want to scream at it, Stop that!

Now what? Why is it I feel so bad? He could have called me. He never did call me. I know they go down to Belle View for Thanksgiving but sometime in there, he might have called me. Well sca-rew you, Bud. I pick up the phone again, relieved that it's still alive, and dial Steve's number. Courage!

Steve says slowly, "Now listen, don't use my lawyer, my ex-wife's lawyer was pretty darn good."

"Anyone," I say wearily.

"That bad," he says.

"Yes," I say.

"Why now?" he says, "after all these years?"

Out tumbles all this stuff about my good self and my bad self until I hear puzzlement ricocheting back at me right over the telephone wires. "It's Jenks," I say at last. "He wants to come back. Can you come for Thanksgiving dinner tomorrow?"

A silence as deep and precipitous as the Grand Canyon. "Do you really want me?"

Uh oh, a trick question, so I ignore it and ask him to bring some wine, red and white . . .

". . . and blue?" he asks dryly.

"Rosé. Bring Roger, come at three, we'll eat at four."

I hang up gently this time, hoping I haven't made yet another mistake.

The Looking-Glass Lover

· · · 1 · · ·

It was the oddest thing. Claire had had no intention of working that Friday. She'd gone out for a walk down to the river — the day was mild, the little brick houses of the Village looked domestically Dutch and rosy, and the sidewalks smelled damp, chalky and clean after the night's rain — but something onerous and cloudy hung in her head. Walking back up West 12th Street, she found she was hurrying, and when she got to the apartment she put away the milk and coffee she'd bought and hastily went to the desk in the living room. She pulled up the roll top and her eye fell vaguely upon its compartments and pigeonholes all stuffed with papers and envelopes — one large manila envelope protruded annoyingly but she ignored its beckoning and sat down. She groped for paper and pen and began writing and when she looked up again it was six o'clock and Jason was due in half an hour.

Damn! She'd looked forward to luxuriously waiting for him, taking a hot bath, washing her hair, making up her face, dressing carefully — now she was empty and exhausted, too tired to care about any of these things. She sighed and rubbed the painful area between her shoulder blades. But the story was good, she thought, yes, *good*. All that feeling! Where had it come from? The story had emerged all of a piece and she had written it out so rapidly, in such a sustained burst of passion that she felt as if she'd just given birth. She sat back with a blissful sigh and reread her favorite line, greedily enjoying the way words and image trailed on and on until dwindling, exhausted, they vaporized into pure thin air. She smiled. So she'd done it. At last after all this time, she had done it.

"Done what?" Jason asked, tossing his coat across a chair and slumping — or trying to slump — into the corner of the sofa. The sofa, an obstinate camelback, with a seat like a slab of rock uphostered in an itchy Black Watch plaid, disobliged him and he leaned forward and filled his wineglass. He wore a white shirt nicely rumpled with sleeves rolled up, and Claire wondered if, all day, between taking phone calls and soothing authors, he had glanced at the clock and thought of her. She felt badly. She hadn't consciously thought of him at all.

"Wrote," Claire said simply and smiled. She sat girlishly, happily on her palms on the straight-back chair, leaning forward, her feet hitched up on the chair's stretcher. "Try the pâté, it's awfully good." She had put cheese and caviar and pâté on the cobbler's bench coffee table in front of him.

"Thanks, I will. What did you write about? Was it about me?"

Claire teased, "Why on earth would I write about you?"

He bit a cracker and said, munching, "Women always write about their fathers or their lovers."

"But you're neither."

"Not yet." He grinned at her and dangled the wineglass. "Excellent wine, I must say. What is it?"

"Pouilly fumé."

"Ah," Jason said, his eyes fixed on Claire's bosom, his brows wiggling. "Delicious."

She laughed at him. "You look awful when you leer. If women write about their fathers and lovers, what do men write about?"

· 230

"Important manly things," Jason said promptly. "War and politics." He hunched over the table and happily engorged another cracker.

Claire laughed, a sharp, clear, merry laugh. "Tripe! They boast about their conquests but give it a global meaningful backdrop. 'Bombs were falling thick as beebees while she gave herself to me on the fender of my war-torn war correspondent's jeep. She was the two hundred and tenth woman I'd had while in Barcelona and I wouldn't remember her name in the morning . . .' "

"Jeeps don't have fenders," Jason said. "Why are you so far away? Why can't you sit on this wretched sofa with me?"

"Men are so full of their own self-importance," Claire said. "It's disgusting."

"You're quite right," Jason said agreeably, "that's why most sensible men would rather spend their time with women."

"Do you know something? I've just had the oddest flash. You *do* remind me of my father."

Jason sighed and fell back (then winced and straightened his broad shoulders). "Claire darling, whatever is wrong? Can't you be a feminist or whatever you're being some other time? If it's incest that's worrying you, I claim no responsibility. I never knew your mother and you're *too old* to be my daughter."

"I loathe the way you say 'too old.' "

"Well, what is worrying you?"

"Nothing, it's just writer's hangover."

"Something you wrote didn't agree with you?"

"Mmm . . . maybe."

He patted the firm seat of the sofa. "Well come over here and we'll talk about it. Come on now . . ." He held out a hand. "That's a good girl. Sit right here. See? That wasn't

· 231

terribly difficult, was it? I must say this is the most distress-
ingly Victorian sofa I have ever come across. Don't you have a
bedroom?"

"Jason . . ."

"Yes?"

"Have you . . . ?"

"What?"

"Nothing. How's your wife?"

"My wife." He'd been holding her hand but now dropped
it to help himself to another cracker. "Actually, I think she's
pretty well. This is lovely caviar, must have cost a fortune
. . ." (He munched.) "She's up in Connecticut this weekend
visiting her sister Mary. Mary drinks like a fish, however, so
every time she sees Mary she gets depressed and starts drinking too. Darling, you don't have a teeny slice of lemon do you?
It goes so well with caviar."

No, she didn't.

Oh, too bad. Once (he went on) his wife had gone seven
years without a drink. Then, for no apparent reason, she'd
started drinking more than ever. It didn't matter much. Their
apartment was old-fashioned and large and they inhabited
"separate spheres, as it were." He had a bedroom, a bathroom,
the library — he needed the library since he'd inherited his
father's collection of books. She had her bedroom, a bathroom
and the living room. Occasionally, they met in the dining
room — common ground. He bent over and slowly began un-
tying his shoelaces, then looked up at Claire and asked if she'd
ever read any of his father's novels.

"No," she said gently, but she certainly would now.

"Oh," he said. Well his father had been blacklisted in the
1950s. "Do you know what he did then?"

"What?"

"He began dating much younger women. Once, for quite a

while he dated one of my ex-girlfriends. I met her at a party a few years ago. Do you know what she said?"

"No."

" 'He was so sweet,' " Jason said mimicking the woman's voice, making it sound high and inane. " 'You're sweet too but he was better in bed.' " Jason laughed heartily, throwing back his head and screwing up his eyes — "Ha ha ha!"

"You're just trying to tell me you're nervous," Claire said, smiling a little and brushing cracker crumbs off her skirt.

"Well, yes," Jason said, reaching for her hand again. She let him have it but narrowed her eyes at him. He said, "Now what's wrong?"

"I think it's an act. You're acting, aren't you! For some reason I feel you want me to *think* you're nervous but I don't believe you *are*."

He looked up at the ceiling and raised his eyes to Jehovah. "Dear God!" Then he sat back against the sofa and said, "You're terribly cynical and terribly smart."

"Which one is it? Look, Jason, we don't have to do this. Maybe we should just skip it." (She wished her voice hadn't quavered like that — she'd been doing so well up to this point — brisk and practical.)

But now, sensing her weakness, he smiled wickedly and domestically eased off his long, black, well-shined shoes. "Aaaah," he said and grinned at her. "This is more the kind of thing I had in mind."

She blurted, "I don't know what you had in mind but I want to be . . . ." She had wanted to say "loved," but instead flushed and dropped her head and mumbled, "happy. Don't you want to be happy?"

He held up his glass. "Very much. Is there any more wine in your kitchenette? If you'll bring it back I can seize the opportunity and you."

She laughed and did as she was told and when she came back into the living room he had taken off his tie and unbuttoned his collar button and he lay half-reclined on the stubborn sofa, with his hands cupped beneath his head and a look on his face like a trap about to spring. "Put the wine there," he said, pointing a long finger at the table, "and you sit there." She sat down with a plunk and virtuously folded her hands in her lap. He grinned at her and pulled her toward him and then they were kissing, long, deep kisses that reminded Claire of senior year in high school. Bits of clothing seemed to be coming undone and shortly thereafter, with her dress held modestly up against her bosom, Claire turned her head to see him (they were in the bedroom now) flying cherublike through the air, with a worried look on his face, and a hand cupped over his genitals. He landed expertly on one side of the bed.

"How sporting," she said. "You're obviously very practiced."

He lay on his side, his head held up on his palm. "Get into bed," he snarled humorously, "and stop fussing. And *stop assuming.*"

Later, lying against each other under the sheet, she kept her arms around him and told him about the house she'd grown up in — she had no idea why. Her mother had lately written that they'd torn the house down. A builder was putting up condominiums.

"I've just bought a condominium," he said.

"You have? Where?"

"In Florida. Do you like Florida?"

"I've never been there."

"Really. You've never been to Florida! That's amazing. Just a farm girl. You know, we owned a farm, many long years ago when I was a kid. I had a girlfriend up there — you rather remind me of her. She was one of those fair, rosy girls — her name was Polly, Polly White. Isn't that a marvelously quaint name? Like a Thomas Hardy heroine. She had freckles . . ." He drew his finger gently across Claire's nose. ". . . just like you. She used to wear her hair in braids and marvelous wisps of whitish hair were always flying about her forehead. Clear blue trusting eyes. *Wonderful* eyes. She looked so terribly innocent, but whenever I so much as sighed in her direction, she'd whip off her bra. She loved, simply loved to fuck. Whenever I'd go up to the farm — summers, school vacations, I was . . . let's see . . . fifteen and sixteen and seventeen . . . my father sold it just before I went to college . . . anyway, whenever I got up there I'd last about ten minutes and then I'd be off on my bike for the torture of a bumpy four-mile ride down the dirt road to Polly's father's farm. She'd come out of the house and without a word we'd go off, usually up to the field in back of the house. Once I was pumping away and I heard a noise and when I looked up there was a very large brown-and-white cow standing over us, placidly watching and chewing its cud." He laughed, and then said regretfully, "A sweet girl. You never had to do anything for her. I think once in all the years I knew her, I took her to a movie. On our first date."

Claire turned on her back and lay looking up at the dirty white ceiling. It had been painted over so often it looked like a giant relief map, with ridges and dents, bumps and stipples. In two corners hung gray hanks of spiderweb, and she felt suddenly as if this entire little world, this plaster subcontinent, was held up by the most tenuously spun strands of silk and would any second now fall and crush her. She had an ache in her chest. When she took a breath it hurt. She said, at last, in a thick voice, "What a dreadful story."

Jason was astounded. "Why?"

"Because no doubt she cared for you."

"Oh rot."

"Why rot? Did she do it with everyone, is that what you think?"

He looked angry and turned away onto his side. "Probably. No doubt she did."

"Well I doubt it. I think she cared for you and you're awful to talk about her that way. What happened to her?"

"I dunno," he said in a muffled voice, his face against the pillow. "Probably married some hick and had a passel of kids."

"Weren't you ever curious about her?"

"Curious?" He turned again and lay flat on his back. "No, not really. I'm not a sentimental type."

He had only three sparse black hairs upon his chest and Claire now suppressed her desire to prod him with her forefinger where these grew — near the breastbone close by a (presumably) palpitating ventricle. Hard-boiled Jason!

"And then after Polly you met your wife?"

"No, not right away. Several years later. Ten years later, something like that."

"How did you meet her?"

"Oh God!" Jason groaned. "You women are all alike, you always need to burrow into everything. Well, she was the editor who hired me. Then I got promoted above her and I fired her."

"You fired your own wife?"

"I had to, she was pregnant. What time is it?"

"Seven. Why?"

"Seven. Good God, I've got to go." He sat up.

"What?" Claire, too, sat up in bed holding the sheet to her breasts. "Go where?"

"I thought I told you. I've got to go to a dinner meeting uptown. I'm sure I told you about it, it's just a business thing."

He looked at her with long green wary eyes; a straggle of brown hair fell across his forehead. "Now what's wrong? I did tell you, I'm certain I did."

Claire turned her head away and closed her eyes. Even now, weeks after she'd met him, she never believed a thing he said. It was exhausting.

He said, "You don't believe me, do you? My God, you're suspicious. Look, tell you what. We'll go uptown and have drinks and dinner. Would you like that?"

She said that would be fine. Getting dressed she thought that she ought to be feeling happy but during most of the preceding half hour, he had managed to make her feel miserable.

Outside, in the brisk November night, her mood lightened and she felt everything was just as she'd imagined it would be. She held his hand in the cab and the city went whizzing past them in a blur of black night, yellow lights. They played "name this tune" with Jason whistling, Claire humming, but someplace between 34th Street and Times Square Jason's mood changed. Sitting in the Algonquin's lobby over peanuts and martinis he was gloomy and self-absorbed. Something — a business deal, he'd said — wasn't working out well. He'd brought out a book that he thought would fly but that same week her old publisher (he said this making it sound as if it were all her fault) had come out with a similar book on the same subject. In the red leatherette chair he shifted his long suit-covered bones and glowered. They were promoting the book lavishly. Jason's book was called *The Layperson's Guide to Plastic Surgery,* and was mainly about face-lifts.

"And breast-lifts and ass-lifts." He studied her and lifted his drink. "Soon Claire will need a face-lift."

"You'll need one sooner," she said and stuck her tongue out at him.

When she'd first seen him she had thought he looked old, much older than she — he was, in fact, ten years older — but the more she saw of him the younger he seemed. Often he could be as balky and self-centered as a ten-year-old and like any young adolescent he hated to be teased, his long face going a dull hurt red. But teasing was the only way Claire could protect herself. His rule was not to take anything seriously and, in fact, Claire felt that as soon as he'd begun to take *her* seriously, he'd begun subtly attacking her, pushing her away, fending her off.

"Sorry," he said crisply, standing up. "I'm really being a bore. Forgive me. Shall we go to dinner?"

A tall blond young woman in boots and a long mink coat now came in through the hotel's revolving door and as he glanced at her, the woman tipped her face at him and her bright red mouth widened into a glistening viscous smile. "Ja-sey!" she cried. She had on a matching mink hat and when she threw her arms around his neck the hat fell off.

"Oops!" he cried and they both bent down at the same moment to pick up the hat and then bumped heads. They beamed at each other and Claire felt a searing wave of jealousy and humiliation. At once she stood up and moved to the door.

"Darling," Jason said to the woman in a deep tremulous voice, "it's wonderful to see you. You look . . . Well, you look . . ." He blushed. "Give me a call soon, we'll have lunch." He raised his hand, the woman smiled at him over her shoulder, then she let her eyes slide ironically over Claire, who stood silently, some feet away. He hadn't introduced her, he hadn't even acknowledged her. Without waiting for him, Claire turned and walked outside. In a moment, he caught up with her, caught her arm, held her back. "Where on earth are you running to?" he asked humorously. "I thought we were going to dinner? Sorry about her — that was my wife's cousin."

Claire laughed. It occurred to her that her laugh — this laugh — had a sour ill-humored tone. "I wish I believed you."

"You never believe me," he said calmly. "You are the most cynical woman I've ever met. What is it makes you so suspicious? I thought we'd have dinner at a little place I like over on the East Side. I made a reservation while you were in the bathroom. Shall we walk or take a cab?"

"Oh . . . walk," Claire said wearily.

"You don't trust me, do you?" Jason asked gaily.

"Jason . . . ," she began and then changed her mind. She said, "Should I?"

He considered as they headed east on 44th Street. Looking up at him, Claire thought he looked immensely pleased with himself. "Probably not," he said and then took her hand and wove it around his arm. "Why gracious," he said, looking down at her hand, "Don't you have your gloves?"

"Yes."

"Well, put them on." And he waited, patient and paternal, while she pulled on her long black gloves.

All through dinner, he talked and she listened, nodding. Later, she took a cab downtown alone. She felt troubled, perhaps even ill. Sitting across from Jason, eating tripes de Caen and drinking red wine, she felt herself caught in a strange metamorphosis. Trapped in a chrysalis halfway between herself and her own fictive creation, she no longer knew if Jason, this Jason, was real or someone she'd invented.

2

"The Looking-Glass Lover"

The summer that I met Jason I was nineteen, a junior at Vassar. I had read a lot and considered myself sophisticated, but nonetheless, I was shocked when, after three dates, he told me he was married. One late-summer afternoon he came by the antique shop where I worked and insisted I have dinner with him so he could explain. We went to a little Italian place and I wanted to cry but instead I drank red wine and ate large soft-chewy mouthfuls of Zito's Italian bread. He said that his wife was sick and he couldn't leave her but that they hadn't slept together in four years.

This came out dryly, little by little, and at last I reached for his hand, thinking how brave he was and how kind and self-sacrificing. He felt that if he left her she would break down again and so he had to stay with her until she was better — well enough to be on her own.

We parted nicely. He called me occasionally after that, at school, and I would talk to him in the dormitory telephone booth. We'd say funny, inconsequential things — talk about the weather mostly — strange conversations with long pauses in them but neither one of us wanting to hang up.

In May, before my exams, he called to wish me luck — I thought it was thoughtful of him — and then he said he'd look for me in the antique shop in June. One rainy day he did come in looking sad and bedraggled, and I didn't hesitate — I agreed to have dinner with him that night.

He told me that night he had a downtown place, an apartment his wife didn't know about — she and the dog and the cat and the toy soldier collection and a library of old books all lived uptown at Park and 84th Street. His downtown place was on Thompson Street in what used to be called a slum but has now become SoHo. Jason had painted his SoHo row house yellow and after that gentrification fell upon the neighborhood like a rainbowed cloud; the Parks Department came by and planted gingko trees and the real estate values zoomed, driving out the block's old Italian families.

Jason kept the third-floor apartment and rented out the others. He was good at making money. He liked money. He had married money, not a lot of it but enough. Monique Payne had gone to Connecticut College and her family was what they used to call socially prominent — is there still such a category? I wouldn't know. It used to mean boarding schools, Ivy League colleges, blue chip investments, debuts, an apartment in New York and a house in Connecticut, good family connections — an undersecretary or two in the present administration, an uncle in a leading New York law firm. Her father was a thoracic surgeon, on the staff of New York Hospital, a large, bald, portly man with a big grin and nimble hands and feet. An excellent surgeon, an excellent dancer. After college, Monique had gotten a job in a publishing house and that was where she met Jason. They were quickly married. A year later she had a miscarriage and then a breakdown.

The second summer I knew Jason I had just turned twenty and felt old and wise and experienced. All that June he courted me. We took long lovers' walks through the Village and held hands over sticky little outdoor café tables. We went to the White Horse Bar on Hudson Street where Dylan Thomas used to pass out and we sat in the clotted dark of the Bleecker Street Cinema watching movies that were many years old: *Wuthering Heights* with a polished Laurence Olivier as dark, savage Heathcliff and films with Anna Magnani. "My God," Jason would say irritably, out loud in the theater, "she's so damnably ugly!" (Somehow his saying this made me feel ugly, too, for what I reckoned important about myself was not mere beauty but my will, my intelligence, my spirit and soul, my gifts not necessarily as a woman but as a human being, the same gifts that shone out of Anna's dark eyes.) We did all the things lovers are supposed to do but there was something missing in it — it was puzzlingly all form and no content, but then his expressive range seemed decidedly limited. He had two moods — if he was cheerful he was fixedly cheerful and when he was dour he was very dour indeed.

Of course I saw at once how insecure he was — he often talked about prominent people he knew or his family had known — and perhaps because I was young I enjoyed this harmless name-dropping — it seemed to me very glamorous. I was bookstruck the way some young girls are stagestruck, and because his father had been a well-known popular novelist (now long forgotten) little Jason had met all my literary heroes and heroines. Scott Fitzgerald had once patted him on the head and he had had dinner with Katherine Anne Porter! His mother had died of heart disease when he was small and he'd been brought up by a whole succession of nurses and governesses. He never talked much about his work as an editor and it didn't dawn on me until years later that he didn't really care much about his work. He'd gotten his job through a friend of his father's and had simply stayed on in editing until he was good enough at it.

Sometimes, in those gritty New York summer evenings, we'd get his car out of the parking garage on Charles Street and we'd drive around the West Village streets, the golden sunset-lit Hudson River glowing like an ingot, with a Venetian sky, streaky blue and salmon colored, suspended above it. We'd drive around a bit on the old streets and end up on West 14th Street where the wholesale meat markets were — they opened at four or five in the morning and closed in the early afternoon. The dark cobblestoned street always had a forbidding deserted air, like a European village in a plague year. We would roll up the windows and lock the doors (we didn't trust the neighborhood) and kiss each other long and hungrily, stretched out and pressed against each other in the front seat of the Chevrolet until we were dizzy and our clothes stuck everywhere.

I had fallen in love with him at once and I wanted to tell him but I waited. Some sort of old-fashioned modesty forbade it — I wanted him to tell me first. He kept asking me to go up to his place on Thompson Street but I wouldn't do it. I wasn't a virgin but the two experiences I'd had had seemed pointless and I'd decided I wouldn't sleep with anyone again unless it was certain we loved each other. But the physical strain got harder to bear and he began to get irritable and my body had acquired a life of its own — my skin became devilishly sensitive and the denial I had imposed on us seemed dangerous: I didn't want to lose him.

My mother was getting ready to move abroad that summer. She had decided to marry an Englishman and she was so distracted that when I told her I was moving out she simply nodded and asked me if I'd taken all my woollens to the cleaners for summer storage. My sister Dora was away at camp in Maine. The small upstate town I'd grown up in seemed to me at least a half century behind the rest of the country in moral depravity (no doubt they have caught up now) but when I was growing up there, people still did not mention the word s-e-x in public unless they were dairy farmers discussing bulls and heifers. Despite these limitations, I had acquired some deep instinctive carnal knowledge and I childishly believed that intimate relations were something you had with someone you cared about and that very possibly they were then enjoyable — Nature being the ultimate expert on the carrot and stick routine. That was almost all I knew. Since he had been married and I not, I was sure he'd had access to a wide body of knowledge but I also optimistically felt that love would conquer all and where there was a will, et cetera. I simply do not remember what happened the first time I went to bed with him and I think in a negative way that says a lot. I do, however, remember the date — it was July 5 and some of the kids of Thompson Street were still popping firecrackers but nothing, not that night (or ever with him), went off for me, and for the longest time I thought that's how sex was.

Nevertheless, I loved him and I lived in his place and I took care of it for him — kept it clean and kept his clothes clean and cooked the meals and bought the flowers — bunches of daisies and clay-potted red geraniums for his sunny front windows. I was careful about presuming, though. I didn't want him to think I was taking over, so I kept my own clothes to one side of the closet and I kept my towels neatly on their own rack. He had been annoyed one day because I'd put one of my towels on his rack.

I don't know why I thought it was going to be so perfect, no doubt because I wanted it to be so. For a long time in the deepest part of myself I had wanted someone to love. Sometimes in those first weeks, despite everything, it seemed to me it might be perfect and I'd wake up in the night and see him sleeping beside me and I would lie there softly stroking his bare bony shoulder and wishing that his wife would die. She was sick anyway, so why couldn't she die and leave us alone?

I was writing that summer, finishing the novel I'd started when I was seventeen. Evenings, he'd go over manuscripts and I would sit on the slablike sofa (covered in an itchy wool plaid), in shorts, with my feet up and the fan on, and I'd write in a large notebook of lined paper. It seemed blissfully domestic, the scratch of two pens, that sort of thing. He was several years older than I but seemed boyish and cheerful. The apartment was painted gray in every room, a pretty pearl gray with a touch of lavender in it.

After we'd lived together for three weeks we had our first fight. I had a friend named Tommy Lewin who had graduated from Harvard and was living on Jane Street. I'd bumped into him on the street one day and we'd had a drink together. This made Jason furious. That was the first time he called me a slut. Then, quick as a thunderstorm, the fight was over and he was cheerful again and went into the kitchen for a gin and tonic, leaving me shaky and in tears with my head in my hands in the little stuffy living room. We didn't have air conditioning, only the fan, and when he worked he sat in an armchair and put his feet up on a hassock and kept the piles of manuscript papers held down on the floor with a series of lead soldiers, miniature Scots wearing kilts of different clans — Stuart, Black Watch, whatever.

I had, as well, a college friend named Joan Sydenham who was living in the Village near Washington Square. She'd been a year ahead of me at Vassar and had graduated in June. We'd worked together on the college literary magazine, and I thought her a very good writer. She was working for a publishing firm and trying to write fiction at night, but she said it was awfully hard. She was a tall, stout, freckled woman, with a big laugh and wiry red hair that she wore pulled back into a frizzy bun. We had dinner together a couple of times, the three of us, at a place on Barrow Street that was in a whitewashed basement, cheap and cool. Afterward, Jason and I would walk home with our arms around each other and he'd say, laughing, "My word, what a great cow! Those huge freckled arms! I wonder if her tits are freckled too? Fascinating." This made me uneasy and it hurt me — I didn't want him to talk like that, and I liked Joan and didn't want to hear her talked about like that. He was already making me miserable.

Already — we'd lived together only a month — something was going wrong. His head would turn continuously after any passing woman as if his long neck were on a spring, but when I mentioned someone — anyone else in my life, man or woman, someone who had been in the shop, an old friend who'd called — there would be a brief electric pause and then, moments later, a piece of sarcasm so sudden and barbed it seemed to hang in my very flesh for days.

The trouble, you see, was I didn't know better. I didn't know what to expect. I'd never really been in love before. Of course I thought it was my fault. I thought I must be doing something wrong. I knew that something was very wrong but I so wanted it to be right.

Things got worse as the summer got hotter and longer. One night when I'd made just a salad for dinner he pushed it away. He asked me, with a snarl, if this was what they ate in upstate New York — fodder? He told me that night that my clothes were all wrong — too cheap looking, and they were cheap looking, they were, in fact, cheap. I was pretty much on my own my last years in college. My father had cheerfully declined to contribute anything and my mother had run through a small inheritance in no time flat.

Later that night he told me, yawning, that he thought I was "cute" but not really pretty. "No," he said, turning out the light, "you're not really pretty but you'll do, of course, because you're here." He said it jokingly but what I felt was that it was true, he had given me the truth in the form of a joke. I lay there feeling ice-cold in the hot night. I kept asking myself, What on earth was it I had fallen in love with?

Yet, when he cared to he could be very charming. He was good at telling funny stories and he had a wonderful rolling laugh. When he laughed, his eyes childishly shut up into wrinkled slits, the lids of which I used to kiss when we lay in bed together. But always, after we made love, he'd cheerfully turn over and go to sleep, as if I were a block of wood or a large, life-sized, rubber-skinned doll. It wasn't until years later that I realized there was possibly something wrong — emotionally not physically — with a man who would just "do it." Worse, I had a vague feeling that he enjoyed my discomfiture — he liked knowing he'd had some pleasure from me but I hadn't gotten any from him. He never touched me below the hips and I began to feel, unconsciously, uneasily, that there was something wrong with me there, too. It wasn't just my face, my clothing, my cooking but my body as well that was all wrong. I began to look in the mirror too much and what I saw depressed me. Yes, he was right, he was certainly right: I wasn't pretty. My eyes were too small, my skin too pale, my features too ordinary. How lucky I was to have him! I began to hate the way I looked and I felt grateful to him — yes, grateful — for putting up with me. Besides, I was poor and no-account. Poor and getting poorer because after the first week he never gave me any money for food and I was buying groceries and household supplies out of my little salary. When I asked him once to repay me for the money I'd spent when I picked up his cleaning he said carelessly that all he had was a fifty-dollar bill. I forgave him because I felt he didn't understand just how little money I had. He couldn't understand that if I didn't save any money from my summer job I would have to get two part-time jobs during the school year. When I tried to explain to him he would look at me and nod benignly and I would think, But of course he doesn't understand. He's never been without money.

He could be cheerful and touching and awfully nice as well. One night he came home waving the September issue of the *Atlantic*. "Damn Joan, that great cow!" he said. "She never told us. She's got a story in here and it's tops."

He was so lovely with Joan. He went out to a liquor store around the corner and got a bottle of Mumm's and I called Joan and we went over to her place. We sat at her Formica-topped kitchen table laughing and drinking champagne and Joan laughed and tipped back her head and smoked Pall Malls. Joan got a little high and giggly and raised her strong-looking freck-led arms — they were pure marble on the underside — and unpinned her hair and the upward movement of her arms raised and rounded her large breasts so that they strained against the white cotton of her short-sleeved blouse and Jason coughed and pinched my knee under the table.

"Oh, Joan," he said and shook his head, groaning, "Oh, Joan!"

He told her how clean her writing was and how precise and that she was sure to have a great future and I sat there smiling, holding my chin in my hand, and looking down at the table, I traced with my finger the pink marble streaks in the beige Formica that also had gold flecks in it. I didn't feel very well and I wanted to go home and I was liking Joan, a good friend of mine, less and less.

It was hot that summer and his apartment got hotter and toward the end of August Jason began staying at his office — it was air-conditioned — to do his work. One whole week in mid-August we didn't make love and after eight days, when I timidly approached him and affectionately put my hand on his shoulder, he looked up from the manuscript he was reading and said in a loud voice, "Do you know you have awfully bad breath? Do you think there's something wrong with your teeth?" I started brushing my teeth five times a day. I bought Listerine mouthwash and I went to the dentist who said, "Why, your teeth are fine," and charged me the last of my savings and pinched my ass as I went out the door.

That night Jason called and said it was so hot he'd decided to stay "at home." He said this so casually I didn't at first know what he meant and then I realized he meant his uptown apartment — that was home. Of course, I told myself dully, that was home. I was not home, this was not home, I had only fooled myself into thinking so.

The next night he came downtown but was surly. He sat in the easy chair and made penciled marks on a manuscript. I pulled up a little needlepoint stool and sat down on it in front of him, knees together, chin in hand. He glanced up from his work and asked, what did I think I was doing? I folded my hands in my lap and asked him nervously, what was wrong? He said, briskly, that I was sitting upon his grandmother's stool, a valuable antique, would I please get off? I got off and sat down on the floor with a thud, sat at his feet like a naughty child. All the while, I felt like a kid who is being punished but doesn't know why. What was it I'd done wrong? I wanted to know. I said, "Jason?"

Silence.

"Jason? What's the matter?"

Silence.

"Are you not speaking to me for a reason?"

Silence.

"Do you want me to go, is that it?"

He raised his head. "Could one possibly be so lucky?"

Some part of me pretended it had not heard or understood. I said, "Pardon?"

He let his head drop backward, onto the high back of the old-fashioned chair that was covered with a lace antimacassar. He took off his glasses and contemplated me with the look of a scientist who is bored with the little animal in the laboratory cage. He said, "You know, Barbara, you're an awful bore. You are simply a boring woman."

I sat there appalled, not knowing how it was I'd been so boring. My face must have been a boring stupid blank.

"Some women have talent and some have looks, but you, my dear, fall into that unfortunate category of pure gender."

I dipped my head, as if to an ax. I knew something worse was coming and I knit my hands together. I must have looked silly sitting there, barefoot, with my legs in the half-lotus position, hands knit prayerfully together and head awkwardly bent. I said, not looking up at him, whispering, supplicating, "What is it you mean?"

"Why," he said cheerfully, "it's perfectly obvious that your real career is sluthood."

I waited. Then I said, timorously, confused, "But a month ago you said . . ."

"What?" he prompted, cheerfully.

"You told me I . . . I was just holding out on you and . . ."

He waved his hand impatiently. "I saw it in the story you showed me, which, by the way, I thought simply obscene. Childishly written, deplorably thought out. Your talents, dear, are not really literary. If you have any thought, still, of being a writer, let me save you a great deal of time and trouble. Try marriage instead. That wasn't, by the way, any sort of proposal since I'm already married." He smiled and peeled off a page of manuscript and put it on the floor under a tartaned Scot.

I got up slowly. I felt perfectly stiff as if, sitting there, I had suddenly aged and my joints had calcified. I went into the bathroom and turned on the shower. I kneeled down on the cold tile floor and while the shower ran full blast, put my face into the fuzzy green tub mat and cried. I didn't just cry, I howled like an animal. I wept for an hour. I wept for what I'd tried to give him, I wept for what he'd never given me. I wept for what had happened to me. What had happened to me? *I was becoming a different person.*

When I came out of the bathroom, he was standing in the little hallway with a gin and tonic — he drank a very great deal. "Good God," he said, looking cheerfully down at me, "What on earth is wrong? You look awful. What's the matter with your eyes, they're all swollen." He put a forefinger on my eyelid and poked it open as if looking for a bit of grit. "Dreadful," he said. Removing his finger and shaking his head, he went off into the little bedroom.

I thought I was going insane.

Twenty minutes later he shut off the light in the bedroom and called for me. "Barbara?" His melodious voice! "Barbara, will you come in here please? Don't be a little sill. Come on, you know I didn't mean it. You take things so seriously. I wish you had a better sense of humor."

And this is how lost I was, I went to him and I lay down next to him and he did what he always did — he simply rolled over on top of me and breathed that hoarsely rattling death breath and at last cried out and got off me and turned over and went to sleep.

I lay in the dark a long while feeling numb, smelling of his sperm. My last thought before I went to sleep was that in the morning he would tell me I smelled bad. And in the morning, tying his tie in front of the bedroom mirror, with his chin lifted above the shirt's starched white collar, he looked at me in the looking-glass and his nostrils flared — I left the room.

After that I didn't let him inside me for a long time and, anyway, he wasn't coming downtown much — he said he had tons of work to do, so many people in the office were on vacation. Then I missed him terribly and remembered his laugh and the charming way he had of telling a story and when he came back downtown one night, he brought me a bouquet of flowers — roses, baby's breath, carnations — from some subway stand. It was the first time he'd ever brought me anything and I was mollified and it was cooler, late summer, only later that night he made me cry again.

You see, I wouldn't admit it — that I'd spent so much time with him crying. I would cry in the bathroom after we'd made love, I would cry at two in the morning when we hadn't. In his tiny kitchenette I cried and ate triple-decker sandwiches slathered with mustard and mayonnaise. I cried and I cooked and I ate. I cooked him dinners reeking of garlic and red wine and I learned how to bake his favorite chocolate cake and I brought him coffee in bed on Sunday mornings (on a tray with croissants and butter and strawberry jam). All summer long, I cried and I cooked and I ate and in the end I had gained twenty pounds — he remained as slim as a strand of uncooked spaghetti, God knows where he put all the food I had cooked, he consumed. While I loved Jason I was always ravenously hungry, with a sick, nauseating hunger, and while my body bloated and my face filled out, the eyes that looked back at me from the mirror every morning were the bleak, bruised-looking eyes of someone who is starving to death.

But oddly, until I'd gained almost twenty pounds, I had no idea I was getting fatter. All the while I lived with Jason I felt myself shriveling, getting smaller and smaller. I had dreams in which I vanished entirely and all that was left of me was my voice and that, too, had been reduced to a whisper. In these dreams, my voice wandered like a sunbeam through the cool geometric spaces of a plain white house, a sunbeam searching for an object — for light needs a defining object just as objects, in order to have visual depth, need light and shadow. My voice, the sunbeam, floated mournfully through the empty rooms like the ghost of the Little Match Girl or as if I, not he, had been made of tin and like Andersen's stout Tin Soldier I lay (used, and then discarded), my joints helplessly rusting, my essence a cloud of reddish dust already climbing the cold celestial highways, condemned for a while to wander, then fading into mist . . . a ferrous vapor . . . a silent thought . . . a memory . . . gone.

The last time I saw Jason was a September Monday many years ago. It was the day before the term began at Vassar and I was packing. I was taking my skirts out of the cleaner's storage boxes and folding them sideways, to go in the trunk.

"What on earth is this?" Jason asked, coming into the bedroom. "There's nothing in the kitchen — is it my turn to cook?" This was a joke — he never cooked. It was a cool evening, he had on a gray plaid suit.

I said calmly, "I'm going back to school tomorrow, you know that."

"No I don't know that," he said crossly. "How would I know that?"

"I told you last night," I said, not looking at him but putting a tweed skirt in the trunk. I felt relieved and yet sick at the same time. He watched me a moment and then he took hold of me by the elbows and shook me a little and when I looked up he said, looking down into my eyes, "Now listen. What is the point of this? You don't have to go. You can stay right here. We'll go on just as we are."

"No," I said, twisting away. "You said your wife was coming back to town this week, from the country."

"Makes no difference," he said and tightened his hold on my arms. "You know what that is."

Looking down at the floor, I smiled faintly. "And what am I?"

He didn't answer but said holding on to me, "You could

simply stay here. You could write here. Wouldn't you like that?"

I said, "I've stopped writing."

He stood looking down at me, holding me by the arms, and then he dropped his hands and shrugged. He began pacing a little up and down the room. He said angrily, "If you go back to college we won't see each other."

"No," I said.

"I'm not a saint," he said.

I shrugged.

"You know I won't get up there to see you."

"You could if you wanted."

"No."

"Yes. You could. You could find a way."

"Impossible. You don't . . ." He stood in front of me and looked down at me. He had his hands stuck in his pockets and he looked cheerful, only under the cheer there was something else — the ghost of another expression; there was a look of pain in his eyes and these two expressions — the habitual fixed cheery look and the look of torment and pain — seemed to be struggling with each other and then for a brief moment the pain won and he said, his face twisting, his eyes filling, reddened, "But you won't . . . you won't really leave me?"

And there he was, the missing person, the one you liked so much and kept looking for; the one you'd known all along was there only he was always sent away like a misjudged child in disgrace, although *he* was (no doubt about it) the one you loved, and this other one, the Tin Man, this walking, talking suit of armor, wouldn't let him out, sent him packing, kicked his ass (the one you loved) so that you'd only ever caught hopeful glimpses of him and it was this naïve hopefulness that kept luring you on until now look where you were, but of course you had to grab it (hope, I mean) one more time, and so you said, desperately now for it was growing late, "Oh Jason, can't you tell me? What is it you *feel?*"

He said nothing and I said, "Can't you say anything to me? Don't you feel anything for me?" but he was silent. I turned away. I was looking down at the floor of his bedroom — it was painted a bright apple green — and I saw a small brown roach run across the floor from under the molding, and his long black shoe lifted and he stepped down upon it. I watched his hand reach down with a Kleenex in it and wipe the squashed bug off the sole of his shoe and then with a look of disgust he threw the wadded Kleenex into the wastepaper basket.

We had a last dinner together. He took me out but he didn't stay downtown, he said he had to go back uptown, there was an important meeting he had to attend. I went back to Vassar the next day. I was ill with longing for him and I hated myself for it.

A few weeks later (I hadn't heard from Jason) I met a girl named Betty Mallon who was a friend of Joan Sydenham's. We were both coming out of the Art Library and decided to have coffee together. I told her I'd seen Joan that summer and she rolled her eyes and said, "Oh, I saw her, too, just before I came up. You won't believe this, you know how naïve we always thought Joan was and how we were always trying to fix her up with 'interesting' " (she curved her fingers to make little quotation marks) "men? Well, good old Joan did it in spades, but, boy, typical Joan, she picked a real prick. Can you believe it?" Something, a trickle of poison, slid warningly down my spine. "Not only is he married but — get this — he has another girl on the side. And Joan has an affair with this S.O.B., of course. Joan the obliging victim! You get the picture, of course. Joan's sleeping with him in his place uptown, the other girl's sleeping with him downtown, and his wife is in the country sleeping with the dog, I guess, who knows. I don't know,

I really don't. How come someone as smart as Joan can be so stupid? You have to want to fool yourself a whole lot. No doubt he's a practiced liar and she wanted to fall for it, but it sure ruins your faith in men, which in my case isn't too strong anyhow. Say something, will you? Tell me the guy was sick, anything. I mean, God, are they all like that?"

I got up and went to the telephone booth at the back of the drugstore and I called Jason at his office. He was very cheerful and said he was terribly upset that I felt so bad but I was young and would get over it. That was life, wasn't it. He'd tried to tell me, of course, in one way or another, but I'd persisted so, I'd just hung on. And he had to protect himself. He had known all along I would leave. And in the end (his voice suddenly rose into real anger) I *had* left him, hadn't I? Then he was Mr. Cheer again and nonchalantly said, well, it was too bad, it was a shame that I'd gotten my feelings so involved. Meanwhile, he wished me all sorts of luck in my senior year and he hoped my writing career went well. If I ever wrote anything and needed help in any way — editorial advice — he'd be only too glad to assist.

Eventually (it took only a couple of weeks) I lost the twenty pounds, but for years after that I didn't write — not a word. He had damaged something in me: my faith in myself. You can write with no money, little time, minimal talent, but he had contaminated the very source: I'd lost faith in myself as a woman, and for me, being a woman, being a writer, have always been inextricably intertwined.

· · · 3 · · ·

All the next day, a smoky pink and gray autumn Sunday, Claire sat at the rolltop desk going over her story, drinking coffee, eating pecan coffee cake and rubbing the crick in her neck. At three, she put down her pen, stretched and yawned and then remembered that she'd promised Jason dinner. Ugh, what a vile thought! She was glutted with work and coffee cake — she'd have to take him out.

She left the apartment and walked down West 12th Street to Hudson and then south on Hudson to Perry, back down Perry to West 11th. There was a funny little French restaurant on the corner of West 11th, but it looked closed. She went back up Hudson to Seventh Avenue but all of the restaurants she passed looked dingy or too chic or were Japanese — she hated Japanese food. She came back to the apartment feeling out of sorts with a kind of fritzed-out feeling as if her wires were crossed. She had the vague sense that Claire-the-writer, or the part of her (Claire) who was her character Barbara, was trying to signal a Claire who wasn't listening. Oh the hell with it! she thought irritably, and then thought, puzzled, The hell with *what?*

She flipped through restaurant reviews in *New York* magazine, then tossed the magazine aside, then restlessly began to clean out the pigeonholes and compartments of the little rolltop desk. The manila envelope urgently extended itself toward her hand and she said to it, "Oh all right," and tugged it out of its niche. She unwound the envelope's string and peered inside — photographs, goody. She dumped the photographs on

· 257

the rag rug and sat idly sorting them. No one she knew. All women. Wait. Wait a minute. What *is* this?

And here it was: her father's final gleeful gloating confession.

There were fifty photographs at least, all in black and white, women of many different ages in so many varieties of dress it was like a costume parade. The parade began somewhere in the late nineteen twenties with a dark-eyed beauty in a cloche and fox-trimmed wrap coat, and next to her a straw-haired woman out of the nineteen seventies in check shirt, skintight jeans, boots that came up to the knee.

She began arranging the photographs as well as she could, by year, according to clothing.

Oh, how interesting. Yes, here was next-door neighbor Janie Mercer in a fifties suit with a nipped in waist, high heels, long gloves, a little veiled hat, veiled smile, round earrings. There were other faces Claire uneasily recognized. A Mrs. Lefeber in a strapless bathing suit that showed off her beautiful shoulders, and here, too — surprise, surprise — young Miss Morrison, Claire's own third-grade teacher, who'd left so abruptly in the spring of that year so that the class acquired instead a cranky old substitute with flabby powdered cheeks and a see-through hair net on her waved purple hair. Also, Andrea Edwards's mother. Claire's stomach gave a sudden twist. Andrea had been her best friend sophomore year in high school, and then her parents had divorced and Andrea and her mother had moved away.

The collection appeared to be some sort of a gallery — not a rogues' gallery as much as a victims' gallery — for, in a way, she knew (because she knew her father) that each one of the women had given him something — love, affection, what-

ever — that he had had no intention, no capacity for returning. He hadn't killed them, of course, or maybe only a little —
killed their pride, their self-respect, their souls — but he was
really not so much a murderer as a thief, taking love without
giving anything back. No picture of her mother, no picture of
them — the children. No picture of . . . wait. Here.

The last photograph — Claire had put it aside to study it —
was a fuzzy snapshot of a child. On her knees, Claire wriggled
over to the floor lamp, pulled its chain, held the photograph
up close to the naked bulb. An angry child aged nine or so in
a pointed wool ski cap with a pattern of lacy snowflakes knit
around it, the cap pulled down past the eyebrows, the cheeks
fat with pout, the eyes in shadow, the chin tucked into a scarf
wound twice around. Is this me? It looks like me yet it doesn't.
I remember the hat, but I don't remember this picture. Is it
me? She stared at it, frowning. Mama made me a hat like that
with a matching scarf. One for me and one for Nikki, and one
for Barbara and her sister Dora. Is this Barbara? We're much
more alike than I'd thought. She stared at the photo again and
then gathered up all the pictures and put them away, carefully
rewinding the string of the envelope. At six the telephone rang
and she did not answer it.

It rang again at 6:15 and 6:30 and 6:45.

Why? Why? At home everything seemed for him, an endless
production with shifting scenes in which he was the main actor. Of course the photographs told stories, too, each one a
different story — as many stories as there were women. Yes,
a different life with every woman, for her father who had
failed in an acting career was in life nothing but an actor. As
for Jason . . . he was rather like her father.

Or was he?

If only she hadn't written the story.

If he hadn't been her father she wouldn't have written the

story, and if she hadn't written the story, she'd be with Jason this minute.

But hey, wait a minute.

Did she want to be with Jason?

She was attracted to him, she wanted to sleep with him, but love him?

Ridiculous! Trying so hard to love someone you didn't trust. It was Gordy who had taught her to trust, to laugh, to love. And this man, this man (no, not Jason this time but the other man, her father), it was he who had tried to turn her into a stone. Don't cry! Chin up! Back straight! Don't cry! You know I'm going to hurt you so don't feel!

DON'T FEEL!

She was suddenly in a rage. She stood up and moved to the desk. With her palm she swept the desk top clean — a clock, a mug full of pencils, a vase spun to the floor. The mantel was next with its pottery candlesticks and row of clay Mexican figurines — there! Take that! She smashed them against the grate. And this horrid picture — this good little girl with the apple — she yanked it down from the wall and slammed it upon her knee. Good, am I?

And then she cried, and then, later, she slept.

When she woke up she thought at first that she'd just had a dream but it wasn't a dream at all, it was a memory. It was summer, twilight, she was three or four years old, she even remembered what she'd had on, a little outfit, something in pink-and-white check that was called a "playsuit."

It was a hazy whitish evening, the mosquitoes were beginning to come out, there was a rosebush nearby that gave off the delicious fragrance of ripe peaches or raspberries. She sat on a chair made of sharp wooden slats that was too big for her and uncomfortable — she had to sit in it tailor-fashion. Her father sat nearby on the stone garden bench. It seemed to her (although she wasn't sure) that he had on white pants and a loose white shirt. He was reading her a story. She was completely absorbed in the story. He had a marvelous deep ringing voice and when he read he changed his voice for every character. There were animals in the story — donkeys, chickens, pigs — they were all in danger, they had banded together to save themselves. The story rushed on. She knew the story well but it was going by so fast. "Don't read so fast!" she'd said to him, crossly. He smiled, went on, it was finished, he stood up, snapped the book shut and she burst into tears. He laughed and picked her up and carried her back to the house at a jog. She rode along feeling pleased that she had him all to herself. She kept her legs twisted around his chest and her arms wrapped around his warm neck and laid her wet cheek on his hair — light hair the same color as hers. There were guests. Oh not again. There were always guests. There was a woman with red lips and a cigarette holder. "Isn't she awfully young for Grimm?" the woman said.

"Not at all," her father said. "She understands everything."

She had loved him so much but he had kept going away and then finally, she understood everything.

"Gordon?" she said out loud, in the dark. No. That's right. Gordon was home. She sat up and put her feet over the edge of the bed. Of course Gordon, the real Gordon, had been missing for years. Well, why not? She'd been a stone. If you live with a stone you turn into a stone.

"But why?" she asked the dark, perplexed, out loud.

With a hissing rush the steam came on, her only answer.

· · · **4** · · ·

On Tuesday, Claire rented a shiny new maroon Dodge from a Hertz rental agency on Seventh Avenue and easing into third gear drove north toward Westchester, up Route 287 toward Hartford on 460.

It was a clear, calm, sunny November morning and she was glad to be getting out of the city. Just east of Hartford, on Route 84, there was a curve after a steep downhill grade of such sudden spinning centrifugal delight that if you didn't precisely accelerate — going into the peak of the parabola — you would be carried off to the left in a cosmic continuum and wake up (or not) in a Hartford hospital ICU. Delicious! Heart thudding, she made it (whee!), eased up on the gas pedal looking around enough to appreciate the steep, root-studded wall of quartz-flecked yellowish stone to her right and, to her left, golden rolling New England meadows that faded off into a distance of smoky blue hills.

How nice. I am alive after all. It's always a moot question as to whether the risk-taker is a life-hater or a death-defier — at some point in one's psychic perspective the two parallels converge. I am running away again, this time from Jason. It didn't work, he's something of a disaster, but I feel so much better. Alive again. Almost cured. Jason made me feel miserable, but writing my stories made me feel great!

(Still, his long green eyes, his rolling laugh, his bony touch, his sharp-edged humor and moody sulks. For many months after that, much longer than Claire would have thought possible, whenever she thought of Jason a flaring pain would singe her peeled heart — he hadn't made her happy but he'd made her feel something. And where had those stories come from?)

And where is it I am going? Up to my mother's house. Now that's real disappointing, that I am all this old and my mother is still "home." Anyway, it'll be interesting to see Nikki. I wish Edward were going to be there, I miss him. I'd go to see him in Paris but there's no money, we've spent it all on detectives. If I could see Evan just once or even know he's all right. I miss his warm quiet presence and his melancholy guitar, wandering "thrums" behind his closed bedroom door. I blame myself, I blame all of us. We didn't see, we didn't see what was happening to him. We couldn't help Evan, we weren't even helping ourselves. It's strange how I always thought our families — Gordy's and mine — were miles apart, yet in certain ways they are so alike. *If it hurts, don't speak of it, pretend it's not there.*

I'll stop soon, get coffee at a Howard Johnson's and a big dish of peppermint stick ice cream, my college favorite. When money ran out at college, I used to live on doughnuts and ice cream, then Gordy would come up and take me to dinner. We used to eat and laugh and walk and eat and make love. We could sell the house. Say, where did that come from? I love the house, my kids have grown up there, but somehow, now, it makes me feel . . . entombed.

I remember sitting in Arthur's kitchen once — we were eating peppermint stick ice cream with his home-made fudge sauce — and he said to me, quoting Santayana, "Waking life is a dream controlled." Then we had a long talk about "real life," whatever that is, and how unreal people's lives are anyhow. People make up stories about their lives — "When I was nineteen I met a man who ruined my life." I liked Arthur, he was a great stepfather. He liked us, he loved my mother. I wish he hadn't died so soon. Listen, Gordon, we need to sell the house. We need a change. We need to have a future together, not just a past. Do you hear me, Gordon?

Arthur Haskins had died two years before and so her mother was a widow, living in the little, weathered, brown-shingle house in the country outside of Concord, Massachusetts. When they'd moved to the old farmhouse, Arthur had insisted that she learn to drive, so now her mother had the Buick and the house and a dog named Pils, a dachshund whose coat was the color of pilsner beer and a cat named Alice for Alice Toklas, because the cat loved delicate tidbits of food. Although Claire hadn't seen Arthur often she had come to like him and was grateful for the love that he seemed to heap upon her mother and to which her mother seemed so indifferent. Claire hoped it was an act of sorts — her mother was always affectionate with those around her but demonstrations of affection toward herself would make her stiff and uncomfortable.

Claire had had guilt feelings about her mother for some time. At Arthur's funeral Claire had felt helplessly cut off — she was still so immersed in Evan's disappearance that within the shell of her private grief she could feel other people's sorrows, even her mother's, only as small sharp stings, as if a handful of pebbles had been thrown against the place within which she endured.

And she wanted to talk to her sister, Nikki, too. They were older now, middle-aged, and she wanted to say something to her sister. But what? And was it possible? She'd never been able to talk to Nikki, whose usual retort was a sharp laugh, whose life — money, parties, glamour — was surely, after all, as much a buffer against interior hurt as Claire's puritanical escape into literature and family life. In the past, when she'd talk to Nikki about their childhood, they'd come up with versions so startlingly different that Claire felt as if she were talking to a creature from a different universe who looked upon Claire with detached curiosity. These talks gave Claire the strange feeling that she was morbid or unhinged. Nikki's nostalgia — all bliss and beatitude — was certainly not her own.

At twelve noon, Claire got off the Mass Turnpike and went north on Route 128. Whenever she was in the Boston area, she had a comfortable feeling that surprised her — she'd never felt comfortable living in New England, she liked it more in theory than in fact. But she loved the countryside, with its stone-scarred hills and shaded mossy hollows, its granite outcroppings, its steep pine woods and sudden lateral sweeps of autumn meadow from which flocks of startled birds, black against the sun, suddenly, raucously, flew into the mild sky. At Perkins Nursery (its painted signs advertising cider, doughnuts, Christmas ornaments) she turned right onto a small one-lane road, and then saw her mother's meadows, now all gold, and at the end of the field her mother's house, a house as small as a toy, with the red barn behind it and, like the upstanding rim of a bowl, a sheltering circle of trees — evergreen (shaggy hemlock, blue spruce, pine) — merging gradually halfway around the circle into leafless hardwoods.

As in a child's fable, the chimney of the little house was peacefully smoking. She drove up the long dirt driveway and pulled around in back to park at the base of the barn's tall fieldstone foundation. She saw in her rearview mirror two white-haired women approaching, one tall and slender — Nikki? — in tight jeans, a heavy black turtleneck sweater; and her mother in a handsome wine-colored suede jacket, gray tweed pants. Claire got out of the car feeling rattled and shy while Nikki, arms outstretched, hugged her. Claire saw, shocked, how much Nikki had aged — her glittering aquamarine eyes were set into a tanned face so wrinkled the area around the eyes looked scored, as if with a branding iron. Nikki wore no makeup while her mother, who delicately lifted her face to be kissed, was wearing blue eyeshadow, black eyeliner and mascara so that Claire, linking her arms with her sister and her mother, had the startling impression that her sister was older than her mother. Her mother looked serene and happy, Nikki looked brittle, scarred and worn.

"Ach, Klärchen," her mother scolded, "look at you, you are almost so thin as Nicole. You two! Nah, I see you are not eating well, so, *gut,* come inside quick, the coffee is fresh and I made specially a wonderful crab salad for lunch."

"Mama's been on a big cooking spree," Nikki said, smiling carefully at Claire.

"Oh wait just one minute!" Claire said. "Before we go in, let me look around. It's lovely, Mama, and you had your deck put on after all. What a handsome job. It's beautiful."

"Today we eat lunch on the deck," her mother said, "it's warm enough, *nicht?* You see I have the table all ready."

But Claire was looking the other way, out at the dry, golden-brown fields that surrounded the house like a shallow sea and that when swept by even the smallest of breezes, bowed and flowed and straightened and bowed again with a rhythm of movement not unlike the ceaseless sweep of ocean waves. It had always seemed to Claire that if there were a God His hand could be seen here, moving with lilting certitude across the face of this piece of earth.

"*Ist einer, der nimmt alle in die Hand.*"

(There is one who takes all within his hand.)

Her mother, standing quietly by her side, now touched her arm. "Claire, come. There is someone I want you to meet." Following her mother inside, up the wide back steps, across the cedar floorboards stained gray and laid in a parquet pattern, through new sliding glass doors, she wondered, amused, who it was, a new pet perhaps. Her mother loved dogs and assigned them distinct personalities. Claire had grown up with Rollo the cocker clown, Herman the hound-hund, and a poodle named Coco who was stylish and witty but temperamental.

"Charles!" her mother called out in her clear, light voice. "Come meet my Claire."

Her father — was it her father? — no, it was not, but a man certainly as tall, as big-boned, with straight white hair. He sat in the Thonet rocker near the stone fireplace and lifted his face in a smile. His name was Charles Hoover, he'd built the deck, and he was, Claire saw, completely blind. Moreover, he was obviously her mother's lover.

· · · 5 · · ·

Immediately after lunch on the sunny deck, Claire's mother and Charles Hoover went upstairs to take a nap, her mother vehemently asserting that she was now so old she could have a nap after lunch.

Charles lifted his listening face and remarked, mildly, "Well who said you couldn't?"

"You see, I often don't sleep well in the night," her mother said, scowling over her shoulder at Claire, who felt like giggling but restrained herself. Charles waited patiently for his lover in the kitchen doorway and then the couple — Charles, tall and bony, her mother small but fierce — linked arms and, with their heads tipped together, went up the stairs. Claire's mother was teaching Charles German and Claire could hear them counting together, "Ein" . . . "Ein"; "Zwei" . . . "Zwei"; "Drei" . . . "Drei."

He was an attractive man, Claire thought, feeling surprised at the little sexual pull she felt toward him. Charles's long bony humorous face (down-slanting hoods shielding his faded useless blue eyes) had a light quality, a kind of spiritual resonance that some old people grew into, an acceptance and grace that made Claire feel if only she held out long enough . . . or was that Oz all over again, that mythical point in the future when all becomes bliss and beatitude? She rinsed off the luncheon plates and put them one by one into the dishwasher's waiting maw.

Nikki sat hunched at the round table in the kitchen, frowning and smoking Marlboros. "Do you think they actually *do* it?" she asked.

"I sure hope so," Claire said fervently, kneeing the dishwasher door shut. "Did you know that sex is good for arthritis? I read it in *Vogue*."

"Yeah?" Nikki said, "what kind of sex? I'm sick of the do-it-yourself variety."

"How long has it been?"

"Three months, two weeks, four days. I threw the little turd out. He brought his boyfriend into the house. I mean, I had heard of this but never actually experienced it. I was giving Jean's friend a home and cooking for him and Jean was giving it to *him* whenever I went out the door. I caught them in bed together. I don't know," she said wearily, "I felt so . . . dumb."

"Did you . . . care for him?"

Nikki brooded, shrugged, stubbed out her cigarette in a chipped saucer — her mother kept no ashtrays in the house. "I don't know. Hell, I don't know anything anymore." With a sweep of her hand, she pushed the saucer away. Her hands, Claire saw, weren't well cared for, the nails broken and chewed. "Yeah," Nikki mumbled, "I did."

"Well," Claire said gently, "whoever it was it would have hurt." She wiped up the countertops with a sponge and said, "I think I'll retire myself. I got up very early this morning." Nikki didn't answer. She sat with her fist clutched in her straight gray hair as if in anger or in mourning she wanted to tear it.

In her room at the back of the house, a sunny room with white walls, whose yellow-curtained windows looked past the red barn into the fields and trees, Claire unpacked her suitcase. She hadn't brought much — clean underwear, shirts, a sweater, the manila envelope. Why did I bring this thing? She stared down at it — damn, damn, she thought — and plopped the envelope on the top of the dresser.

"I can't get over it," Nikki said that night in Claire's room. "How does she do it? She keeps finding these men who are crazy about her. And I guess they do do it because guess what I saw opened up, face down, on the table next to her side of the bed?"

"What?"

"*The Joy of Sex.* God."

Claire smiled and said, "That's sad. It's so long overdue."

Nikki was sitting on the yellow chaise with her feet in big fluffy fur slippers. "What's that?" she asked yawning. She indicated with a lift of her chin the envelope Claire had put on the bureau.

"Some pictures," Claire said. "Do you want a cup of tea or something?"

"No. Who are the pictures of?"

"Nobody much. Nobody you know. Want to see them?"

"Why would I want to look at pictures of people I don't even know? Anyway, Charles seems nice. A little simpleminded."

"Simple but not simpleminded."

"Maybe, but he's certainly not Father."

"Thank God for that. Besides, I think there's more to Charles than meets the eye. He's a New Englander, not your average lurid Californian. He's honest and plain-spoken, but reticent. He used to be the captain of a tramp steamer and he's lived all over the world. Did he tell you that?"

"No."

"He's been everywhere — the Orient, Africa, Australia, South America."

"Oh Jesus, Claire, it was a brief remark, you don't have to make a big production out of it. I like him perfectly well, so let's drop it."

"Okay," Claire said agreeably. She didn't feel like fighting. She was lying on the bed propped up on pillows, wishing Nikki would go away so that she could read for a while, but Nikki sat on, smoking and brooding.

"Anyway," Nikki said, "you never understood about Father."

"Oh gee," Claire said, "I think maybe I got the picture. I sure wouldn't want to know much more."

"Mama treated him like a little kid."

"Nikki. He *was* a little kid. And Mama cherished him. She *adored* him."

"What's so great about that? It's hard to be adored."

"What's hard about it? Anyway, as you said to me once a long time ago, if he hadn't wanted it that way, he would have done something about it."

"He hung in for many years. Then when he did do something, you never forgave him."

"I hated what he'd done to Mama. And the rest of us, too."

"Aw, hell, what did he do that almost every other person in the country hasn't done lately? He was just ahead of his time."

"I'm not talking about sex. That was only how he got at Mama. With us kids he had all those other techniques. Oh let's not do this, we could debate this forever. Tell me about your kids. It's been ages since I've seen them. What's everybody doing?"

"Oh God, the kids, let's see . . ." Cigarette in hand, Nikki rubbed her forehead. "Ann's taking acting classes and Kevin is our nonresident intellectual — did I tell you he's thinking of converting to Catholicism? He met this girl who's in Arab studies. They're so in love." She made a mocking face. "The other two are pretty much the same. When was it we talked, last June?"

"Yes."

"And how are you?" Nikki raised her black brows — a startling remnant of her youthful beauty, those wide black wings over her light jewel-bright eyes.

"Me? Oh, I'm all right." Claire opened the book — hint, hint — and looked at the title page. Why doesn't she go off to bed? Nuts.

"No," Nikki said persistently, "I mean how are you really?"

Perhaps the words registered concern, but in her sister's tone of voice Claire detected — or thought she detected — a menacing mockery. An instinct inside her did a mummer's dance and rattled its silent chains. Watch out, watch out. Claire knew from ancient experience that if she revealed any true part of herself some blow stunning in its sarcasm would knock her off balance: Nikki was, truly, her father's daughter. She said, reluctantly, "I'm fine but I'm not living at home at the moment."

"Oh-ho, Claire the bad widdle girl. Having a time of it with somebody new?"

"Nope."

"Nobody at all?" Nikki drawled, eyes narrowed, wheedling.

"No," Claire said, "I've been working." She stood up, went to the window and looked out at the nighttime blackness, three kinds of black, the taut starless black sky looking oddly transparent like a piece of stretched silk, and the black-black trees, and the field, a solid pocket of black interspersed with long milky yellow gleams — the barn light was on. If I pull down the shades, maybe she'll get the hint. Cheap shades, funny stuff Mama bought for this house, everything cheap and new — the elderly bride without a trousseau.

There was nothing in the house Claire could identify out of

her childhood. Her mother had sold all the old furniture, silver, vases, pictures, rugs Claire had grown up with. She and Arthur had gone to Pier I and bought bedspreads, furniture, rugs — two honeymoon kids on a spree. Claire pulled down the shades — zip, zip and (at the south window) zip.

"It's funny," she said, sitting down on the edge of the bed, "this place doesn't have one thing in it that we grew up with but it's more home to me than that was."

"You think so? Not to me." Nikki was smoking again. She frowned, put a middle finger to her tongue to blot up a bit of tobacco.

"I thought driving up how badly I wanted to come home. I wanted to see Mama and then I felt silly. The big old baby. Still, I love this house. I feel comfortable here."

"And you with your gorgeous mansion."

"Well, as I said, I'm not living there now."

"Exactly where are you living?"

"New York City."

"Huh. That's not like you. You never wanted to live in the city."

Claire reached for the book again, opened it, closed it, put it aside. "I was desperate."

They were silent and then Nikki said rudely, "I have something to tell you."

Claire looked up.

"It's about Evan. I've seen him." Claire felt a pause in her entire metabolism, as if everything — heart, blood, brain — was thunderstruck, listening. Then blood began to flow in her veins again. "He came to the house in June."

Stunned, Claire sat looking at her sister. Nikki dropped her eyes but went on loftily, "I couldn't tell you. I promised I wouldn't."

Why is it I feel ill? Claire thought.

"He was living in L.A. with those people, the Hare Krishnas, but he's left them. He said he had a new job up in Petaluma. He asked about you, anyhow. I offered him money but he wouldn't take it. Actually, I'd seen him once before but" — Nikki shrugged — "he wouldn't speak to me."

Nikki got up and went to the door. She stood in the doorway looking at Claire, and when Claire looked up she saw on her sister's face a naked look of envy and hate. "When we were small," Nikki said, "even when we were older, you always got everything. *You* were the one with the talent. You were his favorite and you never loved him." Abruptly, she opened the door and slammed it behind her.

It passed. After a few minutes, Claire stopped wanting to kill her. The violent wave of anger she'd felt dwindled, curled up, died. She went downstairs to the kitchen where on the raised hearth of the stone fireplace, the dying red embers of the evening's fire sighed at her. She prodded the fire awake with a poker then tossed in the large manila envelope and watched until it burst into cleansing flame.

Gordy! She picked up the telephone to call home. No one there. She let it ring for a long time. I've got to go back, she thought. I've got to tell Gordy. She wanted to see her husband, tell him, watch his face, watch his eyes — his beautiful sad dark eyes — light up with pleasure, watch his face break into a smile. She would touch his arm, take his hand and place it palm out upon her cheek. No one home.

Back in her room upstairs, the imprint of Nikki's body still in the down cushions of the yellow chaise, Claire paced furiously, hugging herself, sat down, stood up, lay down on the bed, shut off the light, turned it on again. Flashes of joy mingled stormlike with flashes of rage. How could she? Claire thought. Almost six months! Back in June . . . if only . . .

doesn't she understand? She's had children. Doesn't she understand anything? Doesn't she have any feelings at all? It's a mystery, I'll never understand her, my own sister. A stranger to me, forget it, go to sleep. She snapped off the light and lay staring up into the dark. Why wouldn't he call us? My child. He's alive, that's the main thing. Gordy! Listen to me! My dearest, he is safe and alive.

But she couldn't sleep and at three she got up again and went down to the kitchen, feeling now exultant. She made herself a cup of tea and sat in the rocker, next to the warm ashes of the fire, sipping and rocking. At four-thirty she heard a noise and there was her mother, no mascara now, a white-faced old lady whose long silver hair hung down her back like the good witch in a fairy tale.

"Mama," Claire said, looking up joyfully. "Nikki's seen Evan. He's all right."

"*Ach Gott sei dank!*" her mother exclaimed and clapped her hands together, an old fairy-tale gesture that always seemed potently magical to Claire. They sat down at the kitchen table close together. "Gordy's not home," Claire said. "I called, I wanted to tell him right away. I'm sorry, I'll have to leave tomorrow."

"Of course," her mother said, "but where could he be? And the children, where are they?"

"Down at Belle View, maybe. They might have left early. We were going down for Thanksgiving."

"You don't know where they are?" Her mother looked at her sharply. Her brows, which without eyebrow pencil were as silver as her hair, drew together.

"I've been away from home."

Her mother was silent, then twisted a ring on her small, gnarled hand. "Na, ja," she said, "I left home once, but I came back."

"He wasn't so good to you, Mama."

"No, but of course that is not the point. He was always to me . . ." Her mother dropped her head and smiled. ". . . so fascinating, I could not tell you now why. And of all my children, you are perhaps most like him."

Claire averted her face and her mother added softly, "You, too, have this talent, to live in your imagination many different lives."

"He didn't live in his imagination. He acted it all out."

"But he was an actor! Yes, with him as with Nikki it was always the next one and the next one."

"It was nonsense," Claire said roughly.

Her mother smiled gently and got up to go to bed. "Ja, ja. But now how long it is over."

Driving in sunshine from New England to New Jersey, Claire
kept a firm foot on the gas pedal but her mind wandered, as
if darting in and out of shadow in a dense half-familiar forest.
She felt, still, intensely happy, but her mood was calmer now
as she planned what had to be done next — the flight out to
California. As for her father . . . she hadn't told anyone and
no doubt never would. Let it, him, all of them, rest in peace.
A final flight, a final abandonment. Why not? He'd done it
before. The bigger mystery, Claire thought sadly, was how,
despite everything, savage hurts of all kinds, you went on im-
placably hating him and at the same time (oh, Nikki, you are
so wrong) irrevocably loving.

Once off the Garden State Parkway, she drove straight to
Belle View, straight to her in-laws' house on Ocean Avenue.
The house, of gray shingle, with sparkling white trim, was as
wide open as if it were July, yet not a soul was in sight. In
the dining room, the long table was laid for the next day's
Thanksgiving dinner — yards of stiff damask, the old Herend
china, sparkling crystal, the heavy silver and, propped up in
front of the massive silver bowl piled high with fruit, a yellow
legal pad with her father-in-law's black scrawl upon it:
GORDON — *we're out for cocktails. Your office called.*

Where was Gordy? Visions of all sorts passed before her
eyes — Gordy with someone else, no doubt Barbara — and then
she laughed at herself and ran out to the car. He'd be at the
club, getting in one last sail before winter.

She drove across town to the bay side, drove through the

Yacht Club gates, parked, walked, half ran to the clubhouse and all the while she scanned the long docks where a few small boats still bobbed at anchor. At the very end of the longest pier she saw a figure, black against the afternoon sun, moving about in a boat, bending, straightening, getting ready to set sail. Up went the jib of the Lightning. The sail began to flutter in the breeze and Claire walked toward it, then ran.

"Gordy!" she called out.

The figure, in a Windbreaker and sunglasses, straightened up, looked toward her shielding his eyes, then turned his back on her, sat, began (she could tell) fanning the tiller.

"Gordy, it's me! Stop. Come back!"

But Gordon sat on while the jib fluttered and then bellied, and the nose of the boat trembled and slowly turned outward toward deeper water.

"Gordy, listen to me. Come back. There's something I want to tell you."

Gordon looked once over his shoulder, then resolutely looked away into the sun, which now, at three-twenty, lay in a spill of fiery gold upon the bay's black water.

"I love you! Come back!"

Gordon raised one hand in salute — goodbye. The little boat sailed on, picked up speed, the prow parted the water with scarcely a ripple, water that seemed not water at all but something molten, black as lava, edged at the horizon with a band of fire. He was hoisting up the mainsail now. It went up slowly, lightly luffing and paused (as Claire knew it would — it always stuck a third of the way up) and then, with a sudden jerk, rose higher.

Gordy's voice, booming out deeply over the water sounded like someone else's when he said, "Don't wait! I'm not coming back. This SHITS, CLAIRE. THIS IS AWFUL!"

Amazing herself, Claire began to laugh and cried out (not

caring that people were stopping now, pausing on the clubhouse dock to listen to the shouted, echoing conversation),
"Oh yes you are. You're coming back all right. We are married, Gordon, we are married forever. We have this BOND.
Dammit, Gordy, you fucking idiot, come back here!"

· IX ·

After

After the leftovers were put away in Saran-wrapped glass bowls, after the dishes were done, the pots washed, the roasting pan left to soak in the sink, after the wineglasses were hand washed and dried and Alicia had gone to bed with a book (instead of a boy, what a relief) and Susan had gone to the movies, glowing at young Roger Moss, and after Steve Moss had kissed me briefly in the kitchen and gone out the back door, and after Nesta had broken the turkey platter, an old blue-and-white export china piece from some remote seafaring branch of the Bigelow family tree, I took a tepid bath (there was no hot water) and lay in the tub smoking one of Alicia's Marlboros and taking sips from a tumbler half full of Jack Daniel's that Steve had brought along with the wine, and looking up squint-eyed at a pie-shaped wedge of plaster in the bathroom ceiling that seemed to be coming closer, I thought: Shit. Everything's all fucked up as usual.

The minute you think things are going to get better, watch out. Life is gonna let you have it with its little ol' sledge hammer.

Anyway, dinner was almost fun.

Except ruined for me of course with Cliff not there.

Steve's so nice, but . . .

Gee, I don't know.

Still, when I told him I'd finished my novel, that was really terrific the way he got so excited, as if it really mattered to him. All these years, nothing I've done for myself has ever mattered to anyone but me. It was funny to hear him say, "Is that right? You finished it last night? Well, what time?"

"This morning, actually," I said. "At four A.M. or thereabouts. Then I went up to the kitchen and stuffed the turkey."

He laughed. He *likes* me. He likes *me*. I told him I'd made a decision — no matter what, I was only going to teach school one more year.

I wish Cliff had come home, though. Was it Nesta, I wonder, or me or something entirely different that drove him away? Gone, they said, but he left me a note: "Maybe Christmas." Packed up last night, was gone after dinner. I felt, oh, I felt . . . okay . . . I felt *heartbroken*. I felt like I had this burned-out crater inside my chest. But never mind: *Maybe Christmas!*

Looking around the table today at everyone eating and talking and laughing — Susan and Roger Moss flipping walnuts at each other and Nesta, red-eyed, downcast, and Steve making droll remarks, I was thinking how ever since I was thirteen, I have spent my life taking care of people. And what scares me about Steve is, he wants to take care of me.

I don't know.

The whole thing makes me uneasy.

What if I, oh, wanted to leave?

And then I would hurt him, wouldn't I? The way my mother hurt my father when she left? And the way I hurt him, too. I mean, I felt *bad* at leaving home. I felt *sorry* for him. I felt like a traitor, as if I'd *abandoned* him.

But I'm not like my mother. I never left here, did I? Why is it I have to keep telling myself?

Spilling sheets of cold water and shivering violently, I stood up and reached for a long frayed pink towel. From down below on the second floor a stereo suddenly boomed out, socking me in the gut, and immediately a door opened and someone — Alicia — shouted, "Shut that dumb thing off, Nesta! I'm trying to read."

Carefully, I laid the (wet but still smoking) cigarette on the edge of the sink and began rubbing myself dry. My legs ached from standing at the stove all morning and my head felt as light, empty and thin-walled as a gourd. The constant pressure of the novel (which I felt as a dim thin tumor on the back of the brain) was gone but along with it I felt that I'd lifted out most of my gray matter. I felt dumb. Dumb and lonely. My characters were always so real to me — much more real than so-called real life — which wasn't so awfully real when you thought about it, filled as it was with hopes, wishes, dreams, myths and impossible longings. Oh that last scene, the tiny boat, black against the sun, Gordy with his back turned and Claire laughing and swearing.

Now listen, Claire, I'll admit it: I used you. I used your life. But before you get all hot about it, try to look at things my way. It's sort of a compliment. After all, on the Island of Aroo-ta-po-pa off New Guinea, the natives ritualistically eat members of the opposing tribes. It's not because the place is barren of vegetation and protein poor, it's because the Aroo-ta-po-paens admire their rivals and think they're ingesting some pretty good qualities!

But I'll tell you one thing — I am glad it's all over with Gordon. He is not for me. It came to me all of a sudden who it was he reminded me of, the clothes and the passivity and the depression . . . my father! Can you beat that?

"Moth . . . Mrs. Bi . . . ge . . . low!"

"Nesta! For heaven's sakes! What is it?"

"There's water down here everywhere! It's coming right

through the ceiling in, like, waves. It's all over the stereo, it's all over this *Kansas* album, and it isn't even my album, I borrowed it from Susan. Help!"

So I sighed, picked up the cigarette, took one last hard drag, and then tossed the butt into the can and, attired Queen Leilakalani style, with one edge of the towel tucked tightly into an armpit, marched barefoot but imperious to do battle downstairs.

"Courage!" I told myself.

Someday, after I sell this house, and after the kids have left, I will buy a Winnebago, and if, by that time, I still haven't zeroed in on Steve or the man of my dreams, I will drive straight across the United States. I will drive to Kansas, right over the rainbow!

Claire sat at her desk in the attic with her chin in her hand and the encyclopedia (volume 11) open before her. On this day, the relaxed Friday after Thanksgiving, three kinds of music drifted up to her from various rooms — Bruce Springsteen, beginning Bach on a hoarse cello and the final quartet from Act III of *The Tales of Hoffmann*. While Hoffmann beseeches his consumptive young mistress not to sing, in the wings evil Dr. Miracle (a basso) conjures her singing. Antonia's voice rises higher, spiraling up against the ghostly voice of her dead mother (transcendent art), Hoffmann (earthly love) and Miracle (the satanic side of artistry — ambition). Antonia dies on a shriek, Hoffmann cries out in despair and Claire pondered the life of her ancestor, Hoffmann, E. T. A. (1776–1822), lawyer, artist, conductor, composer, critic, poet and writer of bizarre tales; well known in Russia and Europe, influenced Dostoesvski, Edgar Allan Poe, De Maupassant; invented the Doppelgänger or Double and no wonder, given his busy life, but did he have children? It doesn't say. Uh huh, just as I thought, some man wrote this, they never think of children as work *or* accomplishment.

From below, the music rose, commingled joyously, momentarily condensed and cloudlike cast a shadow upon the serene violet of her personal mountain range — Michael, she thought sadly. The cloud passed.

She sighed. Someday soon, maybe starting Monday, she was going to write a novel with Barbara in it. Writing that story, she'd seen Barbara in a completely different way, as if, like a demon-spirit, she'd passed through Barbara and come out on the other side. Or maybe — here was a thought — Barbara had passed through *her*. Well, whatever. The point was, she could feel the colors of the novel (dark and light) and she could sense its shape (a braid) and already a few props seemed to want to speak to her (a bathtub, a kitchen knife).

But now, judging from the abrupt decline in household decibels, the music-lovers were breaking for lunch. She, too, would go down to the kitchen, have a turkey sandwich on white with lettuce, and a big bite of Gordy's neck. At the end of her novel she planned to give Barbara everything — everything except Gordy.

Whistling, she went downstairs and her family smiled at each other and said, "Ma's happy."